Also by Amelia Grey

The Earl Next Door

It's All About the Duke

To the Duke, with Love

Last Night with the Duke

The Duke in My Bed

The Earl Claims a Bride

Wedding Night with the Earl

Gone with the Rogue

Amelia Grey

St. Martin's Paperbacks

This is a work of fiction. All of the characters, organizations, and events portrayed in this novel are either products of the author's imagination or are used fictitiously.

First published in the United States by St. Martin's Paperbacks, an imprint of St. Martin's Publishing Group.

GONE WITH THE ROGUE

For information, address St. Martin's Publishing Group, 120 Broadway, New York, NY 10271.

www.stmartins.com

ISBN: 978-1-250-21878-0

Our books may be purchased in bulk for promotional, educational, or business use. Please contact your local bookseller or the Macmillan Corporate and Premium Sales Department at 1-800-221-7945, ext. 5442, or by email at MacmillanSpecialMarkets@macmillan.com.

Printed in the United States of America

St. Martin's Paperbacks edition / May 2020

10 9 8 7 6 5 4 3 2 1

Chapter 1

Being stuck in a tree on a rather precarious and shaky limb wasn't actually an unfortunate position to be in, at least not if you were a boy looking for an adventure. That the person stuck was a female, a lady at that, more specifically Lady Kitson Fairbright, daughter-in-law to the elderly, high-nosed Duke of Sprogsfield and mother to his three-year-old grandson, changed the equation and put her in something of a pickle.

Not that she didn't always seem to be in one. According to the duke, Julia was constantly trampling on the strict rules he and Society dictated for a young widow. He was always itching for her impulsive ways to land her in trouble so he could make good on his promise to take her son and raise the boy himself.

Which was why she never should have climbed the tree in St. James Park. And especially on her first day in London. But what was she to do? When they'd arrived earlier in the day, she couldn't deny Chatwyn's request to play in the park. He'd been traveling in a hot, bumpy carriage for two and a half days. The long journey was torture for an active four-year-old boy.

Unfortunately, the fine webbing of Julia's butterfly net had caught in a branch of the old elm just as she trapped the beautifully winged insect. No amount of pulling or yanking brought the net down. She couldn't let the butterfly suffer an untimely demise in the rare late-summer heat. With an extreme amount of mental fortitude and more physical strength than she thought possible, she had thrilled her son and appalled his governess by scaling the tree. Holding on to the limb above her head for balance, she'd sidestepped out as far as she dared, and reached over. Taking great care not to touch the delicate wings, she freed the butterfly from its prison but couldn't dislodge the net.

Her discovery that the tatted collar sewn onto her dress had become tangled in a cluster of small branches and now held her hostage wasn't what caused her moment of panic, an emotion that wasn't common to Julia. She'd calmly removed her bonnet so it wouldn't get caught and went about trying to free the lace at her nape with one hand while continuing to steady herself with the other. All she'd managed for her struggles was a damp neck from the exertion, raw palms, and a pair of summer white gloves that would have to be thrown away.

Yet, still remaining mostly unruffled, Julia had thought about her options and decided on the only sensible one. She'd sent her son and Miss Periwinkle home with instructions for the governess to return quickly with scissors so she could cut herself out of the knotted mess. Julia had much to do before the duke arrived in London.

Three weeks ago, she'd overheard him talking with his solicitor about a company he owned—one of many that weren't recorded in his name but he controlled. Julia had to get her hands on the documents of one in particular. If she found it, she could prove he wasn't the righteous standard-bearer for how one should obey rules of Society, conduct matters of business, and treat their fellowman fairly—even generously.

Julia looked at her widow's dress. A small collar was all the trim the duke thought a proper widow should wear. He believed he knew better than anyone else what was right and what was wrong. What was acceptable and what must never be said or done. Society had kowtowed to him and agreed there was no other man more fair-minded or respectable than the revered Duke of Sprogsfield. Everyone in the ton believed he had never stepped a foot outside the straight line he drew for how one should conduct one's life, be it gambling, drinking, or dallying with the opposite sex. The problem was that he expected Julia not to either.

The duke himself was a younger son and was never supposed to inherit the dukedom. He had been educated to be a clergyman, and he'd never put aside his strict code of what he considered right and wrong after he became the duke. He made it easy for people to assume he was better, wiser, and saintlier than they were.

While other widows were unregimented by such a pretender and could enjoy the somewhat relaxed freedoms their status availed them, Julia was not and could not. And as soon as she was free from the tree, she would return to the duke's house and begin her quest to end his tyrannical ways.

It was daunting to think about taking on the duke, but she had no choice. The first thing she planned to do was start acquainting herself with the staff's current habits. She'd overheard the duke telling his solicitor that all the papers concerning his secret companies were hidden in his London house. She must find them before he recovered from his illness and joined her in London.

Julia would have to be careful and elude the servants. There was no reason she should be in the duke's bedchamber, dressing chamber, or private book room—the most likely places for him to hide the documents. It would definitely cause suspicions if she were seen in any of those rooms, and she had no doubt that the housekeeper or the footman would make sure the duke was told if she were caught trespassing. And Julia had no doubt the duke would drag himself from his sickbed to get to London if he should ever have an inkling about what she was up to.

Yet the thought of success and confronting him with her findings when he arrived in London heartened her while she waited to be freed from the tree. She desperately needed proof the duke wasn't the pious and honorable man he portrayed himself to be but a charlatan and, in truth, an odious man.

Julia closed her eyes and breathed in the pungent scent of drying bark and sun-kissed foliage. She heard a bee buzzing nearby and laughter from the children she'd seen in the distance. Ever since she heard the duke discussing the secret companies, she'd envisioned finding the proof of his lies and telling him if he didn't allow her and Chatwyn to be free of him and his rigid ways, she would expose his secrets to all of Society.

She opened her eyes and peered through the canopy of leaves to see if Miss Periwinkle was in sight. There was no sign of the governess, but she saw a gentleman walking his horse straight toward her as if he'd known she was ensconced among the branches. Her normal calm threatened to desert her. She hoped he would pass without a whiff of notice. Carefully, she drew her feet closer together, and lifted the hem of her dark plum-colored skirt to the tops of her walking boots to conceal herself further into the tree that thankfully was still in the full bloom of summer.

Julia couldn't see the man's face from her vantage point with the brim of his hat riding low, plus the way he held his head down as if he were a determined man on a mission. He was powerful-looking with wide, straight shoulders and long, lean legs that were fitted into shiny black knee boots that had short leather tassels at the top. They seemed to wink at her with every step he took. There was no doubt he had the strong, confident stride of a man who knew his place in the world, what he wanted and didn't care what others thought.

To her surprise and annoyance, he didn't pass by her but stopped at the base of the tree and patted the horse's neck. The fine cut and fabric of his coat suggested he was a gentleman, but she didn't recognize him. Carefully watching him, she wondered why he tarried. She started imagining what he could be doing. Was he pausing to take a drink from his flask, or a late-afternoon nap in the last sun rays of the day? But then an entirely different idea crossed her mind. Maybe he was waiting to have a tryst with a woman.

Right beneath her!

And that's what caused Julia's moment of panic and the loud gasp that gave away her position.

The horse tossed its head and shuddered.

The man looked up.

Julia froze.

"What the deuce are you doing up there?" he asked incredulously, looking as startled as she was.

"Nothing," she answered defensively, tamping down her horror at being caught, yet somehow managing not to be completely mortified by the unfortunate event.

She was now sure she'd never seen the man before. And even more sure he was no gentleman. Gentlemen removed their hats—or at the very least pushed them farther up their foreheads—when meeting a lady. Even if said lady was in a tree. He did neither.

Focusing on his face, she took in his full, nicely shaped brows, angular cheekbones, and slightly square chin that made him as handsome as any man she'd ever seen. She watched his gaze skim over her, too, just slowly enough to cause a curl of feminine interest to shimmy in her chest. At that, the heat of the afternoon swelled heavily around her, flaming her already flushed cheeks.

Staring up at her with a quizzical expression, he offered, "That's a rather odd place to be standing around and doing nothing."

But true. She'd long since given up on finding the strength to break the durable tatting thread, tear the well-made fabric, or twist in two the branch that held her captive. She must have sworn a hundred times already that she'd never trap another butterfly in a net to give it closer inspection no matter how much her son pleaded.

Realizing she still held the tail of her dress above her boots, she quickly released it and said, "Never mind about me, sir. I don't know who you are and you should be on your way."

Sweeping his hat off his head, he tossed it on top of his saddle without taking his gaze from hers, and with a teasing glint in his eyes he said, "Mr. Garrett Stockton at your service."

Julia almost gasped again. She knew the name and the man's reputation as a rake and a man who didn't obey anyone's rules. He was said to have a mistress on every continent and more than half a dozen in London alone. She could understand why. He was a handsome devil—just as she'd heard. Strangely, their paths had never crossed when he was in London. He wasn't the kind of man she'd forget meeting.

There was a building in St. James that bore the name Stockton Shipping Company, and it was his. She'd heard talk about the intriguing sea adventurer fighting pirates, and having the Spanish armada chasing his ships. Looking at him, she supposed it could be true. The gossip in Society seemed to be that whenever he was invited to parties every young lady in attendance wanted him to take her out on the dance floor. Julia wondered why the gossip wasn't that all the ladies wanted him to take them into the garden for a forbidden kiss.

But now wasn't the time to keep thinking about how attractive he was or peruse her memory for more gossip about him. She had to figure out how she was going to get out of this with some of her dignity intact.

She needed him to go away and forget he ever saw her.

"I am Lady Kitson Fairbright, Mr. Stockton."

He gave her a bow and said, "My lady."

Julia wasn't sure whether he recognized her name as the daughter-in-law of the influential Duke of Sprogsfield. Mr. Stockton pushed both sides of his dark blue coat behind him, rested his gloved hands on decidedly slim hips, and continued to stare.

He wasn't making this easy for her. Did he think a lady wanted to be caught in a tree by a stranger—or by anyone? Usually Julia could control whatever situation in which she found herself. But this afternoon everything had gone wrong.

She attempted to dismiss him again by saying, "Whatever it was you were going to do or whatever secret rendezvous you might have planned, you'll have to move away and find another place."

With a slight, intriguing half smile, he said, "I have no secret plans to meet anyone under this tree. I'm in London because a friend of mine will be marrying soon and I want to attend his wedding. I'm in the park because trees are something I want to see after a long voyage. Now, that branch you're on doesn't look particularly sturdy. I don't think it's safe."

"I'm perfectly fine," she responded confidently, even though there was no truth to her words. She was getting more worried by the moment in her cascade of greenery. Her arms were tired from holding on to the limb above her head, first with one hand and then the other to keep from losing her balance, falling off, and hanging herself. But that was too gruesome to think about. And admitting she'd done something so outlandishly impulsive that she needed any help she could get right now didn't come easily to her nature.

Instead, Julia resisted the urgency and cold hard truth of her peril again, continued to stare straight ahead as if studying something important, and said, "I'm enjoying the view. In the distance I see at least three carriages rumbling along, and a lady and a gentleman are walking with a dog—a spaniel, I think. Another couple has three children with them, and much farther down, I see a crowd gathering around a cart. Someone must be selling sweet cakes, or perhaps there will be a puppet show."

As if to emphasize her jeopardy, her arm trembled as she finished her sentence. Where in heaven's name was Miss Periwinkle? It shouldn't take her so long to get home, grab a pair of scissors and get back to the park.

A rustling noise caught her attention and she looked down. Mr. Stockton was wrapping the reins over a bunch of low-hanging leaves.

Her heartbeat skipped with apprehension. "What are you doing?"

"Securing the horse. I don't know why you climbed the tree, Lady Kitson, but it will be dusk soon. I'm not going to walk away and leave you standing up there."

Why was it that sometimes things that appeared relatively simple in their inception frequently had a way of turning into ill-timed problems for her?

She understood the wisdom of his words, but stifling her very real fears about her predicament, she said, "My son's governess was here with me. She will be returning shortly."

"How is she going to help you to the ground? You must be up at least eight or nine feet."

Julia was hot, tired, and exasperated. A feeling of weary surrender settled over her. "Oh, piffle," she said as a pain of anxiety struck her stomach. She had to believe Miss Periwinkle was only a minute or two away. "I might as well tell you so you'll leave me in peace. If you must know," she began, recounting the misadventure that had her trapped. She concluded, "Thankfully the butterfly is now free."

She watched his eyes scan the tree and knew when his gaze lighted on the dangling net. "You must have been running and jumping to get it caught up that high. Climbing the tree was brave and kindhearted."

"But foolish as well," she suddenly admitted honestly, hating to reveal the seriousness of her situation to this man but grateful he seemed to understand the reason behind her jeopardy. Out of frustration, she reached to the back of her neck and tugged on her clothing again. "When Miss Periwinkle returns with scissors I will cut myself free and climb down. You must leave. The Duke of Sprogsfield is quite rigid when it comes to my following the accepted behavior of widowhood, and I simply cannot be seen with a man helping me down from a tree." Especially such a young and handsome one. "Now, please go."

There was a firm set to his full lips and jaw. He placed his hands on his hips again and in a resolved manner asked, "Can you move?"

Such a simple question. Her temples were beginning to pound from the oppressive heat, from the exhaustion of holding first one hand and then the other over her head. "Very little without strangling myself," she confessed, realizing even the fresh green scent had become stifling. "My collar isn't detachable but I will manage." Somehow. Surely. She would get herself down.

"I'm not leaving you up there."

Grabbing the sides of the substantial trunk with his gloved hands and fine-leather booted feet as if steel spikes were attached to them, he started climbing up. One firm clutch at a time.

"No, don't do that, Mr. Stockton. Please. No."

It seemed only a second or two later he was standing on the widest point of the same wobbly limb with her, but with his back and weight pressed tight against the trunk and his eyes staring intently into hers. She suddenly felt as if all the quivering leaves on the tree were in her stomach as every muscle in her body tensed at his closeness. He stood beside her, tall, confident, and decidedly male. An unmistakable awareness passed between them. What struck her even more disturbingly was that he had ignored her pleas to go away. He was determined to help her. How many times had she asked others to help her break free of the duke's domination so she and Chatwyn could be free to live by themselves? Countless. Everyone had refused her, including the duke's two older sons and his daughter. They were as restricted by him as Julia was. And now this man was helping her when she wasn't even in need of it. Julia knew Miss Periwinkle would return.

Rays of late-afternoon sunshine found a sliver of space between the bouquets of leaves, glistening off his golden-brown eyes and highlighting strands of his tawny-brown hair. She wanted to reach out and brush the wayward strands away from his forehead, but held back that feminine instinct and asked, "How did you do that so fast?"

"I've climbed the mast of a ship many times."

Julia stilled. Her heartbeat slowed as long-ago memories rushed past. The mention of any ship always brought the sinking of the *Salty Dove* to mind. It had taken her husband's life and more than one hundred others. She lowered her lashes over her eyes, as she often did in a show of respect, honor, and memory of all who were affected that day by the passenger ship going down in a violent storm off the coast of Portugal.

"I shouldn't have said that," he offered, with a tone of regret in his voice. "It was careless of me to mention a ship and remind you of the tragedy and your loss."

So he had recognized her name. He knew her story. "Please don't worry yourself," she said, lifting her gaze to his face. "No words are necessary." She didn't mind talking about the disaster that befell the *Salty Dove*, its passengers, and the crew four years ago. Lost friends and family should be remembered.

When it happened, Julia had found herself in the unenviable position of being eight months with child. Perhaps some ladies would have taken to their beds in sorrow and grief, facing the overwhelming burden of suddenly being a widow. Julia had never been one to allow situations to get the best of her. She accepted the blow fate issued and carried on. Besides, she had to be strong for the babe waiting to be born.

Julia hadn't been in love with her husband when she married him or when he died, but she had always been grateful to him and respectful in all ways. Now that he was gone, she honored his memory and felt sadness that he hadn't lived to see his delightful son.

"My mourning is long past," Julia said quietly. "Life goes on, Captain Stockton."

His eyes seemed to take in every detail of her face as if he were delicately searching for something before he nodded once in acknowledgment.

"Not everyone who owns a ship is a captain, Lady Kitson."

"I hear you own many ships."

He ignored her statement, but not her. His gaze

swept down her widow's dress. Dark plum color, long sleeves, high neckline with the proper amount of cream-colored lace trimming it. She didn't mind the sensual way his glance brushed over her. It was purposeful and filled with interest, causing tingles of awareness to tighten her chest and stomach.

"How did you manage to get up here?" he asked, testing the strength of the limb beneath his foot.

"The same way you did, though I am willing to admit it wasn't as easy or as quick for me as it was for you."

"And I will admit you are quite accomplished to have done so."

His compliment was like a gift of fresh air. Unexpected, but heartily welcomed, since she was feeling weak from the heat and exertion of holding herself on the limb. She was certain his praise was sincere and not just flattery. She couldn't let his words pass without giving him a brief smile before saying, "Miss Periwinkle hasn't returned as swiftly as I'd expected. I hope you can save me before I lose my balance and hurt myself with this wretched collar."

"We can't have that."

"Then tell me, sir, how do you propose to get me out of this untenable situation?"

"A man should never offer to rescue a lady if he doesn't have the means to do so." He slowly bent his knees, slid his hand down to the top of his boot, and pulled out a leather-handled knife. Flickering shadows and dancing sunlight glinted off the short blade.

Relief came sweet and cooling as an October breeze. "Yes, Mr. Stockton," she said softly. "That should do it, but will the thinner part of the limb hold the weight of us both?"

His gaze fell to the branch. He was silent for a moment. That worried her.

She held out her free hand toward him. "Why not give me the knife and let me do it?"

"No, Lady Kitson," he answered, taking off the glove on one hand and stuffing it into the pocket of his coat. "You must trust me to do this."

She looked at his mouth, wide with well-defined lips, and thought about his words. If the wood splintered and broke, she would be—well—the possibility was suddenly too real and too horrible to think about. She stared into his warm, golden-colored eyes again. Because he seemed so sure of himself, she said, "Very well. Since I have little choice in the matter and even less patience or strength left to argue, let's get this done."

He reached up and grabbed hold of a different limb than the one she held, then steadied himself, too. "Turn as far away from me as you can and then place both your hands on the branch above you. Rise to your toes and lift as much of your weight as possible with your arms, and hold yourself up for as long as you can."

It wouldn't be as simple as he made it sound. Already her arms trembled from the strain of the last half hour. Yet she must do as he instructed. She couldn't twist very far without tightening the collar across her neck, but she took in a deep breath and pulled up and onto her toes.

The branch swayed down and creaked under his weight. She heard the quick intake of his breath and gripped the limb tighter and gasped, shutting her eyes tightly. Thoughts of dangling from the tree only by her collar, her feet kicking, and never seeing Chatwyn again flashed through her mind. For a moment, she thought she might scream, but then she heard a soft, masculine whisper near her ear: "We're fine."

His soothing words penetrated her fears. Julia's lashes fluttered up.

"It's going to be all right. I'm not going to let you get hurt."

Mr. Stockton was looking at her calmly. His faith that everything was going to be all right flooded her. She sensed a bond developing between them and knew she could trust him to get her down safely. He was going to save her. She gave him a hint of a nod. Cautiously, he took another step, and another, and then he was right beside her.

It had been a long time since she'd been so close to a man. The way his physical presence filled the crowded space between the branches was calming but also wonderfully stimulating. She couldn't help but notice how broad and strong-looking his shoulders were and had to suppress her innate desire to grab on to him for safety and to feel his masculine strength beneath her hand.

"I'm going to reach around you, so don't try to look at me or worry about what I'm doing," he said, in a low voice.

She was attuned to his every breath as he gently placed the back of his ungloved hand on her chin and urged her to turn her head to one side. A faint, pleasant scent of a spice she couldn't identify clung to his skin. She found the unfamiliar fragrance titillating. His touch was tender, sure, and undemanding, so she complied without complaint.

When he slipped his arm behind her, Julia's heartbeat seemed to thrum in her ears. A tantalizing shiver washed over her. She was attracted to this man and had to resist the temptation to lean in closer and take comfort from his nearness.

She felt his fingers lightly touching her nape. A shiver of pleasure washed through her again. Whirls of wondrous feelings spun inside her. She could tell he was assessing the tangle of twigs, leaves, and lace, deciding what needed to be cut and where best to do it, and not meaning to cause such womanly feelings to awaken inside her. They did just the same. It was maddening, really. Bound as she was, completely without defense, she should be frightened out of her wits, but no, she was enthralled by the rogue's touch.

"Tell me about your son," he said, his machinations squeezing the collar tighter around her neck for a few seconds.

Determined to stay steady, she fortified the strength in her arms and toes and rolled her eyes toward her rescuer. There was an easy-going charm about him that was irresistible. "Are you trying to distract me from what you're doing?"

Mr. Stockton ignored her question and asked his own. "What's his name? His age?"

"Chatwyn. He's just turned four, with hair as dark as mine. His eyes are a bright blue. He's quite inquisitive about all things but especially butterflies. He loves to be outside and running free, as I do, and—"

"Shh," he said, interrupting her as she felt the first thread break, giving her a little more moving room.

"What is this? You just asked about him and already you're tired of hearing—"

"Someone's coming," he whispered as the last thread broke, freeing her so she could move her head at will. She lowered her feet and rested one arm by her side. "Shh." With the tip of the knife, he pointed toward the ground.

Suddenly Julia heard the voices, too. Ladies' voices. Neither of them Miss Periwinkle's. They were coming closer. Apprehension gripped her with its cold, icy fingers of dread. She was no longer trapped but might still be caught.

"Look over here," one of the ladies said excitedly. "Don't you think this is the horse we saw Mr. Dryden riding?"

Julia cringed. She recognized the voice as Miss Lavinia Etchingham. Of all the people in London who could have stopped to check out Mr. Stockton's horse, why did it have to be her? She was thought to be the person who fed gossip to the scandal sheets.

"I have no knowledge of horses," a softer voice answered.

"You know some are brown, gray, or black, and some are this reddish-brown color which happens to be the color Mr. Dryden was riding when we saw him."

It sounded as if the ladies had stopped right under them, still Julia didn't dare look down. She was hardly breathing for fear they'd be noticed. "I don't know why anyone would want to ride such a big beast, though most gentlemen seem to enjoy the opportunity."

"Of course they do," Miss Etchingham remarked. "It makes them feel more powerful to have such a magnificent animal beneath them and to be in total command of it."

"How like you to be so truly improper."

"Whenever I look at Mr. Dryden I feel rather naughty."

A loud giggle from one of the ladies startled the

horse. The mare snorted and nickered restlessly. Dizzying fear ripped through Julia again. She felt her heart might beat out of her chest. Her gaze locked with Mr. Stockton's. His brow furrowed with concern.

"Oh, never mind about this horse. We're wasting time and it's probably not Mr. Dryden's animal anyway. And do walk faster, or we'll never find him before dusk overtakes us and we must return home."

After more than a few seconds ticked past, Mr. Stockton lowered his head and looked down at his chest.

So did Julia.

His shirt front and the ends of his neckcloth were rumpled into her tightly curled fist.

Chapter 2

A tremor of arousal slammed through Garrett Stockton and his pulse soared as he stared at the feminine hand fiercely clutching his chest. Lady Kitson's
touch was as explosive as lighted gunpowder to a man
who had been at sea a very long time and had only this
day put his feet on English soil. The pull of pent-up
desire made his body throb, and no amount of deep
breathing was helping to curb the ache or the force
of it. It didn't matter that she was a lady and should
be treated like one. Like the legends of the sea sirens,
she silently called out to him, and his body reacted.
It made no distinction between lady and mistress. It
only felt need.

That Lady Kitson hadn't jerked her hand away from
him the instant she realized she was holding on to him
was testament to her inner strength and keen sense of
control. For now, they would both have to endure their

vulnerability and not move until the ladies below them were far away. Not that he was in a hurry to shift away from her touch.

His gaze eased up from her soft hand to her beautiful lips, and then to her intriguing eyes. They were a rare and vivid shade of dark blue-violet, and staring straight into his. Her complexion was flawless and the color of pale parchment, except for the bright flush of heat in her cheeks. Bits of leaves and tiny pieces of twigs were scattered throughout her lush, chestnut-colored hair. Long damp strands had escaped from her chignon and framed her face.

Oh, yes, she was a beauty.

Lady Kitson's fingers slowly relaxed. She gently slid her palm down the buttons on Garrett's waistcoat until she dropped her arm to her side. His skin pebbled deliciously as he felt every inch of her light caress. It sent a hard throb of pulsating heat directly to his lower body. The madness of what it did to him threatened to overwhelm his control. His hand tightened around the limb above his head. She was making it too easy for him to imagine the hunger of his lips crushing against hers, and the thrill of his hands skimming her bare skin in passion and pleasure, the need to—Garrett swallowed down the primal desires warring inside him, fighting to take control of his common sense.

There were usually two things Garrett wanted to do after his boots touched London soil. His first stop was to visit a mistress and his second was to ride in the park. Today, he'd reversed that order. At the time, he didn't know why getting on a horse seemed more important. Now he knew. She was standing right beside him.

Seconds continued to pass. The voices faded away.

Garrett gave Lady Kitson a nod and slid his knife back into the sheath sewn inside his boot.

"That was close," she whispered, her breaths sounding as labored as his.

He hoped she didn't know how close. It wasn't only the appealing way she looked to him right now that enticed him. He was drawn to the fearless spirit that must have sent her into the tree in the first place, and the inner strength that kept her from panicking while she was there. Whether or not she'd ever admit it, that made her an adventurer, too. And she was obviously as impetuous as the day was long. How else could she have managed to get herself tangled in a tree?

"You were upset I discovered you up here."

"Yes," she whispered under her breath as she lightly rubbed the whiplashed skin on the back of her neck. "But in doing so, you saved me. Your skills with a knife are exceptional and appreciated. You knew exactly where to put the blade."

Garrett shrugged casually. He'd already received gratitude enough from the trace of her hand and the ensuing thoughts it encouraged. He cautiously moved some leaves and took a sweeping glance around the other trees and slopes near them. There were still several people enjoying the late afternoon but none venturing nearby.

"Let's get you down." He held out his hand to her.

Without further ado, she took a firm hold of his hand and quickly stepped toward him, but in her haste, one of her boots slipped off the edge of the limb. Her weight yanked her hand off the branch above her head. Garrett instinctively tightened his grip on her hand and caught her around the waist with his other arm, while quickly falling back against the trunk to keep them from tumbling out of the tree. His breath stalled, his heart thumped, and his lower body took a heady jolt of desire as Lady Kitson fell against him.

Garrett's heart was beating fast against his chest. They had come very close to hitting the ground, but she was safe, in his arms, her lips inches from his. Her breaths were as deep and rapid as his. Neither of them moved.

From beneath long, full lashes, her gaze searched his. Attraction and wanting were pulsating between them. He had no doubt she could feel the distinctive proof of his desire for her. The necessity to act on the tension and danger the moment had created was evident as they gave each other second and third looks. There was an exotic, sensuous atmosphere settling around them. The inviting scent of crushed leaves mixed with the smell of her freshly washed hair. A sheen of moisture glistened lightly across the bridge of her nose. His gaze swept down her face to linger on her lips.

Garrett felt as if all the sounds around them suddenly went silent. There were only the two of them in this space, this park, and this world. His hand pressed firmer against her back, compelling her forward. Her body was solid, but soft against him. Thin but muscled, and warm as the sunshine that flickered through the leaves. His lower stomach and body tightened with need. With his ungloved hand he gently cupped her soft cheek and cautiously let his forearm rest between her breasts. She didn't flinch. Instead, she relaxed and leaned toward him, her lips moving seductively closer to his.

He could see her features softening. Her dark lashes lowered and her mouth formed a beautiful enticing bow. Garrett bent his head ready to claim her for his own, but just before his lips touched hers, a masculine shout and the harsh snap of leather rang through the air as a carriage rolled by.

Letting out a sighing breath, Lady Kitson moistened her lips. "We almost fell." She pushed away as she reached up and grabbed an overhead limb to steady herself. Her gaze stayed steady on his. "Thank you for saving me once again."

Garrett had had a few exciting dreams in his lifetime. A few wild moments, too, but it had never entered his mind that he could one day be in a tree on a sultry afternoon with a lady who would tempt him to forgo civility and kiss her until they were both dizzy. He'd wanted to ravish her. He still wanted to.

He was sure her contemplations had been going in the same direction as his, that she'd felt the same rush of intense desire, but she was being levelheaded. They were in no position for a kiss. But to feel her lips on his, somehow he would have managed.

Garrett strengthened his stance with his feet and legs. "Take hold of my wrist with both hands and don't let go until you feel comfortable doing so."

"Stop worrying, Mr. Stockton," she said softly, grasping his forearm. "I know exactly what to do."

Garrett wasn't easily impressed anymore, but the confident lady standing beside him was making a sizable dent in his cynical perspective. Taking him to task was a refreshing change from women who usually wanted to please his every desire.

He bent his knees and lowered her as close to the ground as possible without endangering his position. As soon as she let go of him and her feet touched soil, he grabbed hold of the limb they'd been standing on and swung himself down—too close to the horse. The mare yanked her head a couple of times, nickered, and sidestepped restlessly.

"Easy, girl," he said calmly, rubbing the animal's neck with one hand and controlling the bridle with the other. "Nothing's wrong. Settle down, now."

"Is she all right?" Lady Kitson asked as she cautiously scanned the park from east to west and then looked around to the other side of the tree.

Garrett continued to pat the mare, but his attention was on Lady Kitson. "She's fine," he answered. "Just startled. How about you? Any twisted ankles or wrenched knees?"

Lady Kitson touched the damp tresses at the back of her neck and then brushed the skirt of her dress. "Nothing is hurt other than my pride." She scoffed out a soft laugh. "In her haste, Miss Periwinkle left with my bonnet, so I am in the park without a headpiece or a companion. Other than those two forbidden things, I am in perfect order."

Garrett liked the way her straight, slender shoulders moved a little when she talked. She probably wasn't even aware that she did it, but he was noticing every little detail about her. She was a widow, a mother, yet still there was a wholesome innocence about her.

Though Garrett hadn't been in London at the time, he knew Lady Kitson Fairbright's story. The sinking of the *Salty Dove* had widowed her and two friends, Lady Lyonwood and Mrs. Brina Feld. To their credit, they had overcome their loss and started a small charitable boarding school for daughters and sisters of the workers who'd lost their lives.

Garrett unrolled the horse's reins from the branch. "I'll walk with you to meet the governess. You shouldn't stay here. The ladies who stopped by might return before she does and question you. You would be at a greater risk of ridicule from being alone than being seen with me. I will walk with you."

She glanced around the park again, obviously still worried someone was close enough to recognize her. "I'm afraid the duke would see both as equally damaging to my reputation."

Garrett's mouth twitched sardonically. Her answer was proof that wealth could not equal a title and social standing in Society. Most members of Society believed that Garrett had breached the threshold between gentleman and tradesman after his father had passed. Obviously the duke was one of them.

First sons of a third son were welcomed in Society—as long as they never gave an appearance of having anything to do with what was commonly known as work.

Most of London's peerage was fine with a gentleman inheriting, buying, or winning at the gaming tables a company as prosperous as Garrett's, but what kind of gentleman could he be if he actually worked to build it into an empire? That wasn't what a proper member of Society would do, no matter how far removed he was from a title or how light he was in the pockets. It was far better to be at the mercy of a distant relative for a small house to live in and a meager yearly allowance, yet maintaining social status as a gentleman, than to earn money and prosper oneself.

Garrett's father, Alfred, had held to that belief all his life and tried his best to instill it in his son.

But he hadn't.

Barely twenty at the time of his father's death, Garrett had decided against accepting an allowance from his titled third cousin in favor of seeking his own fortune with a ship his father had won in a gambling match but had never sent to sail. Garrett set out to change that.

The old captain who lived onboard the vessel was happy to have a mission—teaching Garrett the ways of the sea. Because of the sea dog's wealth of knowledge, garnering contracts to ferry the shipments had been easier than Garrett expected. He learned quickly that smaller ships carried less cargo but reached their destination faster, which pleased traders. Undercutting his competition's pricing and carrying dangerous cargo was lucrative, too.

He'd taken foolish chances in the first couple of years of his sea life, carrying armaments of varying kinds that perhaps weren't legally sanctioned but the freights made him a lot of money quickly. Garrett didn't ask questions when the pay was good. The risks were great, but they had given him enough income to pursue more respectable shipments of wines, fabrics, spices, and all the things that made people comfortable and happy.

Then, Garrett's only goal was not to return to London as penniless as when he left. Now, ten years later, Garrett had built a burgeoning shipping empire. The hell of it was that some in Society considered that achievement unacceptable for a gentleman.

So be it.

Recriminations or regrets weren't emotions he wanted to have hanging around. He did what he had to do then, and he would now that he was back in London.

"I won't leave you unaccompanied in the park, Lady Kitson. I will walk with you," he said again.

She continued to stare into his eyes. Her caution was real. He didn't know much about the Duke of Sprogsfield, but the man certainly had Lady Kitson worried.

"My hesitancy isn't because of you in particular, Mr. Stockton," she offered. "I didn't mean to imply it was. It would be any man, I'm afraid. But that said, I do believe you were right in indicating I can hasten an end to this debacle I've found myself in by going to meet Miss Periwinkle. If the duke hears rumor of me walking in the park in such a state, I will tell him a gust of wind took off my bonnet and Miss Periwinkle had to fetch it for me."

Garrett smiled at her. The afternoon air had been as still as sea glass lying on a deserted shore. It wasn't likely the old duke would believe a puff of wind ripped off a bonnet on this day. But he liked the fact that she'd try to convince her father-in-law otherwise.

"How would you explain being seen with me?"

"With the truth, of course." She smiled, too. "You saw me at a difficult time and took advantage of me by introducing yourself."

It was worth coming back to London just for the encounter with Lady Kitson. He had a feeling he wouldn't feel the need to seek other adventures if she were around. She could give him more than enough to satisfy the wanderlust in his soul.

Fitting his hat onto his head, Garrett chuckled and then said, "Let's go in the direction you expect Miss Periwinkle to be coming from."

"Yes. Hopefully, we'll meet her before seeing anyone we know. If not, it won't be the first time I've not lived up to the duke's expectations of proper widowhood. It's just that especially now I don't want to give the duke any cause to—well, never mind about that."

Garrett wondered what she'd started to say but thought better of it. They started walking, and after a tug or two on the reins, the reluctant horse fell dutifully in line behind them. A curricle came up over the rise in front of them, but the young man driving it was in too big a hurry to pay them any mind.

"What did you do to garner the duke's ill favor?"

"I upset his plans by eloping with his youngest son. After that it didn't take much, I assure you. For a time, all I needed was to have one too many flounces sewed on my skirt or for a bow on the sleeve of my dress to come untied and he would be looking severely at me. He is a very pious and rigid man, and holds everyone to his standards."

"That must be difficult to accept for someone as independent as you seem to be."

"Yes, but it's best for my son," she answered without looking at him. "For Chatwyn, I've learned to stay on somewhat agreeable terms with the duke."

Garrett looked over at her. She had a troubled, determined expression on her face. More was going on with the duke than she wanted to talk about. She was being prudent again. Still, she'd said enough that he was curious. He wanted to know more about Lady Kitson and her father-in-law.

"I don't know much about you, Mr. Stockton, but I've heard you return to London every year or two, only long enough to break a few young ladies' hearts, and then you are off again."

"If that's true, my lady, it wasn't my intention. I return to check on my businesses here and see no reason not to enjoy the dinners, parties, and conversations when invited."

Her eyes held steady on his once again as they

walked. "It does seem Society as a whole can't make up its mind about you. Are you a gentleman or not?"

"It's a question I hear every time I come back to London. I leave that for others to decide." He pulled on the reins when the horse wanted to stop and graze. The animal shuddered a couple of times but gave up her protest and continued to clop along behind them.

"You are clever to remain silent on the issue."

Her eyes sparkled with amusement. He liked the way he felt when she looked at him. It teased him with the possibility they would have another opportunity to explore the desires that had sparked between them when they were in the tree.

Lady Kitson then looked straight ahead, and so did he. They were nearing the area in the park where the family with the three children was playing. Their high-pitched voices rent the air with youthful chatter and laughter. Not too far away from them was a man driving a wagon that looked to be loaded with baskets filled with vegetables. Garrett took it all in. Enjoying the sounds of life was always important to him when he returned to England. Through the greenery of the trees in the distance he could see the western sky melting into calming shades of orange, pink, and dark blue. The sky had grown darker while they walked, but the air stayed heavy with heat.

In the distance, he heard even more shouts from other children playing and, even farther away, the sounds of a dog barking and carriage wheels rolling over the uneven terrain of St. James. He always found the more common sounds of life cheering after so many days on a ship where all he heard was the flapping of sails in strong wind, riggings banging against the mast, and masculine voices.

"What are some of the countries you've seen, Mr. Stockton?" Lady Kitson asked when silence between them stretched.

"Turkey, India, the Americas. Too many to mention."

"According to the maps I've seen, all of them look to be very far away."

Garrett remembered the seemingly endless days and nights he'd spent at sea before land would appear as if it were rising out of the waters. "They are."

"And what cargos do your ships carry?"

"Silks for clothing, porcelains for tables, and jade for jewelry. Teas, and spices. Horses from Arabia. The East India Shipping Company can't ship everything the English, the Europeans, and the Americans are hungry for. Smaller companies like mine are needed to help them."

"I suppose I should be more thankful there are those who make the journeys." Lady Kitson looked over at him with curiosity gleaming her eyes and curving the corners of her beautifully shaped lips. "You must enjoy your life as a sojourner, Mr. Stockton."

Garrett chuckled under his breath. *Sojourner* was the ton's favorite word for him. That gave the impression he was simply a traveler and hadn't participated in the work of building his shipping company. Nothing could be further from the truth.

On his last voyage, Garrett had realized the reason he never stayed in London very long was that he didn't have a home. He intended to change that. He was going to purchase a house in London. Not just any house, but the one where he had grown up. The one that his father had said could never be theirs. Garrett wanted *that* house. And he didn't care what it cost him to get it.

"It's rumored your ships have brought secret artifacts into the country for the Prince to display in his
lavish homes."

Lady's Kitson's interest in him seemed genuine, but
he gave her a wry grin of doubt. "If it was a secret, it
obviously wasn't a well-guarded one."

"So, then it's true," she said with a breath of astonishment. "You don't deny that you have sailed for the
Prince."

Garrett sensed disapproval by her tone, but he wasn't
about to make apologies. He couldn't deny her ac-
cusation. His company had brought shipments of the
Prince's plunders to England. Garrett had never met
the Regent and had no idea what he did with his bounty.
Garrett always worked through an emissary.

He kept a steady gaze on her face as they walked.
The side of his mouth twitched with a slight smile. "Do
I hear a note of scorn in your voice, my lady?"

Their exchange of looks lasted long enough for him
to believe her attraction to him was real, no matter that
it was clear she didn't support some of the things he'd
done.

She answered with a feminine shrug, and then, as
if to give herself time to collect her thoughts, she
scanned the horizon and then to her right and left
again. He wondered what made her so skittish concerning what the duke thought about her.

"It's well-known how carelessly and lavishly the
King's son spends on his homes, for trinkets, gambling
debts, and probably other things that only a few are
privy to," Lady Kitson said.

Most everyone knew the Prince had a flamboyant
lifestyle. He'd never bothered to hide it. He had an in-
satiable appetite for many things; food, wine, women,

and gambling. He also had a keenness for beautiful and rare paintings and extraordinary art objects. Garrett wouldn't call the artifacts he brought into England trinkets. The King's son appreciated his share of oddities, for sure, but he also coveted other countries' priceless treasures.

The Prince was often vilified in articles and illustrations for his proclivities and his expenditures for furniture, renowned paintings, delicate china tureens, plates, and vases. And more porcelain than even a prince's house could hold. That was just the start of the plunder he had garnered for his extravagant collections. However, Garrett wasn't one to judge the way someone else lived his life.

"I have no firsthand knowledge of the Regent's gambling, but one thing is sure, Lady Kitson: the Prince will not take any of the treasures he's bought or otherwise collected to the grave with him when he dies. So, in the end, England will be the bountiful beneficiary of a great number of priceless artifacts one day."

"You know you are saying the end justifies his questionable acts, don't you? I probably can't even imagine half the things you have done."

She stopped walking, looked at him, and laughed softly. The merriment in her eyes and the whispery sound echoing from her tempting lips made Garrett's heartbeat trip. She was heavenly tempting when she looked at him like that. His desire to catch her up in his embrace and kiss her was strong but also impossible. He probably could have held her spellbound with tales of storms so fierce he wasn't sure he'd live to take another breath, but he didn't want to talk about himself or the Prince's lifestyle. He wanted to know more about her—a widow confident enough to start a charitable school for girls, brave enough to climb a tree, and kindhearted enough to save a butterfly.

"You were telling me about your son earlier."

"I delight in talking about Chatwyn, but don't think I don't know you asking about him is your way of changing the subject."

He affirmed her statement with a nod. "I would never expect I could fool you about anything, Lady Kitson, and I'm sure having a four-year-old son in the house would be just as adventuresome as sailing the seas."

"You are probably right about that. Chatwyn surprises me every day. He's old enough we can now have conversations—on simple subjects, of course, like birds and butterflies. But only for a short time. He doesn't like to tarry with anything. Especially with his dinner."

Garrett noticed the way her eyes brightened and her features relaxed contentedly when she talked about her son. "I don't know much about children, but I would think most boys are that way."

Lady Kitson looked away from him again and brushed her mussed hair, securing an errant strand behind her ear. The innocent gesture stirred his lower body again. The hunger inside him was as real as the early twilight and humid air. And it was more than just the long absence of a willing woman in his bed. He and Lady Kitson sensed the mutual attraction and the possibilities it would bring. He kept wanting to feel the warmth of her in his arms and the taste of her kisses lingering on his lips.

Garrett had enjoyed the companionship and pleasure of beautiful, desirable women on his travels, but his time with them was always brief. It never included leisurely strolls, inquisitive questions, or long-lingering looks. Certainly not the kind he and Lady Kitson were exchanging. In each country he visited, his main focus was always to secure cargo. He scoured markets, streets, and shops where everything from ordinary clay cups to exotic orchids were on display and could be bought, sold, or bartered. From the time he dropped anchor until he set sail again he was making agreements to fill his ships with things people wanted.

Now it was time to have something *he* wanted—the house on Poppinbrook Street. And to see Lady Kitson again.

"Perhaps I could—"

"Lady Kitson!"

At the sound of a feminine voice, Garrett turned and saw a petite young woman in a dark gray dress waving frantically at them.

"Thank heavens Miss Periwinkle remembered to bring my bonnet." Lady Kitson acknowledged her and then turned to Garrett.

A strange sensation rippled through his chest and changed the rhythm of his heart. A masculine possessiveness rose inside him. He wasn't ready to part her company.

"Thank you for your help, Mr. Stockton. I trust I can count on you to remain a gentleman about this incident and keep *my* secret."

"It's *our* secret, my lady, and it is safe with me."

She seemed to adjust her shoulders slightly in frustration because he hadn't said exactly what she wanted, but then she lifted her chin in acceptance. "Since you have traveled the world, I assume you have knowledge of a great number of subjects. I have a question for you, Mr. Stockton. If you don't mind?"

That intrigued him. "You can ask me anything, Lady Kitson."

She held her hands together tightly in front of her. "If you wanted to hide something in your house that you didn't want anyone else to see, something important. Where would you put it?"

Garrett's gaze held fast to hers. What did she have that was important enough to hide? Jewels? Money? "That depends. How big is this something I would want to conceal?"

She'd tried to sound casual, but the way her eyes narrowed when she glanced away from him showed that she was serious about this. Garrett wondered what she was up to.

Giving her full attention back to him, she answered, "Rather small, I should think. Letters, documents. That sort of thing."

That made him even more curious. What kind of documents could a duke's daughter-in-law want hidden? Property she didn't want him to know she had seemed the most reasonable thing.

"I'd probably put them in a leather pouch and bind it tightly to keep out moisture. A good place to stash something small is in a secret compartment under the floor. Cover it with a rug and then place a large piece of furniture on top of it. Another good place would be behind a wall of books on a high shelf, or if there are a lot of books in the room you could even cut out the pages and hide the items inside a very dull volume on the chemical sciences."

Her quizzical gaze connected with his again. "Yes, all of these sound very clever. What about a false-bottomed or secret drawer in a desk?"

"That would work." He nodded. "But it would

probably be the first place someone would look. If you are going to hide something, you need to make it difficult to get to. Usually, people who are looking for an object have very little time. The harder you make it for them, the better."

"Yes. I see what you mean. Thank you for sharing your insights on this with me."

Lady Kitson smiled at him and Garrett's stomach tightened. "Do you need my help with something, Lady Kitson?"

Her lashes fluttered and she took in a deep breath before she spoke. "No, not at all."

Garrett knew she wasn't as convinced she didn't need him as she indicated. He didn't want to pressure her, but asked again, "Are you sure?"

"Yes, of course," she responded more confidently. "I was just wondering for no particular reason. Now I really must bid you good day, sir."

He bowed.

Garrett watched Lady Kitson hurry toward the governess. She stopped and quickly donned a wide-brimmed straw hat, taking time to shove wayward strands of her hair beneath it before making a hasty bow with the ribbons under her chin. She then turned and looked back at him, causing another surge of wanting to tighten in his lower body. He hadn't expected her to give him any more consideration but was glad she had. He tipped his hat to her and turned away.

He didn't imagine the way she looked at him. She was as attracted to him as he was to her. Though her words didn't bear that out, he'd felt it as surely as he could feel the wind in his hair when a storm was brewing at sea. Yet she'd made no indication she'd welcome his attentions.

He couldn't blame her for being cautious about him. Probably none of the things she'd heard about him would woo a sensible lady. Why would a jewel like her want to get involved with a man who was known for being gone a year at a stretch, or sometimes longer? She had a son and would be looking for stability in a man.

Garrett felt the tug of desire again. His body was eager, but his mind ruled. He didn't want just any woman. He wanted one who was brave enough to climb a tree and turn down his attentions when he knew she wanted them.

The saddle creaked as he put his foot into the stirrup and climbed onto the back of the horse. He turned the mare around and headed back toward the tree.

Being a rogue had its benefits. Garrett would see Lady Kitson again, and propriety be damned.

Chapter 3

From her bedchamber, Julia heard boyish squeals, laughter, and the sound of small feet running down the hallway. Bigger footsteps followed, and then more delightful shrieks. Sometimes Miss Periwinkle acted as young as Chatwyn. He was supposed to be learning his letters and numbers, but clearly the young governess didn't yet have control of her charge. He was teaching her—to neglect her duties.

Which made Julia realize she was forgetting hers. She tapped the freshly trimmed quill into the ink jar and turned her concentration back to the sheet of foolscap in front of her. Promising to write the duke a few words each day about what she and Chatwyn were doing was a small price to pay for the precious freedom to be in London without the duke so she could search for his secret documents. It would be so much easier if she knew in which room they were hidden.

She assumed his private book room was the most likely place and was concentrating her efforts there, but really they could be hidden anywhere.

She bent over to sign her name and the feather of the quill tickled under her chin, instantly reminding her of Mr. Stockton's light touch at the back of her neck when they were in the tree. For those few moments in his arms she had forgotten her fear of falling to the ground—and her fear of the duke. The only thing she'd been aware of was her need to feel the rogue's lips on hers.

The heat had been stifling, and her heart had pounded at the possibility of his kiss. After four years, Mr. Stockton was the first man to have her thinking about testing the duke's directive that she restrain from any man's attentions. According to the duke, shunning all men was the only proper way for Julia to mourn her husband. It was what he expected from her—if she wanted to remain in her son's life. And that was what she'd done since her husband died.

But Mr. Stockton didn't have her feeling proper. She wasn't even feeling like a widow. His brief touch made her feel as eager for attention as a young belle attending her first ball. Why he was the first man she was attracted to since Kitson, Julia had no idea. She only knew he stirred and provoked her passions in a way she couldn't deny and hadn't wanted to ignore.

She wanted to experience and explore once again the inexplicable delight that occurred when a man and woman came together for intimate pleasure, and she wanted to do it with Mr. Stockton. There was no doubt she'd caught his eye, too. She'd felt the current of awareness that passed between them when they looked at each other a little too long. She'd felt the tremble of desire in his body when her breasts pressed against his chest and his arms tightened around her waist. She'd been so tempted to allow the kiss, and she was certain he knew it. Even thinking of the possibility of it caused an erratic beating of her heart.

Julia placed the quill in its holder and whispered, "No."

Much as she wanted to, she couldn't find a way to see Mr. Stockton and encourage him. The risk was great and she had much to do. What lay before her wasn't going to be easy. She needed to stop thinking about the rogue and kisses and be content to enjoy this time of having her son all to herself without the duke's watchful eyes. She'd had to give up so many things concerning Chatwyn to the duke's orders. Decisions that should be hers to make—when he could play out- side, what foods he should be allowed to eat, and when he left the nursery for the governess's teachings.

Julia always had to bow to the duke's will because of his threat to take custody of Chatwyn. The duke prided himself on his reputation of being a devout family man even though his second wife had run away with another man. She remembered hearing that he became all the stricter about obeying his rules after that.

The past couple of days, Julia discovered neither of the servants entered the duke's private chambers when he wasn't in residence which was good to know. He kept a minimum staff at the London house when he was away: Mrs. Desford, the housekeeper, and Mr. Leeds, the footman.

Both of them had been with the duke a long time, and Julia had no doubt they were loyal. She wasn't in a position to befriend either of them.

For all his virtuous standing in London and how

properly he treated everyone, the duke had never accepted Julia into the family. Perhaps he had just cause
for that. Julia and his youngest son, Kitson, had foiled
the duke's plans for a wealthy family merger and had
eloped. The reason wasn't that they were passionately in love with each other. It was more a defiant
matter for Kitson and a desperate one for Julia. The
duke had selected a young lady for Kitson to marry,
and Julia's uncle had his heart set on her marrying
an older viscount who already had three children.
Eloping with Kitson had been an easy decision for her
to make when he'd suggested it.

She'd never regretted that impulsive act. Their union
gave her Chatwyn.

For members of the ton, it appeared the duke had
accepted their elopement with the dignity and fairness
he showed everyone. Only Julia knew different. When
they first returned from Gretna Green, he told her he'd
never forgive her for coercing his son into marriage,
though for a time she'd thought he had. But then Kitson died at sea, Chatwyn was born, and the duke's true
feelings for her emerged. She discovered he not only
disliked her, he intended to punish her for marrying
his son. He considered she had ruined Kitson's life and
now he was trying to destroy hers by his strict rules
and the threat of taking her son.

After folding and sealing the missive to the duke,
Julia pushed away from the secretary and walked over
to the open window that looked out at the back garden. Still, tepid air met her. An uncommon and oppressive heat had gripped London for the past three days.
Windows and doors were thrown wide up and down
the street. Everyone was suffering from the effects and

hoping for a vagrant breeze to flow through their houses and shops to cool down the rooms.

Below her in the garden, she caught sight of a butterfly flittering around the withering blooms. Mr. Stockton came to her mind again. He'd never left her thoughts for very long since she'd watched him climb on his horse and ride away. How could she forget such a rousing man?

Besides, she welcomed the memory of him. How could she not when she enjoyed and longed for the feelings thoughts of him provoked? The strength that was so evident in his quick actions and his body, the unrecognizable spice that clung to his skin and teased her senses were still so real. It had been far too long since she'd pondered so intensely about kisses and caresses. Now they came so easily to her mind. She would never forget how he looked at her, as if he desired her more than any other woman in the world. He made her want to forget where they were, who he was, what was at stake and just follow the delicious feelings and sensations that welled up inside her.

Oh, it had been exciting. It had washed her with such unbelievably wondrous feelings. She had never felt such impatient spirals of desire as when she'd realized she hadn't fallen out of the tree but had landed against Mr. Stockton's solid chest. His lips would have covered hers with kisses if not for the man shouting to his horses.

Even now she wished she'd forgone her fear of being caught and allowed the kiss anyway. If she had, she wouldn't have to be daydreaming about how Mr. Stockton's kisses felt. She would know.

Julia closed her eyes and forced the pleasant feelings

away. Time to put thoughts of Mr. Stockton out of her mind. She had something much more important to think about than her feminine wishes. There would be time for that in the future. She had to focus on her goal of ridding herself of the duke's choking control before he returned. But even that now reminded her of the rogue. He would probably be off on another voyage by the time she was free to pursue the life she wanted.

However, she'd taken his advice and searched the book room floor for a secret compartment last night after everyone went to bed. Barefoot and in her night robe, she'd slowly, carefully crawled on her hands and knees from one side of the room to the other and back again, hoping to feel a lose board, raised nail, or something to indicate the wood might have been compromised and a hidden compartment may be under the floor. She'd quietly moved chairs and lifted rugs. She'd felt a few rises in the wood in some places and had checked them carefully but could find no sign of anything amiss other than aging of the wood.

The only place in the floor she hadn't surveyed was under the duke's desk, and that was because it was too heavy for her to move. Tonight she'd start the painstaking job of removing each book from the shelves, one at a time and feeling for a crack, a seam, or anything in the wall that might be suspect.

"Pardon me for disturbing you, Lady Kitson?"

Julia turned toward the open doorway and smiled at the housekeeper. "You never disturb me, Mrs. Desford," Julia responded kindly.

"Thank you, my lady." The short, slightly robust woman with gray hair and doe-like brown eyes gave her a reserved smile of appreciation. "Mrs. Brina Feld is here and wants to know if you'll receive her."

"Yes, of course," Julia whispered excitedly. She'd been anxious to talk with Brina about her plans. "There's a letter to the duke on my desk. Would you please see it gets posted to him today?"

With that, Julia lifted her skirts, then hurried out of the room and down the stairs. She rounded the doorway that led into the drawing room where she stopped abruptly. Her dear friend stood in front of the large window that overlooked the front lawn of the house. Shards of sunshine streamed across her face and silvery blond hair. Julia's old foxhound stood beside her, slowly wagging his tail. Brina seemed in such deep thought that Julia hesitated in calling out to her.

Brina Feld was the youngest and most wounded of the three widowed friends who had started The Seafarer's School for Girls two years ago. Sad as it was for Julia to admit, Brina was the only one of the ladies who had deeply loved her husband. In the nearly four years since his death, her mourning hadn't seemed to lessen. Nor had the heartbreak that losing him had caused her.

Brina was tall and slender, with a straight, graceful carriage. Everyone took notice when she walked into a room. To most of Society she was the embodiment of all a widow should be. Quiet. Proper. Staunch. Yet there was a beautiful, feminine appeal about her that any lady could envy, and some did. Most every eligible man, and many who weren't, had tried to court her since her mourning passed. Like Julia, she always kindly, but firmly, let them know she wasn't available. Their differences rested only in the fact that Julia wouldn't have minded the attention of a gentleman or two, if not for her father-in-law's promise to take her son from her if she didn't stay a proper widow. And Julia hadn't met the man who would tempt her to risk losing her son.

Until now.

Mr. Stockton entered her thoughts again. The rush of longing to have his strong arms surrounding her, pulling her up close, and his lips covering hers with kisses wouldn't leave her in peace. There was a hunger inside her that wouldn't stay away.

Julia defiantly shook the images from her mind and said, "Brina."

In a rush, the friends met with welcoming hugs and kisses to each other's cheeks.

Feeling a brush against her skirts, Julia glanced down. York woofed softly. She reached down and patted his black head. He didn't hear very well anymore, and recently she'd noticed his voice wasn't nearly as deep or strong. She bent down and gently took his gray muzzle in her hand. Looking directly into his cloudy dark brown eyes, she said, "I've already said hello to you today. No attention for you right now." Julia looked back to Brina. "I didn't expect you to come so soon, but I'm so glad you did."

"I had to. It's been over three months since we've seen each other. I wanted to dash over the minute I received your note saying you'd returned, but restrained myself to give you time to settle in."

"Tell me how you've been."

"Except for the heat these past few days, I have been well, and I do have something I want to share with you, but we are going to talk about you first. I'm dying to know how you talked the duke into letting you come to London without him. That's never happened before! Did you give him a dose of laudanum in his brandy and make him groggy enough to say yes to anything you said?"

Julia smiled. "No, but I probably would have if I had thought about it." She glanced toward the doorway behind her. "Let's move farther into the room and sit on the settee by the window. I don't want anyone to hear us so we must speak softly."

"Yes, of course. You now have me anxious, but before we begin . . ."

Brina reached over to a chair and picked up a package York was sniffing. "I can't give you one of these right now," she told the dog, and then presented Julia with a bundle of cloth that had been pulled up by the ends and tied together with a blue ribbon. "I had plum tarts made this morning for Chatwyn." She looked down. "And York, too."

"Oh, you are no friend at all," Julia admonished with a smile. "You know what an utter mess Chatwyn makes of himself and his clothing when he eats."

"I do and I insist you let him have one of these while I'm here so I can watch him eat every bite of it. York will enjoy every crumb that falls to the floor."

Julia laid the package on a side table—and out of the foxhound's reach. "Of course. I'll bring him below-stairs in a few minutes and you can give him one."

Brina made herself comfortable on one side of the deep rose–colored velvet settee and Julia the other. York, sensing he wasn't going to get a treat or any more attention, turned and slowly wandered out of the room.

"Now, tell me," Brina said softly. "What's going on? Your note said only enough to intrigue me."

Julia had needed to talk to Brina since she overheard the duke's conversation. "It's really two different stories, but I'll be brief with each."

"Don't be for me." Brina laid her hand on her chest. "I have all day."

Julia did not. She planned to spend some time in the duke's book room on the pretense of looking for a book to read.

"First, I'll tell you how I managed to get to London without the duke. He hasn't been his spry self all summer. He didn't complain, of course, but I noticed he'd sometimes wince in pain when he bent over or when he'd rise. He lacked his usual vitality in chasing Chatwyn around the house and garden. A few days ago, the duke made the comment he might be feverish. I became concerned and quite innocently asked if he thought he might have something that Chatwyn could catch. Once that fear was spoken out loud, there was no taking it back. The possibility he might have a serious condition that could pass to his grandson concerned us both. Naturally, he doesn't want Kitson's son coming down with anything. I saw this as the chance I desperately needed to come to London without him."

"It's a dream come true for you," Brina said in a normal voice, but then caught herself and whispered, "To be free of him. To be on your own."

"Yes, for more than one reason, which I'll tell you about, too, but I want you to know I don't wish a grave ailment on the duke. I only want to be allowed to live my life the way I want, but I can't wish him severe harm."

"You don't have to say that to me," Brina said sympathetically. "I know your heart."

Julia nodded. "After the duke agreed we needed to get Chatwyn away from Sprogsfield to spare him whatever was ailing the duke, I wasted no time. We left early the next morning. I didn't want to give him opportunity to change his mind. I do want him to recover. Eventually." She sighed. "But not for at least a couple of weeks or longer. A month if possible. I must be ready when he returns."

Brina clutched her hands together tightly and scooted closer to Julia. "Ready for what? I see concern in your expression."

"That is the second part of the story. I've always known the duke had two faces. The righteous one he relishes and everyone in Society and the rest of his family sees, and the coldhearted one I must endure every day. But now I have the chance to prove to everyone he isn't the man he's always claimed to be. As distasteful as it is for me, I'm going to search the duke's private rooms, every drawer, every pocket of every coat, under every rug—" Julia paused and shook her head in earnest. "I will leave nothing untouched and will not stop until I find the confirmation of his own wrongdoing and confront him for his deceitful ways."

Worry etched in Brina's face. "What wrongdoing? What will you be looking for?"

"Documents," she answered firmly. "A couple of weeks ago, I was in the garden reading. I heard the duke and Mr. Isley, his solicitor, approaching on the other side of the tall hedge. There was no reason to alert them I was there. I assumed they'd continue walking and never know I was nearby. And they did, but not far past me they stopped. I could hear them clearly." Julia paused and glanced toward the doorway again. She had no reason to believe the housekeeper or the footman would eavesdrop on her conversation, but she still needed to be careful. "Mr. Isley asked the duke where the documents on the Eubury-Broadwell

Gaming Company were kept. He replied that they were safely hidden in the London house with all the rest of his secret companies."

"Secret?" Brina asked.

"Yes. Mr. Isley responded that the duke should destroy all papers concerning that company the next time he was in London because fifteen people were killed in 'the explosion.' The townspeople were asking for help in locating the owner so they could force him to pay restitution to the victims' families. The duke said, 'Poppycock. They can look all they want. We know they will never find the owner because there is no such man. But I will dispose of the papers.' He laughed as they walked away."

"What explosion?" Brina asked. "I don't read newsprint every day. I must have missed it."

"I don't know any more than I've told you. I must find out. Most explosions happen in mines and there are many all over England. It could have occurred anywhere." Julia squeezed her eyes shut for a moment at the thought of finding that evidence and what it would mean for her. "The important thing is that I get my hands on the documents for the Eubury-Broadwell Company. No one knows he owns it and the papers would prove the duke isn't the standard bearer for how one should treat their fellow man justly. He wouldn't want everyone in Society to know he lives a lie and that he doesn't treat people fairly. It would ruin his credibility and topple the pedestal he's put himself on. I'm going to find that proof, and when I do, I'm going to tell him if he doesn't allow me to live as I choose with my son, I will make sure the true ownership of the company will be made known to everyone in Society and all of London, too."

"What can I do?" Brina asked anxiously. "Should I help you search the house?"

"My dear Brina." Julia smiled and shook her head. "Do you really want to sneak over here at midnight, slip into the house to help me look through the duke's personal chambers?"

Brina shook her head, too. "No, but you know I will do anything for you."

"It has helped tremendously just talking to you. I will manage the search on my own, though." Julia looked toward the doorway again. "After everyone went to bed last night, I took a candle into the duke's book room and carefully inspected the floor for loose boards. That is, every area except under the duke's massive desk. It's no ladies' rosewood secretary with spindle legs. I tried to move it so I could look under the rug it sits on, but it was impossible to budge. It will take someone much stronger than me to lift it."

Brina frowned. "Why did you want to look at the floor?"

Mr. Stockton's words flashed through her mind again. Julia considered telling Brina about his suggestion, and she would. Later. "For a compartment where he might have hidden his secret papers."

"Oh, yes." Brina's expression brightened with understanding. "I can see where hiding something under a big desk that isn't easy to move would be a good idea for the person hiding it. So what are you going to do?"

"I don't know." Julia inhaled deeply. "I can't ask Mr. Leeds to help me. He's not very strong, anyway. Maybe if I solicited the help of Miss Periwinkle and my maid we could move one end at a time. But I'm not sure I want them to know what I'm doing. Right now, I still have many places I can look."

"But his book room is the most logical place because he would keep all his correspondence there, right?"

"That is what I'm thinking, which is why I'll start looking behind the books for secret places in the wall."

"I wish I could help you!"

"Of course, I'll call on you if I think of anything you can do. I'm watching Mrs. Desford and Mr. Leeds to see if they have set routines. If they go up to their rooms at a certain time each day to rest, or if they leave to purchase food—anything that will give me a few minutes in the house alone to enter the duke's bed-chambers."

Julia could search his rooms at night, but the thought of being in his chambers in the darkness sent a chill over her. In truth, she'd never felt in danger from the duke, but the fear of him keeping her from ever see-ing her son again was much worse than any physical harm he could do to her.

"In any case, I will take whatever opportunity pre-sents itself. But there is something you can do."

"Anything."

"Ask your father if he knows of a recent explosion that resulted in deaths."

"I will as soon as he returns. He's visiting his brother and isn't expected back for a few days. I will ask Mama if she remembers hearing anything about it. You know she's of the mind that ladies shouldn't read anything other than poetry and the scandal sheets."

Julia laughed lightly. "I do. I've probably told you that after my uncle caught me reading *The Times* he started throwing it in the fire when he finished with it so there would be no possibility of me getting my hands on it again. He thought I was far too young to be exposed to things that were written in it. I was seventeen."

Sighing, Brina relaxed her shoulders a little. "We have been treated far too delicately most of our lives, haven't we?"

"Yes, but as you know, men are very powerful and controlling."

"Stewart was never that way."

"I remember."

A knock sounded on the front door. York barked once, but she didn't hear his nails immediately clicking on the hardwood floor. In his old age, he seemed to have lost all curiosity about who was paying a visit. And once he lay down, she knew it was a struggle for him to get up again.

Julia took in an exasperated breath and gave her attention back to Brina. "I don't know who the caller is, but I would bet my favorite slippers the duke sent a letter to someone asking them to pay me a visit to make sure I'm behaving myself." From the corner of her eye, Julia saw Mrs. Desford pass by the drawing room. "We've talked enough for now about me and my troubles. Let's talk about you. What have you been doing this summer?"

Brina brushed her hand down her skirt absently, and said, "I've been doing the usual. Reading, painting, writing poetry, and—" She stopped and sighed. "There is something that's been on my mind and I've wanted to—"

"Excuse me, my lady," Mrs. Desford said from the doorway. "There is a gentleman here to see you. Mr. Garrett Stockton."

Chapter 4

Julia's heartbeat increased rapidly. A prickle of apprehension and anticipation burst inside her. The sojourner, at her house?

A gripping sense of eager anticipation shuddered through her. He'd come to see her. She'd hoped to see him again. Even wanted to see him, but he shouldn't have come to the duke's house. That was asking for trouble, and she already had more than enough to deal with.

She glanced at Brina who looked as shocked as Julia felt. "I have no idea why he is here."

"Is he who I think he is?" Brina asked, clearly intrigued by hearing his name.

"Yes," Julia answered honestly. "I met him yesterday in the park."

"You saw him yesterday? Why didn't you tell me this?"

"I was going to, of course," Julia whispered defensively. "But I thought the other information more important. It doesn't matter. I must send him away. He can't be seen at the duke's house."

"No," Brina said emphatically, in a normal voice, and then catching herself, whispered, "For now, tell Mrs. Desford you need a moment to consider this and let's talk about it."

Julia hesitated. Her heart was racing even faster. She wanted to see Mr. Stockton again but knew the peril of doing so. The duke would never approve of her conversing with such a man. But then she saw Brina's expression tighten with determination.

Looking back to the housekeeper, Julia said, "Please ask Mr. Stockton to wait in the vestibule until you have word of whether or not I'm available."

Mrs. Desford nodded.

"Tell me everything," Brina insisted. "Now."

Though she'd hoped no one else would ever know she'd been stuck in the tree, Julia had now been caught yet again. But Brina was the one person Julia didn't mind telling.

Starting with, "I met Mr. Stockton in the park quite by accident yesterday." She quickly told Brina the most relevant information about what occurred. But, of course, how the man had stirred her with wanton feminine desires and the near kiss between her and the adventurer weren't part of Julia's confession. For now, she would keep those things from her friend. They were too intimate to share.

Brina's blond brows rose slightly, and she leaned forward slowly, as if patiently, carefully considering everything Julia had said. "I've never met him. He left

England before our debuts. I've heard he's quite a dash-
ing captain and that he may actually be a pirate."

"I don't think he's either of those things. He's just
a man." But as soon as Julia said the words she knew
they weren't true. He wasn't *just* a man. If he was, her
heartbeat wouldn't speed up to an alarming rate every
time she looked at him. Every time she thought about
him. She wouldn't be trying to convince herself she
wasn't feeling what she *was* feeling at just the thought
of him coming over to see her.

"Oh," Brina said, seeming a little disappointed he
wasn't a pirate or a master of a ship.

"You can understand why the duke must never know
about the encounter I had with him, and why—" Julia
stopped when Chatwyn let out a high-pitched, jubilant
squeal as he ran from room to room abovestairs.

Brina smiled wistfully. "I know it thrills your heart
every time you hear him."

"Yes, of course it does," Julia said softly. "I simply
couldn't bear it if the duke ever kept me from seeing him. And Chatwyn is the reason I can't encourage Mr. Stockton. I must find evidence the duke is not
who everyone thinks he is, that he has misrepresented
himself time and time again and confront him with
the truth. I can't continue to live in this kind of fear."

"You will find what you seek," Brina said confidently. "But you can't search the house right now, so
you might as well find out why Mr. Stockton is here.
Mrs. Desford already knows he's here. Either she will
tell the duke or not. Perhaps it's something as simple
as you dropped your handkerchief in the park and he's
come to return it."

"That can't be," Julia answered on a breathy note

of eagerness that crept into her voice. She did want to know why he'd come. Was it that he'd felt all the things she had yesterday? "I didn't have one with me."

"Perhaps he found someone else's and he *wants* to think it's yours."

"What are you implying?"

Brina folded her arms across her chest and gave Julia an expression that seemed to suggest she knew exactly why he was at Julia's door and it had nothing to do with handkerchiefs. "I can't believe you're going to make me say this. The only other reason I can think he might be here is because you caught his fancy and he wants to see you again. If only to make sure you have no lingering effects from being stuck in the tree for so long on such a hot day."

Julia frowned, though tingles of anticipation were washing through her at an alarming speed at the very thought of it being he simply wanted to see her again, and she had no hope of suppressing them. "Whatever his reason, it doesn't matter," she said reluctantly. "He can write a note if he wishes to inquire about my welfare."

Brina's brow furrowed again. "Though I'm not privy to anything about Mr. Stockton other than gossip I've heard over the years, I don't think he's the kind of man who writes notes to anyone. It's perfectly fine for you to invite him in and see what it is he wants. I am here to be your companion, so you aren't seeing him alone. Besides, I want to meet him."

"Really, Brina?"

"Not for romantic reasons, of course. I certainly don't have designs on him. Whether true or not, I've heard stories about him fighting pirates as well as being one. It's rumored he once stole an entire ship that was filled with grain and sailed it to starving—"

"I've heard all those stories, too," Julia interrupted her friend, and then huffed out a breath as she noticed Mrs. Desford waiting just outside the doorway for an answer about whether to turn the man away or to bring him into the drawing room.

"Mr. Stockton couldn't have done all that was gossiped about him. That would be impossible. But since you are eager to meet him, I will do you the favor and invite him to join us."

Julia looked over at Mrs. Desford and nodded.

"That's all I asked. Why did it take you so long to agree?"

"Because I wanted to put my poor judgment of saying yes to this mistake squarely on your shoulders. I can't let him stay long. He'll have his say—whatever that is—and then leave."

The sound of masculine boots walking across a wooded floor sounded down the corridor. Curls of expectancy danced in Julia's stomach.

"Just remember," Brina said. "He is interested enough in you to seek you out. No matter the reason."

Brina's words sent ripples of excitement flowing through Julia again. She wanted it to be so yet feared the thought of it, too. The duke had never minced words with her. She could continue to be a part of her son's life only if she continued to be his son's widow—a proper widow who stayed true to Kitson's memory. Right now her future was dependent on finding the information on the Eubury-Broadwell Gaming Company. She couldn't allow a handsome man to make her lose her focus on that.

"I hope I don't regret doing this," she added, more to herself than to Brina.

A moment or two later, Mr. Stockton rounded the corner and sauntered into the drawing room as comfortably as if he'd been a welcomed guest there many times. Julia savored the sight of him as he strode across the room. A warmth of fluttering excitement swirled in her chest. If possible, he seemed taller, more imposing, and more magnificent than he had yesterday. The fawn-colored coat he wore matched his golden-brown eyes and fit perfectly across his shoulders. His neckcloth wasn't fancy with lace or tied into an elaborate bow or intricate knot. His one bit of frippery was the short leather tassels that hung on the sides of his boots near the knee.

He stopped near her and bowed. "Lady Kitson, pardon me for intruding on your afternoon and your guest."

"You're not," she said honestly, embracing how wonderful it felt just to see him again. Brina was right. The deed and its damage were done. He was already at her door. Right now she could enjoy talking to him. Later she could worry about the possible consequences if the duke heard about this visit and the job she had yet to accomplish. "I'd like to introduce my friend, Mrs. Brina Feld. Brina, Mr. Garrett Stockton."

The two greeted each other politely and, no surprise to Julia, Brina didn't offer him her hand. Since the death of her husband, she was particular about whom she allowed near her. Julia knew Brina definitely wanted to examine Mr. Stockton closely, but from afar.

He turned his attention back to Julia. "I won't take up much of your time, Lady Kitson. You are looking well. It doesn't appear you've had any ill effects from the heat of the past few days."

Julia's hand automatically lifted to rub the back of her neck, where Mr. Stockton's fingers had touched her skin so lightly as he held the knife and cut the threads of her collar. "None at all, Mr. Stockton." She let her arm drop to her side. "As you can see, I'm quite well."

"I'm pleased to know that. I wanted to let you know I retrieved your butterfly net from the tree in the park."

Surprised, she looked at his empty hands. "You mean you went back to the tree and—"

He started nodding before she finished, so her voice trailed off.

Keeping his voice low, he said, "From our brief encounter, I had no doubt you are quite fearless and filled with a considerable amount of will. I thought you might go back and try to get the net out of the tree yourself. I wanted to save you the trouble and do it for you."

Julia struggled to fight the very real attraction that was developing between them. Mr. Stockton seemed to know just what to say to make her feel confident in herself, and she desperately needed that right now. It pleased her that he considered her strong and capable and filled with determination. And there was a time she would have gone back for the net. But that was before the duke had used her son to take control of her life. She had to remember that even now he could have recovered sufficiently to be on his way to join them in London.

She must keep her thoughts, her focus, her very being on finding the incriminating documents on the Eubury-Broadwell Company. Then, once she was free of the duke and his plans for her life, she would be able to enjoy and pursue the feelings Mr. Stockton stirred up in her. Her heart sank a little. If he was still in London and hadn't returned to the sea.

"That was very kind of you, sir. I had no idea you were going to do that."

After her experience yesterday, Julia had sworn off catching butterflies or any other kind of insect to amuse her son. Chatwyn would have to be patient and look at them in flight or wait for them to settle on a flower or shrub before examining them.

"Unfortunately, the netting was tangled to the point it couldn't be saved and the webbing had to be cut away. I took the liberty of taking it to a shop to have it replaced. I'll see it's returned. I hope that's acceptable to you."

"Yes, yes, of course." She felt her expression soften even more as she looked at him. If Mr. Stockton was a pirate, he was a thoughtful, heroic one. "I—it was nice of you to trouble yourself."

His gaze stayed on her. It was as if he were drinking in every detail of her face. It was odd but his attention made her feel warm and cared for. His interest in her was appreciated more than he could ever know.

"It wasn't any trouble, Lady Kitson."

"All the same, I should have thought to send someone to cut it down myself. I'm sure it would have been unsightly hanging there after all the leaves fall. Or heavens, I hadn't even thought about the possibility until now, but some other insect or even a small bird might have become tangled in the netting and not been able to get away. I should have had more consideration about it, but I'm afraid I had other things on my mind. I'm grateful you remembered. Thank you."

He nodded and turned to Brina. "Mrs. Feld, I was

sorry to hear about the loss of your husband. About everyone who was lost at sea that day." He glanced briefly to Julia and then back to Brina. "Stewart was well respected by all who knew him."

An inquisitive softness fell across Brina's face, and she took a step toward to Mr. Stockton. "You knew him?"

"Before I left London the first time, and before he met you, we spent many evenings together playing cards. He was more skilled than I at hazard and roulette, all the games. He was an expert at the billiards tables, though that didn't stop me nor anyone else from trying to beat him every chance we got. I don't know of anyone who ever had a complaint about him. You get to know a man when he sits across a card table from you. Stewart was fair-minded and even-tempered whether winning or losing. He was the kind of man everyone wanted as their friend."

"Yes, he was, Mr. Stockton," she said quietly. "He enjoyed life and took pleasure in watching others enjoy it, too."

"That's the way I remember him, too. He was a worthy opponent shooting a pistol, musket, or bow, and he could fence better than most of us."

"Stewart loved all his pursuits, especially when putting his money on a successful race." Brina breathed in heavily and smiled. "He always believed he had a good eye for a winning horse and was quite proud of all his horses."

"He was never boastful about it."

"No, he wasn't," Brina agreed. "He was quite respectful about his attributes and accomplishments. Thank you for letting me know your memories of him, Mr. Stockton. That means more to me than you could possibly know. It's been a long time since Stewart's death, and not many people take the time to even mention his name to me anymore. I appreciate that you did."

Listening to Mr. Stockton converse with Brina about her husband touched Julia deeply. His voice was even, genuine, and considerate without a hint of placating. He believed what he was saying about Brina's husband. There was nothing Mr. Stockton could have possibly said or done that would have pleased Julia more than his comforting words to her dear friend. And by Brina's sweet expression, Julia had a feeling he'd just made a friend for life.

Mr. Stockton nodded to Brina and then focused his attention back on Julia. She felt another tug at her heart as he looked at her, and she would love to be free to explore it and act on what she was feeling. Most any lady would be drawn to such a man. The difference was that Julia was no ordinary lady. She had boundaries the duke had put around her. She had to be sensible about Mr. Stockton.

He'd said what he'd come to say. Much as she would like, she couldn't let him linger.

"Thank you for stopping by, and for removing the net from the tree."

"I was happy I could do that for you, Lady Kitson."

"If you'll tell me the name of the shop where you left it, I'll pick it up and save you the trouble of having to go back and worry with it."

He was silent for a moment and seemed to be seriously considering her suggestion, but then to her surprise, he said, "It's no trouble for me. I left it there. I should be the one to pick it up and bring it back to you."

Julia's breath fluttered in her throat. She would like

that, too. But it was dangerous for her to encourage him no matter how much she liked the idea of doing so. "Perhaps you could return it to The Seafarer's School for Girls. There's a house in front of the school. I can pick it up from there."

"I'll let you know when I'm going to do that."

As if sensing Julia's frustration over the situation she was in, Brina walked over to stand beside her. "Lady Hallbury is having an afternoon tea on Saturday," she informed Mr. Stockton. "Her parties are always a delight. Julia and I will be attending."

Brina looked at Julia and smiled so innocently Julia had no choice but to return her pleasant expression and say, "Yes. We will."

"Perhaps we'll see you there, Mr. Stockton," Brina added.

Mr. Stockton nodded to Brina before his gaze swept over to Julia once again. A deep warm glow seemed to fill her. Yes. She would love to see him there.

"It was my pleasure to see you, Lady Kitson." He bowed, turned, and headed toward the doorway.

"What are you doing?" Brina whispered. "Don't just stand there." She made brushing motions with her hands. "You must at least see him to the door. Go."

"I don't need encouragement to do something I shouldn't do."

A wild squeal of merriment startled Julia. The shrieking was followed by childlike laughter and little feet rushing down the stairway.

Julia huffed. "Chatwyn knows better than to run down the stairs. I've told him a thousand times he's going to fall and hurt himself one of these days." She picked up her skirts and marched toward the corridor. "Chatwyn!" she called. "Slow down!"

She entered the corridor in time to see her son careen into Mr. Stockton at the front door. Chatwyn giggled, wrapped both his arms around one of Mr. Stockton's legs, and looked up at the man gleefully.

Chapter 5

Gasping in horror that her little boy would be so familiar as to lock his arms around a stranger's thigh, or anyone's, and be happy as a puppy while doing so, immobilized Julia. Mr. Stockton seemed completely calm. He looked down at Chatwyn, ruffled his hair a couple of times, and asked, "Who are you running from?"

"Miss Periwinkle is after me."

Julia could only manage a whispered, "Chatwyn, what are you doing?"

"Playing chase," he answered loudly, looking around Mr. Stockton's long, sturdy, and quite powerful-looking leg to stare at Julia. A gleam of youthful mischief shone in his bright blue eyes. He giggled again. "And I caught him. It's his turn to chase me now."

"What?" Julia almost sputtered the word. "Absolutely not! Mr. Stockton isn't playing with you. He is a guest in this house. Let go of him this instant!"

Miss Periwinkle made it to the bottom of the stairs and assessed what was going on. "I am very sorry, my lady," she said hastily. "I told him it wasn't playtime but he can get past me so quickly. Master Chatwyn, you must come with me at once."

Chatwyn paid no mind to Julia nor to Miss Periwinkle. He continued to stare up at the man he held hostage, seeming captivated by him. Spurred into action, Julia rushed forward, and the timid Miss Periwinkle reached for Chatwyn.

Mr. Stockton stayed the governess's hand and glanced back to the distraught Julia. "He's all right. He's just being a little boy."

"A very naughty boy," Julia whispered under her breath, stopping beside the two.

Mr. Stockton looked down at him, smiling. "It looks as if you won the game. I'm caught and can't go anywhere."

"I'm fast and strong," Chatwyn said. "Do you want to play chase with me?"

Julia listened to her son in stunned disbelief, quite humiliated by his refusal to obey her command and let go of Mr. Stockton. "He's not the duke, Chatwyn. He can't play games with you."

"Your mother's right," Mr. Stockton said goodnaturedly. "I can't play with you today, but maybe another time."

"When?" her son asked.

"I'll have to discuss that with your mother and she'll let you know."

Mr. Stockton glanced at Julia. She gave him a grateful smile. He was being kind and patient to a little boy who was misbehaving badly. Her heart softened even more toward the sojourner. "Chatwyn, you must let go of him now."

"I'm going to be tall like you when I get older," Chatwyn said, continuing to ignore his mother completely. "When I turn five, I'll be as tall and big as you are."

"You probably will."

"What's your name?" Chatwyn asked.

"That is none of your concern, young man," Julia said sternly, having had enough of her son's deliberate disobedience. "Let go of him this instant or you won't be allowed to go outside for the rest of the day and maybe not for an entire week."

"Chatwyn," Brina said, walking up to him with York ambling slowly behind. The old dog looked as if he had no clue as to what was going on in the entryway.

Brina stopped beside Chatwyn and bent down to his level. "Look what I have here in my hand. I brought you something I think you will like very much."

Chatwyn's blue gaze searched the pretty wrapped package she held. "What is it?"

She placed it close to his face, and with a smile she said, "Smell this and I think you'll know."

He leaned in and put his nose against the cloth. So did York, who had nudged in between them. There was no doubt when Chatwyn caught the scent of baked pastry and fruit filling. His eyes grew wide with delight. York's tail started wagging and he licked his chops. He might have lost his hearing but not his sense of smell.

"Mama, can I have one?" Chatwyn asked.

"Of course, but you must—"

Chatwyn didn't wait to hear more. He let go of Mr. Stockton and reached for the tarts.

Brina pulled them back just before his little hands closed around the fragrant bundle, and rose. "Not yet, my little friend. You can't eat them here in the entryway. That wouldn't be the polite thing for us to do. You must come with me and I'll give you one—or two or maybe three if you are a good boy."

"I'll be good." He looked at Julia. "I love you, Mama."

Julia's throat clogged with emotion.

"Come on," Brina said. She held out her hand to him. In an instant he reached up for her. Brina smiled at Julia. "No need to thank me. We'll be in the breakfast room if you need us."

With a bob of her head, Julia motioned for Miss Periwinkle to go with them before taking in a deep breath and facing Mr. Stockton again. Their eyes met and held. What had just happened left her feeling drained, and strangely moved by how he'd talked to her son and how he'd looked at him so calmly and didn't seem perturbed at all. She was grateful he wasn't as horrified as she was by her little boy's behavior.

Instead of following the food as a younger dog would have done in hopes of a dropped crumb or two, York decided to sniff around Mr. Stockton's boots. She reached down and tried to brush the old hound away, but he didn't obey her any better than Chatwyn had.

"I'm sorry for that display of childish behavior and his wanting to be in control," she finally managed to say and hoped Mr. Stockton didn't hear the catch in her breath. "Chatwyn is still learning his manners and, apparently, has further to go than I realized."

"He was fine. He behaves better than some of the men I've sailed with."

His words comforted her and she whispered a laugh. "I remember you saying yesterday you didn't know much about children. That can't be true. You certainly showed you know how to handle a rambunctious little boy. You didn't blink an eye at his overactive behavior."

Mr. Stockton looked thoughtful, as if he were weighing whether or not he wanted to say what had entered his mind. He must have decided against whatever it was because he looked down at York, who acknowledged him with a woof.

"What's this fellow's name?" he asked, and knelt on one knee to rub the foxhound's head, behind his ears, and down the back of his thinning fur.

"I call him York, but I don't think it matters. He doesn't hear very well and no longer bothers to be inquisitive about most things."

"He has a few years on him."

"Yes," Julia agreed softly, thinking of her fondness for the old hound. "I have no idea how many."

"So you haven't had him since he was a pup?"

"No, only a little over a year. I'm glad to see him moving around today. The journey from Sprogsfield this week was hard on his bones. But he's getting up and walking better now that he's had time to recover from being curled upon the floor of a coach for the better part of two days."

Mr. Stockton gave her a quizzical look and rose. "Does he belong to the duke?"

As if sensing he'd gotten all the attention he was going to get, York turned away from them and slowly walked down the corridor toward the breakfast room.

"Heavens, no. I found him on a street here in London. He was so thin, dirty, and hungry, of course. I brought him home with me. Since I was a child I've had a fondness for old dogs. They're so gentle and seldom seek attention like the younger ones. I only take in strays who are older and can't take care of themselves anymore. I enjoy giving a little comfort to them in the last years of their lives—no matter how long that might be. When York is gone, I'll find another to care for."

Mr. Stockton's steady gaze didn't give away his thoughts. All resolve she had not to be tempted by the adventurer fell away from her as easily as rose oil gliding across her skin.

She didn't know why, but she felt as if he wanted to reach over and touch her cheek, brush his thumb across her lips, and then let his fingertips trickle down her neck while kissing her softly. And she would have let him, but he made no move to do so. It was odd, but she had the feeling he wanted her to make the first move. She was tempted to do just that even though it was foolish to think about the possibility of doing such a dangerous thing. Mrs. Desford could walk past the doorway at any moment.

"I'm not sure I've ever met a lady quite like you before, Lady Kitson. Freeing trapped butterflies and saving old dogs. You obviously have a very tender heart."

She did have a love for all animals and couldn't bear to see them mistreated or neglected. "You forgot educating girls, Mr. Stockton," she said with a hint of pride in her tone. "With the school, I'm helping improve their lives now and for their future. They will have the skills of a seamstress when they finish and will be able to take care of themselves, should they ever need to do so. I'm quite pleased about that accomplishment, too."

He stepped in closer to her. "I don't know how I could have forgotten that."

"You probably have no idea why I'm so interested in the school, do you?"

"I know," he answered softly. "I wasn't without news of London while away. I received mail in India and Turkey. I mentioned my childhood friend who will be getting married, Wiley Calder. He and my manager, Mr. Urswick, keep in touch with me when I'm away. Whenever letters or financial papers were sent to me, newsprints and other readings from home they thought might be of interest were always included."

Julia puffed out a soft laugh. "By *other*, do you perhaps mean the gossip pages and scandal sheets? Do you dare admit you read them?"

He met her teasing with all the confidence a rogue should have. "I read each one and was happy to get them. No matter how far away I was, how eager I was to see different places and experience the different customs in the world, I was always eager to receive news from England."

"I'm sure I would be that way, too. Why do you stay away for so long each time?"

"There has never been a reason not to. Mr. Urswick is the most intelligent man I've ever met. He's a genius with numbers and details. I trust him to manage the day-to-day business of my company."

"You are fortunate to have him and such trust in what he does for you."

Mr. Stockton nodded.

With conflicting emotions, she said, "You didn't come over here just to tell me you went back to get the butterfly net, did you?"

"No," he said with remarkable ease, taking a step closer to her. "I wanted to see you again."

A delicious tingling sensation rippled through her chest and spiraled down to her abdomen. She'd wanted to see him again, too, and was glad he'd admitted it even though she couldn't. He was a rogue with no ties and no restrictions. He could be forward. She liked that.

She didn't need to have what he was implying spelled out for her. It was probably scandalous of her to want to know. Yet she couldn't seem to stop the word "Why?" from slipping off her tongue.

He remained at his comfortable stance and offered, "I wanted to know if seeing you today would make me feel the same way I felt when I first saw you standing in the tree."

Unable to bear not knowing, she asked, "What is the answer to that?"

"I do feel the same way." His gaze was intense but his voice soft.

Her throat tightened, shortening her breaths even more. His answer led to more questions she didn't need to ask, didn't need to know the answer to. He admitted his attraction to her was as real as hers was to him. That should have been enough. She didn't need to fuel the fire going on inside her, but one thought was saying, *Don't ask anything else. He is nothing but a danger to you. Show him the door.* But another, stronger voice was demanding she ask him, *How do I make you feel? Tell me everything you are feeling and make me yearn for your touch.*

Their gazes stayed locked together. The seconds tumbled by, one after the other. Neither of them moved. There was a warm glow in his eyes that made her feel exceedingly precious, wanted and longed for.

"What did you feel when you saw me yesterday, Mr. Stockton?"

"Desire for you. I still want you in my arms. I want to feel your lips on mine. You felt the same for me, too."

Yes, she'd felt heavenly desire for this seafaring man who had reportedly fought pirates, dueled gentlemen, and dined with monarchs around the world.

All of that made him an exciting man to think about, to wonder what his touch and kisses would be like, but that wasn't all that drew her to him. She had no knowledge of whether those stories were true. She desired the man before her now, who understood a little boy's eagerness to be tall and brightened Brina's day with a few kind and simple words about a husband most had already forgotten.

Julia's heartbeat went from slow and steady to hard and fast. She had no idea how long Mr. Stockton would be in London. It might be only a short time before he headed back to sea. If she was ever going to defy the duke's decree she rebuff all men, Mr. Stockton was exactly the kind of man she needed to be involved with. He wouldn't court her openly, with thoughts of marriage on his mind—something she couldn't possibly consider. His sojourner's way of life would never fit in with that. Their desire was mutual. Could she dare think about a safe and secret way to be with him so she could feel the strong, sure touch of his hand against her skin?

He wasn't hurrying her for an answer, only waiting for an invitation he had to know she wanted to give. That made him even more attractive to her.

Julia wanted to ask him to meet her where they could be alone and share those kisses he spoke about.

She opened her mouth to let him know she would consider a secret rendezvous with him, but then she heard Chatwyn laughing. His gleeful boyish sounds pulled at her heart.

What if she were caught and the duke found out? She couldn't take the chance of losing her son to spend a few moments, a few hours, or a few evenings with *this* man, no matter how tempting he was. For now, fear of what the duke could do would continue to control her.

Julia sucked in a deep breath and walked over to the side table. She picked up Mr. Stockton's hat and extended it toward him.

"Thank you for stopping by, Mr. Stockton."

He gave her a long, hard look but didn't take the hat. "I meant it when I said you could trust me, Lady Kitson."

She believed him. Perhaps it was because of the bond she'd felt with him when he'd saved her from that wretched tree and their near fall. She sensed he'd felt it then and again now, too. Thoughts started churning in Julia's mind.

"In that case, if you don't mind, I do have another question for you, Mr. Stockton."

"I am at your pleasure, Lady Kitson."

Julia cleared her throat. "I know you haven't been in London very long, but have you heard anything about a recent explosion in a mine? A dreadful accident where lives were lost?"

He quirked his head and gave her a questioning expression. His interest was clear.

"It's an odd question, I know," she hurried to add. "I thought there might have been something in the morning's newsprint, or perhaps you heard talk in one of the clubs or—wherever you might have been last night."

"In a mine, no."

Julia's spirits plummeted.

"There was a short article in *The Times* this morning about an explosion in Manchester about six weeks ago that brought down several buildings. More than a dozen people were killed."

"Yes, that must have been the terrible accident I heard about," she said. "The entire town must be in mourning. Did the article say anything more about it?"

"They discovered that one of the buildings—a gaming house—was storing barrels of gunpowder. No one knows what ignited it and there was no reason to believe it wasn't an accident. The men who worked there and several patrons were killed in the blast. They're still trying to locate the man who owned the building. He seems to have vanished. And no wonder, the amount of gunpowder it would have taken for such destruction should never have been stored on a busy street. Could that be what you're referring to?"

"Yes," she murmured softly. "That must be what he was talking about."

"Who, Lady Kitson?"

Julia blinked. "It was a conversation I overheard. I didn't have the details of what happened. That's why I was asking about it. I hope they find the man who owned the building and he's forced to help the town recover. Thank you, Mr. Stockton. What you told me has helped me tremendously. I didn't know what kind of explosion it was. Only that it was recent and people were killed. Do you remember if the article reported

the name of the company that was storing the gunpowder?"

"Eubury-Broadwell Gaming House."

Julia suddenly felt lightheaded.

"Why don't you tell me why this information is so
important to you?"

Should she confide in him? Could she trust him
to keep her secret? If she did, was there anything he
could do? She couldn't ask him to help her search
the house for the documents and see to it that the
duke took responsibility for the tragedy and helped
the victims. Yet, because of a twist of fate, she felt an
uncommon bond with the adventurer, but she didn't
know if it was wise to act on that. She wanted to accept she could trust him. Suddenly the doorknocker
sounded, making her jump. No, it was best she keep
this information about the duke and his hidden companies to herself for now.

"Thank you, Mr. Stockton. You've been very helpful." She looked down and saw that her hands had
made tight fists on the brim of his hat. "Here you go,"
she said, giving it to him as Mrs. Desford came down
the corridor toward them.

Julia and Mr. Stockton moved to the side of the vestibule for the housekeeper.

"If you should need me, Lady Kitson, I'm staying
at the Holcott-Fortney Inn. Send me a note."

She nodded once as Mrs. Desford opened the door.
"I hope that won't be necessary."

He smiled at her. "I hope it will."

A man of average height, dressed in black except for
his shirt and neckcloth, stepped into the vestibule and
removed his hat. He had a round, full face with large
green eyes that seemed to pierce Julia. He carried a

well-worn brown leather satchel. He bowed to Julia and dipped his head toward Mr. Stockton. She didn't know why but she took an instant dislike to the man.

Mrs. Desford continued to hold the door open, no doubt expecting that Mr. Stockton was going to exit through it, but he remained by Julia's side. He must have perceived that just the appearance of the stranger unsettled her.

"I'm Mr. Oren Pratt, here at the request of the Duke of Sprogsfield, my lady. I'm to tutor Master Chatwyn."

"Tutor?" Julia asked anxiously as a feeling of foreboding curled inside her. "I don't understand. For what?"

"I am to take over instructing the duke's grandson in his lessons during the day."

Julia stared at the man, astounded. "What do you mean? He's just turned four. He's too young to have such strict structure in his life, and if the duke doesn't know that, you should."

With an air of superiority, the man lifted his chin. "One is never too young to begin learning. The sooner he starts, the more advanced he will be. I'm to start his formal training."

"Formal? That will begin when he goes to Eton." She glanced at Mr. Stockton. He was intently listening to every word that was said.

Mr. Pratt reached into his coat pocket, pulled out a letter, and handed it to Julia. "This is from the duke. I assume it will explain everything to your satisfaction."

A dizzying swell of anger replaced astonishment as she took the letter and squeezed it in her hand. Julia felt as rigid as the tutor looked. "No, Mr. Pratt. I can assure you it won't."

He merely smiled condescendingly and said, "I have

my instructions from the duke, my lady. If you'll introduce me to the child, I'll begin."

Instructions indeed! Despite the warm day, she shivered. A deep, suffocating weariness stole over her. Even in sickness the duke intended to maintain control over her and Chatwyn. This was madness. Her little boy was too active to be made to sit in a chair for hours a day. He still needed the relaxed instructions Miss Periwinkle gave him. It was unfair that the duke allowed her no say in Chatwyn's life.

Sick or not, she should have known the duke had something up his sleeve when he agreed that she could come to London without him. This was just the duke's way of making it clear to her she would never be free of him, never be allowed to live her own life as she chose. Who was she to think she could take on the duke and win?

Not knowing exactly what she was going to do, Julia turned stiffly toward Mrs. Desford. "Would you please show Mr. Pratt into the drawing room and have him wait for me there?"

"Yes, my lady."

Mr. Pratt stared at Julia. For a moment, she thought he was going to take her to task or refuse to leave. But then, after a parting glance at Mr. Stockton, he turned and followed the housekeeper.

Julia tried to hide her seething anger when she gave her attention to Mr. Stockton once more. The way he studied her face intently, she knew he wanted to make sense of what was going on. She knew he wanted to help her. But what could he do about the tutor or the duke? What could he do about any of her troubles other than make them worse? If that were even possible.

"That man seems determined to do the job the duke sent him to do."

"Yes," she answered tightly. "For now, anyway."

"Would you like for me to have a word with the man?"

"No, no, of course not. I will post a letter to the duke immediately and hopefully be able to clear this up quickly."

The corners of his mouth tightened. "I think you need my help in some way, Lady Kitson, and you are afraid to ask me."

His words stole over her like a warm shawl on a chilly night. Once again she had an overpowering need to reach out to him. He would only be in London for a short time and then be on his way to another country. Surely her secrets would be safe with him.

While she contemplated a way to respond to him, his eyes continued to search her face, encouraging her to trust him. But how could she? Mr. Pratt wouldn't stay away just because Mr. Stockton asked him to. She was sure the duke was paying the tutor a handsome sum. In fact, he probably wasn't just a tutor but also a spy sent to watch her every move each day.

No, as much as she would like to see Mr. Stockton again, confide in him, it was best she not be seen with the sojourner.

"Thank you for the offer, Mr. Stockton, but I am fine. I must bid you good day."

Chapter 6

Garrett stood on Lady Kitson's front steps and crushed the brim of his hat in his hands almost as hard as she had. She not only stirred his passions, she stirred his desire to protect her. He didn't like the idea of Mr. Pratt trying to teach Lady Kitson's little boy, either. And when to hire a tutor should be her decision. Not the duke's. Garrett was tempted to turn around and walk back into the house and insist she tell him what was going on. Why was the duke forcing this tutor on Chatwyn? What kind of documents was she trying to hide, and what did an explosion have to do with any of it? And what had her so frightened at the thought of asking him for help?

Lady Kitson wasn't a lady who lacked courage or resolve. Something vital was at stake for her and he wanted to know what it was. The problem was that she wasn't ready to confide in him and trust him to help her. He could understand that. Maybe. She was cautious. He could appreciate that, but surely she couldn't consider him a stranger anymore. Something kept her from confiding in him.

Placing his hat on his head, Garrett walked down the steps to the street. He untied his horse, climbed onto the saddle, and headed toward St. James Park. He hadn't expected to arrive in London and be immediately and totally consumed by thoughts of an alluring lady and her intriguing state of affairs. He was used to planting his feet on dry soil and immediately taking his pick from a number of women willing to satisfy a seafarer.

After his encounter with Lady Kitson, he hadn't wanted to pay a visit to a mistress. He'd only wanted to retrieve the widow's butterfly net. She was the only lady on his mind.

He'd settled into the Holcott-Fortney Inn and had sent a message to Wiley that he'd arrived in London, asking him to meet at their usual place for a ride through the park. After that, he bought a bottle of the inn's finest brandy and found an empty chair at one of the tables in their card room. That's where he'd spent most of the night.

At first awakening this morning, his head pounded and his body ached with unfulfilled desire. He cursed himself for deciding to pursue gaming and an over-indulgence of brandy instead of the comforts of a soft, willing woman. He'd planned to rectify that mistake today. Now, after seeing Lady Kitson again, he knew why he'd come to that surprising conclusion yesterday. And difficult as it was to endure, it was still the right one for him. Strange as it was to admit, Lady Kitson was the only one he desired. And for now, he was going to have to live with the pain that caused.

Bright sunlight made the sky blue as a sparkling gem, but it also made the air still and hot as Hades. He passed a man in a rumbling wagon filled with rattling milk cans, baskets of vegetables and firewood as he entered the park. Garrett tipped his hat to the farmer, and then nudged his horse to go faster. Obviously, the midday heat hadn't kept anyone inside. The park was bustling with people strolling about, sitting on blankets, and riding in their carriages.

Garrett had never returned to London to win favors or to reacquaint himself with anyone in the ton other than Wiley Calder, though oddly enough, Garrett was usually in Town less than twenty-four hours before the first invitations to dinners and parties started arriving. He always assumed Wiley was responsible for making it known the sea adventurer was back. Interest in him was always the same. There were those who sought him out to hear about his travels and those who questioned his right to continue to be a part of Society's small circle.

His friend since childhood, Wiley had always understood Garrett's desire to make his own way in life, and his fascination with the world that lay beyond England's tight shores. But Wiley never had the inclination to visit any of the places Garrett had been. A third son himself, Wiley was content to live in London, enjoy the fringes of the lifestyle that befitted an untitled son, and stay a gentleman—living off the allowance his older brother handed out to family members who had no lands or other income-producing properties to sustain them.

Garrett's father, Alfred Stockton, had been that way.

Alfred had no problem accepting the pittance of allowance and a house to live in from his second cousin, an earl and the patriarch of the family. To Garrett's father, it wasn't money that counted; it was lineage, upbringing, and family standards that were important. He'd been happy to live in the small house where the two Stockton men had been granted a home. Alfred never understood why his son didn't feel the same way.

For Alfred, gambling had always been a dependable source of extra income. Not only was he good with a deck of cards, the roll of dice, and at the billiards tables, but he also had an uncanny ability to read people and know if they truly had a winning hand. Luck always seemed to follow him, no matter what game he chose, but he had no desire to even think about using his skills to start a business. He was affronted when Garrett had suggested it.

That was for tradesmen. Not gentlemen.

Garrett's horse galloped up and over a gentle slope in the terrain. In the distance he saw Wiley waiting under the elm where he'd rescued Lady Kitson. The old tree had been his favorite to climb when he was a youngster. Its low branches were wide and sturdy. It amazed Garrett that she'd managed to climb high enough to reach the spindlier limbs.

Wiley was a tall, lanky man with thin brown hair as straight as a board. For as long as Garrett had known him, he had worn it longer than fashionable and was often seen brushing the front length of it away from his forehead. The almond shape of his eyes, long bridge of his nose, and generous, big-toothed smile made him look as friendly as he was.

When Wiley caught sight of Garrett, he mounted and rode out to meet him. He maneuvered his horse to fall in beside Garrett's. They shook hands firmly and then hugged briefly across the horses. The skittish mare snorted and sidestepped, tossing her head, not wanting the other animal to crowd her.

"I was beginning to think you hadn't received my answer that I'd be here," Wiley said in his calm, good-natured way.

"Something came up that delayed me. It's good to see you, my friend. You're looking fit. Obviously, life's been good to you."

"Better than I deserve," Wiley said with a wide smile.

"I have no doubt of that."

His friend wasn't a man who wanted much more out of life than what he already had. That kind of contentment was difficult for Garrett to understand. He'd asked Wiley to sail with him and be his partner, but Wiley had no interest in the life Garrett wanted.

To Garrett's knowledge, Wiley had never traveled much farther than a day's ride from London. He was occasionally asked to spend a week or two in the summer or at Christmastide with his oldest brother, who was a viscount. The greater portion of the year he spent in London, doing the same things most gentlemen of leisure did each day: reading the newsprint in the morning and then discussing all that was of interest with the gentlemen at one of his clubs.

On any given day, if news and gossip were scant, the gentlemen would play cards or billiards. They would attend weekly fencing matches, horse races, and cock fights, or pay a visit to their mistresses. If it was a busy day, a gentleman could manage an appearance at more than one or two events. Late afternoons and evenings would more or less be a repeat of the day, unless someone was hosting a dinner party in their home. Only then might their routines change. Garrett wasn't interested in such a sedate life.

"I know you usually find your way back to London in the spring," Wiley offered. "I'm glad you made an exception this time, but you realize there won't be as much trouble for us to get into with most of our debauched friends off to their summer homes and the clubs and gaming halls empty of their best card and billiards players."

"Chances are we'll find someone who wants to start a row." The two men laughed. Garrett hugged the mare with his knees, urging the lazy animal to keep going.

"To tell you the truth, I'm not going to the clubs as much as I used to," Wiley admitted. "I want to take care of Miss Osborne properly after we wed, and if I have to give up wagers on daily card games and drinking until dawn, I'm willing."

"That's probably a good way to keep her happy."

"So, if we're going to get into a little trouble while you're in Town, we should make it soon. I doubt Miss Osborne wants me to be wearing a black eye when she returns to London."

Garrett chuckled. "I remember the days when both of us would wear them quite often. I promise not to lead you astray. One of the reasons I'm here is to make her acquaintance and to see you are wed. That includes making sure you look your best on that day and with your pockets plump."

"I think you'll like Miss Osborne," Wiley said with an innocence in his voice that seldom showed.

"I already do. She had the good sense to see through all your faults and decide to marry you anyway."

Wiley snorted a laugh and nodded a greeting as they passed an older gentleman who was also riding. "That she did. Some days I still can't believe she agreed. I'm not sure when she'll be back in London. How long are you staying this time?"

That question made Garrett think. He didn't usually stay in London more than a couple of weeks. A month at the most. He didn't want to think about leaving right now. He knew Lady Kitson needed him whether or not she was ready to admit that. "As long as it takes to see you wed."

"Good. She'll write once her parents have decided when they'll be returning."

"But before Christmastide?" Garrett asked with a grin.

"You can be sure of that."

They rode in silence for a few moments before Garrett said, "There's another reason I came to London."

"My wedding wasn't reason enough?"

"Of course, but I want to buy a house."

"Really?" Wiley's eyes narrowed suspiciously as he looked over at Garrett. "In London?"

"Why does that surprise you?"

"Why wouldn't it? You've never wanted to stay in London long enough to have a home. Does this mean you're finally ready to put your traveling boots under just one bed and keep them there?"

For now? Yes. Forever? Garrett didn't know. He couldn't explain it to himself and he wasn't going to try to make Wiley understand. Garrett was all right with that uncertainty for now. Buying the house where he grew up was what mattered. Not what brought him to that reasoning. Lady Kitson crossed his mind. Yes, right now he only wanted his boots under her bed. He didn't know when that would happen, but he was willing to wait for her.

He gave Wiley the only answer he could. "I don't know."

"Fair enough. It's always good to have you in London no matter how long you stay."

"I want to buy the house on Poppinbrook Street from my cousin."

Wiley brushed his hair from his forehead and tucked it under the brim of his hat. "You look serious about this."

The sun beat down on the back of Garrett's neck. "I am."

"You can buy any house in London you want, but believe me, you don't want that house."

"I do want to buy that house."

"Then you'll need to talk to someone other than your cousin. The house was sold to Mr. Peter Moorshavan over a year ago."

Garrett took in that information. It hadn't crossed his mind that the house might now be owned by someone else. That could be a wrinkle he hadn't expected but he hoped not. "I don't know of the man, but it might be easier to buy from him than from the old earl."

"I'm not sure about that."

Wiley pulled his horse up short and stopped him so Garrett stopped, too. Both horses nickered and pulled against their bridles.

"I never met him, but from what I heard everyone thought Moorshavan was simply a wealthy man from the Americas when he moved into the house. Many of his neighbors befriended him. Until, according to rumor, it was learned the man had opened a hidden brothel in the house."

Garrett digested that bit of information as he remembered the house where he was raised. It was small—the drawing room, the front lawn, and the back garden. All of it. But it was something that his father had said could never be his. Did it bother Garrett that the house had been turned into a brothel? No. It wouldn't change his plans.

"I'm not one to judge any man or woman about how they choose to make their living," Garrett said.

"Most would agree. And while many gentlemen in Society might on occasion have reason to visit such a place, none of them want to be associated with anyone who actually owns one—and they especially don't want one on their street. I heard the Lord Mayor and a few other gentlemen paid Moorshavan a visit and he and his women were gone the next day."

"So he should be willing to sell?"

"I don't know. Others have asked about him, but no one has heard from him since it was discovered what he was doing."

"Then he's probably ready to get rid of it." After being a sojourner for so long, needing a home wasn't something Garrett could explain. He had stayed in inns as grand as the Holcott-Fortney, run-down taverns with rooms only big enough for a makeshift bed, and slings in the bottom of a ship. Now he wanted his own home. He wanted his first house to be the one his father could never have dreamed of owning, because of the life his father chose to live at the mercy of his wealthy relatives.

"I want the house on Poppinbrook Street," Garrett said again.

"All right. I can ask around the clubs about the man and see if anyone has heard from him, if you want to buy it and live there."

"I don't want to live there," Garrett said. "I want to tear it down." It wasn't something he could rationalize and he didn't try to. Perhaps it was that in doing so he would also demolish the old guard rule that a man couldn't be a gentleman and a tradesman. It was time for him to move beyond the past. He was committed to removing every board of it and replacing it with a house that reflected the man he was today.

Garrett nodded. "Yes. See what you can find out."

Wiley rested his forearm on the horn of his saddle. "I'll keep you posted."

Garrett knew Wiley had questions but he kept them to himself. "What do you know about Lady Kitson Fairbright?"

"As much as anyone, I guess. Why are you asking?"

Garrett's horse snorted and shuddered beneath him. He nudged the mare to start walking again. "I met her here in the park."

"Hmm." Wiley brushed his hair again and moved his horse alongside Garrett's. "I didn't know she was back in London. I haven't seen the duke at White's or heard about him being in Town. Usually everyone is on their best behavior when the Duke of Sprogs-field's around."

Garrett wasn't interested in the duke. "What do you know about Lady Kitson?" he asked again.

Wiley looked away and seemed to ponder what Garrett asked. They passed a lady and gentleman walking and acknowledged them by lifting their hats off in greeting.

"I probably don't know much more than you, since you saw her. She's lovely, widowed, and has a son. She and two of her friends are benefactors of a girl's school in St. James."

"What else?" Garrett asked, eager to hear something about the intriguing lady that he didn't already know.

"She's fond of animals." Wiley chuckled. "Why don't you just come out and ask me if she's available to pursue?"

Fair enough. "Is she?"

"Not from what I understand."

Garrett's stomach squeezed and his hands tightened on the reins. "She has a lover?"

"I haven't heard about one if she does."

"Then what the devil would make you say she's unavailable?" Garrett asked, feeling a sudden rise of impatience to know all he could about Lady Kitson.

"Because she brushes off every man who's tried to openly court her or have a secret affair with her. I've heard the talk. Believe me, men have tried. I mean—why wouldn't they? She beautiful, young, and from what I understand has quite a substantial amount of property in her own right."

"What are the rumors as to why she rejects all offers?"

Wiley shrugged. "It's anyone's guess. Some say it's because the duke controls her life and forbids it."

That comment made Garret's stomach twist. He didn't like the idea of anyone forbidding Lady Kitson to do anything. And he'd wager a gold coin she wouldn't like it, either. She wanted to hide something— probably from the duke. Garrett was more determined than ever to find out what it was and to help her.

"Everyone knows how devoted the duke is about all his family following the strict dictates of Society," Wiley continued. "He's disowned more than one nephew for not living up to the high standard he expects. But

I think most agree Lady Kitson is involved with only one male and that's her son."

"What about her marriage? Was she happy?"

"As far as I know." Wiley shrugged again and gave Garrett a sideways glance. "How am I to know? I wasn't a close friend to her husband. I only know that her uncle wanted her to marry a man twice her age, but she eloped with Lord Kitson instead."

Nudging his horse to move, Garrett smiled at Wiley's comment. He could see Lady Kitson having the courage to elope with the youngest son of a duke. And he could also see the duke being extremely upset about that.

"Can you get me an invitation to Lady Hallbury's party Saturday afternoon?"

"Did Lady Kitson just happen to mention she'd be there?"

"No. Someone else did."

Wiley laughed. "I'll see what I can do."

Chapter 7

"Thank you for going slow," Julia called up to the driver before stepping into the coach.

She was a fusspot when it came to how animals were treated. If it were in her power to see it done, she wanted them given the same care and provisions all people should receive. Pulling a carriage all day was tiring for horses, so she always insisted the driver take his time—even if she was running late for an appointment or an event.

Julia settled her skirts around her as the coach took off with a lurch and a rattle. She looked over at Brina and smiled. "Thank you for coming by for me."

"It was the least I could do after I said you'd be joining me for Lady Hallbury's party when you didn't even know about it. Besides, I always want you to be my companion when you're in Town. It gives me an opportunity to be away from Mama for a while."

"I know, and I am looking forward to the party," Julia said earnestly. "It's just that the past three days have been difficult."

"I know you were searching for the duke's documents. I take your comment to mean it hasn't gone well and you haven't found them." Brina leaned forward. "But please tell me you didn't get caught."

"No. I've been very careful. It's frustrating I haven't found the incriminating deed to the property so I can prove the duke owned the Eubury-Broadwell Gaming House." Julia sighed quietly. "I've managed to thoroughly search one section of the duke's book room walls, and the flooring—except for the space under his desk, which is impossible for me to get to."

"What about his private chambers?"

"Not yet, and I still have hope I'll find a hidden space behind the books on a high shelf and won't have to go into them. It would be difficult. Mrs. Desford never leaves the house. Mr. Leeds takes care of all her errands outside the house. For now I'm still opening each book and looking at the wall behind it. It's time-consuming as some of the books are quite large and difficult to move and there are so many."

"Oh, Julia, you must let me help you search the house," Brina insisted. "You can invite me over for dinner and I'll come up with a reason to stay late."

"I doubt I could persuade Mrs. Desford to retire before you left. I am making headway through the books, but it's just not fast enough for me because I don't know what day the duke might return." Julia pressed into the back of the plush velvet cushion and sighed. "The worst thing is that now I am having to cope with the tutor the duke sent for Chatwyn's lessons. It's been an absolutely disastrous situation."

"I was there when he arrived but, of course, didn't meet him and you couldn't say much about him before I left. I don't understand this. Chatwyn should be under Miss Periwinkle's care for a few more years."

"Yes, and he will but Mr. Pratt brought me a letter from the duke saying he thinks it's time to begin a more formal education for Chatwyn to start preparing him for Eton. Including his religious training. The man he sent is simply a beast, and unrelenting in wanting Chatwyn to sit in a chair for six hours a day and practice lettering and numbers. We've had more than one row about it and, of course, Chatwyn cries and clings to me. This perturbs Mr. Pratt. He tries to insist I leave the room but I've refused to leave Chatwyn alone with the man."

"I didn't know all this. I'm so sorry and don't blame you for being upset. He sounds like a monster. But, oh, what about today? Is Chatwyn alone with him?"

"No. Never, if I have anything to say about it. When Mr. Pratt arrived this morning, I told him Chatwyn had a stomach issue and he couldn't possibly be expected to sit still and endure lessons today. He said he'd return on Monday. So between my searching the book room, the tutor, and my wayward thoughts about Mr. Stockton—but no, no, Brina, enough about me and my troubles. Please let me hear something about you for a change."

"But I want to know—what it is about Mr. Stockton that has you on edge?"

Julia smiled softly just thinking about him. "He reminds me of how I long to be free so I can have a man call on me. He has me thinking of kisses and caresses. Being held, and—no man has made me feel the way he makes me feel when he looks at me. He reminds me just how desperately I want to be free to enjoy my life on my terms." Julia moistened her lips and took in a steadying breath. "But again, I don't want to talk about me anymore. Tell me something about you."

Brina looked down and smoothed the gloves on her hands. "There is something but I haven't wanted to tell you because I'm not sure you will approve of what I've been doing."

Brina's matter-of-fact tone caused a slight chill to flutter over Julia even though the coach was quite warm. "I'm surprised that you think I wouldn't support whatever it is. You wrote to me that you were going over to the school once a week to read to the girls, much to your parents' angst. I heartily agree with that, so what is it you think I won't approve of?"

"This has nothing to do with the school." Her blue eyes turned pensive. "I couldn't mention this matter to you in a letter, but now that you are here, I would like to talk with you about what I've been thinking."

Julia felt a sudden tension in the back of her neck. "What's disturbing you? You know you can tell me anything."

"I hesitate because of the seriousness of my thoughts." She paused and looked out the window for a few moments. "I'm thinking about the possibility of joining the Sisters of Pilwillow Crossings."

It took a moment for the meaning of Brina's words to sink into Julia's mind and when they did, she stared at her, truly unable to say anything for a few moments. "But that is a—a—"

"A convent, an abbey," Brina said without hesitancy,

"are probably the best names for it. Though not all the women who serve there are nuns, and it's really so much more than that. It's a community of women. Good women who unselfishly do good works for unfortunate people here in London. Their doors are open three days a week to serve a cup of soup and a slice of bread to those in need. Two of the sisters spend those three days attending anyone with wounds and handing out poultices and tonics they make. All of them sew, knit, and bake bread the other four days. I suppose they have time for their services and readings, too. But they have a purpose to their lives, and that appeals to me."

"All right," Julia said calmly. "You want to help them. How? You don't know how to bake bread."

"But I can learn," Brina argued, unapologetic and a bit defensive. "I want to do something more than just get up in the mornings and dress for a walk in the park, or dress in the evenings to sit at someone's dinner table and make idle conversation."

"But that is what you're supposed to do. You are well read, and because of that you're quite engaging with your knowledge on many subjects when you are a guest at someone's house and sit down at their table. You play the pianoforte so beautifully and with so much feeling everyone wants to listen when you entertain. I've read your poetry. It's thoughtful and inspiring. You helped start The Seafarer's School. Why would you think you have no purpose in life?"

Brina turned away from Julia and glanced out the window before looking back into Julia's eyes. There was a sadness in Brina that Julia knew was always there but she seldom let it show. Julia remained quiet for a few moments as the carriage rumbled over a quiet street in Mayfair dotted with white houses.

"If I do have a purpose," Brina finally offered, "I don't know what it is. I don't want to marry, so I'll have no children to love and care for as you do. Mrs. Tallon has two helpers and really needs no more assistance at the school. Reading a book to the girls is the most I can do there."

Feeling great concern for her friend and the seriousness of what she was considering, Julia moved over to sit on the cushion beside Brina. "Why do you think you would be happy at Pilwillow Crossings?"

Brina faced her. "Because I'm not happy where I am."

Those were chilling words. "But you would have to take a vow. You would be giving up all that you were born into."

"No." Brina smiled softly. "I checked into that. You need not worry that I am losing my mind. I'm not considering taking a vow of any kind, and it's not necessary at this convent. There are women who live there who've never taken the vow and don't intend to. That doesn't mean they don't have to obey all the rules that are set forth. They do. I know the solemnity of this action and that's why I'm not rushing into a decision. It's something I'm thinking about, and you should know I haven't mentioned this to anyone else for now."

"You know I'll keep your feelings quiet. And I agree it's best not to tell your parents. Doing this would alter your life drastically, and there's no reason to burden them with your thoughts until you have this more settled in your mind."

"That's why I haven't told anyone but you."

"You're still so young, Brina, you—I truly want you to make the choice that's best for you, but if you do decide to do this, and then later change your mind, would you be able to leave?"

"Of course." Brina laughed softly. "It's not a prison. They only want women who want to help others." A faraway look glistened in Brina's eyes. "I do think I made the right decision when I returned to my parents' home after Stewart's passing. It's been so easy to let them coddle me."

"And now you are wanting something more."

"Something different," Brina corrected. "I just don't know what it is yet. Why don't you go with me to talk with them? I really need your help with this. Observe is all I've done, and only for short periods of time when I could escape from Mama."

"Yes, I'd very much like to go with you. Just let me know. I'll find a reason to tell Mr. Pratt that Chatwyn isn't available for instructions that day. I welcome a chance to do that."

"We'll have to be very careful not to let anyone see us."

"We will. Just let me know when you have your date set. But tell me, how do you know so much about the abbey if all you have done is watch the goings on from afar?"

"I sent my maid with a list of questions to ask and swore her to secrecy. She would never breathe a word to anyone about what I do."

"It appears we both have our secrets this summer."

"Yes," Brina said with a resigned smile. "I'm glad you've returned to London so we can share them."

"So am I. It reminds me of when we were meeting with Adeline to plan for the girls' school. We were so afraid someone would discover what we were doing and stop us before we could get it started."

"But no one did."

"That's right," Julia said as the coach rolled to a stop in front of Lady Hallbury's house. If only they could be as successful now as they'd been with the school.

Lady Hallbury always greeted her guests at the entrance to her formal garden. Most everyone in the ton, including Julia, considered the older countess eccentric. But no one would miss one of her parties—if they were fortunate enough to be invited.

She wore a halo of fresh-cut flowers in her ringlets of graying hair. It wouldn't have seemed odd except for the fact that they were large pink mums. The same flower in a smaller size had been sewed onto the low neckline and high waistline of her flowing gown. There were four flounces on her skirt and the hem of each had been adorned with a row of fresh peonies. Julia had never seen anything like it, and by the expression on Brina's face, neither had she.

The spacious garden was no less lavish and spectacular than the hostess herself, with its array of decor. At the entrance to her back lawn were three white arches decorated with colorful shades of tulle, ribbons, and more flowers placed at the entrance. Guests had to walk under the arches to enter. Past where their hostess stood, Julia could see rows of vibrant flowers lining the stone pathway that led to tables and chairs that had been swathed with white linen. Not surprisingly, a ring of pink posies had been laid in the center of each table. Inside each ring stood a five-tiered silver tray filled with dainty confections and delicacies.

Scattered in between tables were beautifully dressed ladies still wearing pale colors and summer blends of lightweight muslin, crepe, and silk. Their hats and bonnets were the height of fashion and lovely, with netting and organdy coverings. Gentlemen were splendidly clothed in dark coats and waistcoats as colorful as the flowers in Lady Hallbury's garden.

The muggy air was still. Gray skies didn't dampen the enthusiastic hum of chatter or the melodious sounds coming from a violinist, a cellist, and a pianist.

"There you are at last, my dear Lady Kitson," the countess said as Julia and Brina approached. "I was beginning to think you weren't going to make it after all. Delighted to hear you are back in Town. September is the perfect time to be in London, though few agree with me on that. And after the heat earlier in the week, who can blame them. Though it was simply dreadful to hear that the duke wasn't feeling well enough to make the journey."

"It's good to be in London," Julia responded when her hostess finally took a breath. "I'll mention in my next letter to the duke that you asked about him. He'll be pleased."

"Oh, yes, do. It never hurts to have one's name mentioned to a duke."

She looked over at Brina. "Delighted to see you, too, Mrs. Feld. You're looking lovely, as always. Perhaps you'll play a score for us later in the afternoon. It's wonderful to have a pianist, but someone who's hired simply can't play with the feeling of someone who plays only because it comes from her heart. Don't you agree, Lady Kitson?"

Julia smiled at Brina. "Yes, few can play as beautifully as Brina."

Lady Hallbury turned and motioned for a server to come over.

"Mr. Garrett Stockton is back in London, too. I know it's rather brazen of me having him here, but he adds a touch of mystique to a gathering, don't you think? Viscount Rumbly has been giving him the evil eye and hasn't let his daughter anywhere near the man."

Lady Hallbury gave them each a glass from the server's tray. "Do enjoy yourselves," she said and then walked away.

"I always feel as if I've been in a windstorm after talking with her," Brina said.

"I think everyone does," Julia agreed, thinking more of how she felt when she heard Lady Hallbury mention Mr. Stockton's name. "Have you seen him yet?"

"Yes. I saw him before the countess mentioned him."

Julia scanned the group of people over her champagne glass but couldn't find him. It was impossible to see around some of the big urns filled with flowers, stuffed birds, and motionless butterflies. "What's he wearing?"

"A deep green coat with a fawn-colored waistcoat. He's talking with Miss Lavinia Etchingham and Miss Myrtle Jackson. She is standing very close to him but she won't be for long. Her mother keeps scowling at her. Myrtle is oblivious to her mother's warnings to get away from the man."

Julia could understand Miss Jackson's feelings. Mr. Stockton had made her feel as if she were an eager young miss wanting to feel her very first touch from a man. She didn't want to admit it to Brina, but she was feeling more than a little apprehension and sheer anticipation at the thought of seeing him again. Julia hadn't come to London looking to find a man to fill a void in her life, but something had happened between the two of them their first meeting. She sensed he felt it, too.

He was different from all the gentlemen who'd let her know they'd be interested in courting her or having a secret encounter with her. But more importantly, she had felt differently about him almost from the first moment she saw him. Mr. Stockton was the first man who had her contemplating the possibility of going against the duke's stated rules of what she should and should not do.

Julia liked how he'd made her feel so womanly again. How it made her feel to think about being alone with him. It intrigued her that he had the courage to give up the settled, envied life of a gentleman to become a voyager.

It was madness to consider it, but it didn't stop Julia from wondering what he would say if she told him she'd like to be with him. Alone. In an intimate way. But how would she even say it to him if she mustered the courage? Maybe she wouldn't have to say anything. Maybe he would just know—by the way she looked at him that she wanted to be with him.

Thinking about it was all she could do. She believed the duke when he told her he would take Chatwyn and raise him if she wanted to be with a man. And she knew he could. The laws gave him complete power over her and her son. She would only have Chatwyn with her until he went to Eton. That was still four or five years away, and she couldn't give up her time with him until then.

"Wait," Brina said with a satisfied smile. "You don't have to worry about Miss Jackson anymore. Her mother just walked over, took her by the arm and is leading her toward the arches. I assume they are heading home already."

"Is he watching her leave?"

"No. Clearly he has no interest in her or he would. But Miss Etchingham will not have him all to herself. Miss Chesterfield just joined her and Mr. Stockton."

Julia blew out a soft laugh. "I'm not surprised all the lovely misses are lining up to spend a few minutes with him. I'm sure I would be, too, if I thought I had a chance to—"

Julia's voice trailed off. She'd caught sight of the sea adventurer from across the garden, and he saw her. It was as if a beam of sunshine had broken through the gray clouds. Everything in her vision seemed to sparkle. She felt as if he were pulling her toward him.

She didn't know how or why but was certain in her heart that every time they saw each other more than their eyes had connected. An eagerness to indulge in what she was feeling for him seemed to dig its way into her soul. She felt he had the same experience. There was something about him that triggered emotions inside her that were far too raw and intense to consider— especially at a garden party where he was surrounded by young belles who were innocent, younger, more beautiful and didn't have Julia's troubles.

"Of course you have a chance with him," Brina said, bursting into Julia's thoughts. "Why would you even think such a thing? It's all right for you to be cautious. You should be. It's wise. You have to think of Chatwyn, but you can't neglect yourself."

"I know you are right." Julia turned away from Mr. Stockton. She didn't want to watch him chatting and smiling with the two adoring young ladies. "Which is why I'm going to enjoy this glass of champagne and say hello to everyone who's here."

"Right," Brina agreed. "Let's start with Viscount Rumbly. Lady Hallbury said he'd been giving Mr. Stockton the evil eye since he arrived. Maybe he'll tell us something about Mr. Stockton we don't know."

"If he does, it will only be gossip."

Brina smiled. "I know."

It was sometime later and after Julia had participated in several conversations about the hostess's flower-trimmed dress, the possible reasons for Miss Camilla Wangle's sudden marriage to Mr. Bradley Fowler, and the conflicting explanations about what exactly had set off a fire that burned down three buildings on the east end of Harold Street that Julia found herself standing alone.

"What has captivated you about this table, Lady Kitson?" Mr. Stockton asked as he eased up beside her. "You've been staring at it and looking pensive for at least a full minute."

Chapter 8

Julia looked at Mr. Stockton and instantly took note of the way his eyes narrowed just enough to give him a roguishly handsome appeal. It was ridiculous how fast the sight of him could make her heartbeat start racing. She wanted to smile and let him know she was happy to see him, but she didn't dare show interest in him at such a public place.

Instead she drew in a wavering breath and turned back to the table. "The food. I was just thinking how sad it is that no one is eating this deliciously prepared food while there are so many people who go hungry."

The silver serving tray was filled with miniature fruit tarts, glazed tea cakes, lemon confections, toast points covered in sugary butter, and other tiny delicacies. None of it had been touched. It was still as beautifully arranged as it had been when Julia entered the garden.

"It's not just this table," he answered. "I haven't seen anyone eat a bite."

She looked at the trays on the other tables. They all appeared untouched, too. "They probably haven't. It's life in Society."

"I've heard men say they were thirsty when sitting down to have a drink at their clubs, but they don't know what thirst is. Nor do they know what true hunger is. If they did, they wouldn't let one morsel of this food go to waste."

Turning toward him again, she looked into his eyes. "I don't know why, Mr. Stockton, but as impossible as it seems, it sounds as if you are talking from experience."

"Me? Real thirst? Hunger? No. Not even the times when I was on a ship adrift at sea for weeks on end. We rationed our food and fresh water and made it last. I won't say we had all we wanted, but we had enough."

"After traveling the world, I'm sure you've seen people who are truly in need of food and clean water, haven't you?"

He didn't answer, but Julia could tell by the way his brows pinched that he was sensitive about the subject. Sadness swept over Julia. All her life she'd been sheltered from most of life's harsh realities. She thought of Brina and how she wanted to help the unfortunate people who visited the Sisters of Pilwillow Crossings. Julia renewed her commitment to help Brina in any way she could.

"It's not an easy subject to talk about," he answered diplomatically. "Certainly not with a lady and at such a grand affair."

"Ah, yes." She quirked her head and gave him a

puzzled expression. "I'm afraid most gentlemen think ladies should be shielded from such things as talk of the poor or downtrodden. They consider us weak, fragile, and in need of their protection—even from ourselves. A lady's independence isn't something they recognize. You don't feel that way, do you, Mr. Stockton?"

"I've never been one to conform to what was expected of me." He smiled. "However, I would shield you from anything I thought might harm you, Lady Kitson, and I will talk with you about anything you want to discuss. Including this food. I take it you are one of the many here who haven't eaten anything."

"No, I haven't."

"Neither have I." He started removing his gloves. "There's no reason this food shouldn't be enjoyed. Don't you agree?"

"Yes."

He stuffed his gloves in one of his pockets, picked up a serving fork, and placed five of the dainty pastries on a plate and extended it to her.

"Oh, no, I don't usually—" She stopped. He was challenging her, and she wasn't going to be outdone by him. Besides, this situation was of her own making, as was usually the case. She glanced about the gathering and didn't see anyone paying them particular notice. "Very well," she said, pulling on the fingers of her wrist-high glove. "You've made your point. Perhaps if others see us eating they will, too."

"My thoughts exactly."

Julia took the plate from him and placed a small pastry with what appeared to be a dot of apricot preserves on top of it into her mouth. It was flaky, sweet, and delicious. The next looked to be a small square of toast dusted with cinnamon and topped with a droplet of honey. It was delicious, too.

She watched Mr. Stockton enjoy one of the small tarts. He ate with the relish of a man who enjoyed food.

"The rumors about Lady Hallbury's cook being the best might be true," he said, adding more pastries to their plates.

"I agree," she said, and watched him eat another confection. As she watched him, she couldn't stop the sudden desire to feel his lips on hers and his hands touching her skin.

His gaze met hers again and held. "I like the way you are looking at me, Lady Kitson."

Curls of pleasure tumbled inside her. Julia liked the way he held his gaze on her, too. He looked comfortable, contented to be by her side. She enjoyed thinking about being alone with him, kissing him, but then, loud laughter sounded behind her. She couldn't forget where she was so she moved farther down the table. Mr. Stockton followed her. Her heartbeat fluttered. Like most of the ladies at the party, she was flattered by the attention he was showing her, but she had to be careful.

"You can't run away from me, Lady Kitson. I intend to pursue you."

His words fell upon her as softly as a cherishing caress, but she had to give him a quick, "No. I'm afraid I'm not available."

"Why?"

Julia looked around the small gathering and cleared her throat. If they were alone she might have been tempted to tell him the reason so it was probably best they weren't. Brina was nearby, watching her and keeping Miss Etchingham busy. It seemed safe to continue her conversation with Mr. Stockton for now, but she changed the subject by saying, "I was just wondering—is it true that you once commandeered a shipment of grain from a band of pirates and gave it to some villagers up north because their farmland was suffering from a blight?"

"I didn't know that story had been told."

"Then it's true."

"Somewhat true," he said.

A whisper of a laugh passed Julia's lips. "How can it be somewhat true, Mr. Stockton? Either you did it or you didn't."

His gaze swept softly down her face sending a shudder of delight racing through her. "I once took some grain knowing it wasn't mine to take or to give away. We came upon a ship listing at sea. The few men onboard were dead. From a fever, we assumed. We found no survivors. We had space, so we loaded their cargo onto our ship and sailed away."

"Did you try to find out who the shipment rightfully belonged to?"

"No. I could have but I didn't look for the manifest. Once I made the decision to take the grain, it really didn't matter at that point who it once belonged to. I considered it salvage."

"I suppose your actions saved a lot of lives."

"For a time, anyway. There will always be people among us who are in desperate need, Lady Kitson." He looked down at his empty plate before his eyes met hers in earnest. "We can't help them all. Sometimes we can't help any of them—if they won't let us."

Julia knew he was talking about her. There was no doubt he was intuitive. He knew she was in some kind of trouble and not willing to share it with him. It was clear he didn't understand her reluctance and he didn't like it. Her fear was that the risk was so great.

"How is Chatwyn managing with his new tutor?" he asked when he realized she wasn't going to respond to his attempt to wrangle answers from her.

"Not well," she answered truthfully, pleased he'd asked about her son. Julia lowered her head and sighed. "The first day was so horrible I can't bear to think about it and the second no better. Chatwyn cried hysterically most of the day and no amount of reprimands from Mr. Pratt or soothing from me helped him. I tried to explain to Mr. Pratt he's simply too young and not ready for traditional schooling."

Mr. Stockton's eyes narrowed into a frown. "He didn't try to discipline Chatwyn, did he? He didn't put his hands on him?"

"No. I would never have allowed that. He threatened to tie him to the chair if he got up again so I moved to the small chair and held Chatwyn. You've met my son. He is a rambunctious little boy. It's so difficult to keep him still. He's not patient and neither is Mr. Pratt."

"You didn't leave the man alone with him today, did you?"

"Of course not. I met Mr. Pratt at the door this morning and told him Chatwyn was ill. There will be no instructions on Sunday but he said he'd return on Monday to resume lessons whether or not Chatwyn was better. I've written to the duke to ask him to dismiss the man. I explained how stern, overbearing, and completely unsuitable he is for such a young child."

"Do you think the duke will agree?"

"I have little hope he will ever listen to me. He considers himself Chatwyn's guardian and that he knows what's best for him. For the most part I stay quiet because I've been threatened with never seeing Chatwyn again if I don't."

Mr. Stockton took in every word she said and nodded.

"The only thing the duke ever agreed to that I wanted to do was the girls' school. I know he only allowed me use of my inheritance for that because it made him look benevolent to do so. With Brina and Adeline already invested, he knew he'd look stingy withholding money that is rightfully mine for such a worthy cause. Appearance is most important to him. He glories in how everyone praises him for the good man he is." After she was finished, Julia realized she hadn't kept her disdain for the duke out of her tone.

Mr. Stockton seemed to study on that for a moment, and then asked, "Have you resided in the Duke of Sprogsville's home since your husband's passing?"

Julia stilled as she remembered the night she told the duke she wanted to move into a home of her own with her son. Chatwyn was only a few months old. She didn't think it would be a problem. The duke had two older sons and a daughter with seven children between them. They all had their own houses. But it wasn't to be so for her. She was his son's widow. The duke had told her she was free to leave his household, and she could do it with his blessing, but she wouldn't be taking Chatwyn with her. He reminded her he knew every judge in Chancery Court. She couldn't fight him. So she had stayed.

Most widows lived alone, where they were free to go and come as they wished, to entertain whomever they wished at whatever time they wished. She wasn't allowed to be like most widows. She had to be the kind the duke wanted or face the consequences of his threats.

"Yes. I've lived in his house since the day I married his son. I know it's difficult to understand for someone who is free to make his own choices in life. Ladies don't have that luxury. You know the rules, Mr. Stockton. Once I married, everything I owned became my husband's. And once he died, his father was given control of it and of me and guardianship of my son. Society deems women too delicate to manage their own affairs. When you are not allowed access to your own money, it leaves you few choices and even fewer freedoms."

"I think I'm beginning to understand the complexity of your life. Something tells me you'd like to be free of the duke."

"Desperately," she whispered as she looked from Mr. Stockton's strongly built chest and arms to his powerful-looking legs. She felt a leap in her breath. Brina was right. She needed help and she had to trust someone. He could move the duke's desk for her. The documents she needed could be hidden in the floor under it and she didn't need to leave one stone unturned. Mr. Stockton could reach the taller shelves with ease and help her with the larger books, so why was she hesitating?

Julia's throat tightened at the real possibility of her thoughts. How could she get him in the house without anyone knowing? She had no idea but now that the idea of help from him was born, nothing kept the confession from tumbling from her lips. "I'm reluctant to admit it for several reasons, but I do need your help again, Mr. Stockton."

Focusing his gaze intently on hers, he leaned in toward her and asked, "What do you want to hide?"

"Not hide, find," she answered determinedly. She laid her plate on the table and cautiously looked around them again. "I need you to help me find something in the duke's house."

His eyes stayed tightly focused on her. "What kind of trouble are you in, Lady Kitson?"

Probably more right now than she actually realized if Mr. Stockton agreed to help her steal the duke's documents, but she couldn't back out now. She needed someone who would be as fearless as she had to be in order to outwit the duke and free herself from his unrelenting control. She believed Mr. Stockton was that man.

"It would take too long to explain everything right now. I'll meet you at the back door at half past midnight and let you inside."

"Wait." He laid his plate on the table beside hers. A server approached with a tray of champagne but Mr. Stockton waved him away. "Let's take this a little slower so I understand. You want me to slip into the duke's house tonight and help you find and take something that belongs to him?"

Julia looked around again before saying, "I know it's outrageous, not to mention dangerous, but yes. I need you to move the duke's desk in his book room so I can see if he has a compartment hidden beneath it. I've tried. It's simply too heavy for me to manage, and for obvious reasons I can't ask his footman."

Amusement slowly settled in his features. "So you think because I took grain from a foundering ship, I'll help you steal something from the duke?"

"Yes," she answered without hesitating. "Documents. Very important ones about the company you and I discussed—where the explosion took place. I have reason to believe the duke secretly owned that company."

He studied her so closely, she feared he was going to deny her.

"Why would he need to own anything in secret?"

"Because he's not the honorable man everyone thinks he is, and I'm going to prove he isn't. I know it's a lot to ask, Mr. Stockton. Believe me, it's more dangerous for me than it is for you. I would lose my son if you were discovered in his house, but I am running out of options. If I could trust anyone else not to alert the duke as to what I'm doing, I would ask them. But there's no one. Will you do it?"

His gaze swept down her face and then back up to her eyes. "Of course. I've been waiting for you to ask me to help you."

Julia sucked in a deep audible breath as her legs trembled with relief. "Thank you," she whispered.

"Lady Kitson, Mr. Stockton," Lady Hallbury said as she sidled up between them and looked down at their plates. "Do tell me how were the pastries?"

Julia looked down at their plates, too. They were both empty. She quickly glanced over at the silver tray. To her horror, it was empty, too! They had stood there talking and had managed to eat every pastry on the table.

"My compliments, Lady Hallbury," Mr. Stockton said with a nod. "In all my travels, I've never had more delicious sweets."

Lady Hallbury beamed with a satisfied smile. "Don't stop now. Move on to another table and have more. I'm quite delighted. I didn't expect anyone to eat a morsel. They usually don't. I do love surprises."

Chapter 9

A pale shaft of moonlight shone from the one window near the back door. Julia trembled inside as she held her black velvet robe tightly under her chin. It wasn't cold, but she felt chilled to the bone. If Mrs. Desford or Mr. Leeds should see Mr. Stockton in the house, there would be no hope they'd stay quiet. She must have wondered a thousand times why she'd asked the rogue to help her. Truly it was madness to sneak him into the duke's home. There was no answer other than that she trusted him, and she was in dire need.

He'd saved her once. Maybe he could again. Without the deed to the company, she had no hope of getting out from under the duke's strong hand.

She'd tried to think of every possibility that might come up. She had excuses ready if she were found

downstairs. It would be easy to say she was looking
for yet another book to read. She'd made sure she was
never without a book in her pocket or her hand so
Mrs. Desford wouldn't have reason to question the
amount of reading she was doing should she find her
in the book room in the middle of the night. When
Julia slipped belowstairs earlier, she'd stopped by the
book room and left a single candle burning on a small
table.

There was no soft knock, as she'd expected, but she
heard the door creak. Julia held her breath. Slowly it
pushed open. Mr. Stockton stepped inside and gently
closed the door behind him. She stifled an audible sigh
as her heart pumped wildly with hope and fear of what
could happen. "You came," she whispered. "I wasn't
sure if you would."

"I would never disappoint you, my lady."

His words comforted her and she offered him a
grateful smile. "Follow me."

Julia led him down the darkened corridor toward
the book room. A fine woolen carpet kept their footsteps silent. Once inside, she cautiously closed the door
and turned the key with shaking hands before facing
him. With only the one candle, it was dark but she
could see enough of him to know she wanted to look
at him at her leisure and drink in the sight of him. That
was a foolish notion for now. She couldn't waste a
moment on such romantic matters. The less time he
spent in the house, the better.

"Perhaps now is the time to tell me why you are interested in finding these documents you search for?"

"I believe they will give me freedom from the duke
and force him to do what is right for the families who
had loved ones killed or injured in that explosion. I

need to find the deeds or something to show that the property or company was transferred into the duke's name."

"Freedom is something I can understand. What do you want to do first?"

"I've checked everywhere you suggested I look a few days ago—except under the desk and the top shelves of books." She looked over at the two walls of books. "You should be able to reach those with ease and help me see if anything is behind them."

He nodded. "You've looked carefully for a hidden space under the rest of the floor?"

"Yes. Even under the chairs and side tables. There are no loose boards or nails that seem to be loose or raised."

"What about the walls?"

"Every inch," she answered desperately. "Behind the paintings, the sconces, the draperies, and even that tapestry."

Mr. Stockton took no time surveying the layout of the room. The desk was at the back of the library in front of a wall of books. He shrugged out of his coat and laid it on a nearby chair. With light steps, he then strode confidently over to the desk and moved the un-lit lamp, ink jar, and quill to the middle of the desk.

"I'll move it forward one side at the time and then we'll toss the rug back and see if we can find anything under it."

"All right." She walked over to stand beside him, and when he put his hands on the edge of the desk, she placed her hands beside his.

He looked down at her and smiled. "I can manage this without you, Lady Kitson."

The warmth that shone in his eyes was like a

soothing balm to her troubled soul. "I know, but I want to help."

As if sensing how important it was that she be involved, he said, "One, two, three."

They lifted the end of the massive desk and moved it forward three steps before setting it back down. Going over to the other side, they did the same.

Mr. Stockton then bent down on his hands and knees and felt around the fine wool. "The indentations the wood made in the rug are here." He motioned to a spot in front of the desk. "If we push it back to here, we should be able to see all the floor that's been covered. Bring the candle over while I move the rug."

Julia did as he asked and then knelt down beside him. Her stomach quivered and her fingers trembled a little. "Do you want me to hold the candle while you search the floor?"

His face was mere inches from hers. They were as close as they'd been when they were in the tree. "I trust you to do it," she whispered.

Mr. Stockton went to work and Julia watched. He was so close she heard his breaths, caught the scent of his shaving soap and the fresh washed smell of his hair. Through the linen of his shirt she saw the firm muscles in his back working as he bent over the floor. Holding the light close to him, Julia watched his strong, sure hands skim the seams and joints of the wood. Suddenly she was imagining the palm of his hand gliding over the plane of her hip, up to her waist, and gently caressing her breasts.

"Damnation," he whispered after a few moments. "I think I've found something."

For a moment Julia felt paralyzed, but then her breath leapt in her chest. "What?"

He moved farther into the alcove of the desk where the chair would sit when pushed tight again the desk.

Julia crawled to get closer to him, bumping his shoulder with hers, letting her thigh rest against his. "Let me see."

"Give me the candle," he said.

She gave him the round brass holder with a shaking hand.

He took the light in one hand and with the other showed her where to touch. "Start here and follow my hand up to this point and back to here. Do you feel that?"

"The seam of the wood is raised," she said, beginning to believe they might have found something. "How do we get the boards out so we can see if anything is inside?

He handed the candle back to her. Reaching behind him, he pulled his knife from his boot. He started knocking the blade into the seam with the hilt of his hand. The noise reverberated around the room. Julia felt as if a gong was sounding throughout the house. Her heart jumped to her throat.

"Wait. It's so loud I'm afraid it will awaken the housekeeper or Mr. Leeds. I don't know if they are sound sleepers."

Garrett stopped and laid the knife down between them. He reached over and cupped her cheek with his warm hands. His touch was soothing. She wanted to melt against him and let him take this fear and burden from her.

"I'll make as little noise as possible. It's your choice, but I can't break this open silently. There must be a little sound if you want to know what's hidden beneath the boards."

Julia didn't know what to do. It was torture to be so close to possibly finding the evidence she needed, but the noise to get it was terrifying. What good would it do her to find the papers if the housekeeper found her? Mr. Stockton stayed calm. His hand was steady, comforting against her skin. He didn't rush her to make a decision. It was as if he knew she had to be sure what they were doing was worth the risk they were taking. He was right. There was no way to remove a board silently.

She really had no choice. "All right," she said. "Do what you must. I'll leave the candle here with you and go to the door to listen for footsteps from above."

"It's not as loud as you think it is." He gave her a gentle, brief kiss on her lips and then another just as short on the side of her mouth. The contact was startling but calming. Her breaths slowed.

"Everything will be fine. I'll be as quiet as possible." He kissed her forehead. "Now go listen from the door."

His hand moved to the back of her neck and gently squeezed before he let her go. With her heart pounding in her ears, Julia rose and hurried over to take up her post. She unlocked the door and eased it open just enough to get her head through the space. She focused her gaze down the corridor that led to the back stairs which ended up on the servants' floor. She inspected each shadow on all the walls so she would know if a new one appeared. Every creak and crack of wood she heard behind her made her wince in fear that someone would hear and come to investigate.

Seconds turned to minutes, but she dared not leave to see what Mr. Stockton was doing. Her eyes were dry from lack of blinking. Her chest ached from holding herself so rigidly, and her stomach felt as if it had been twisted into knots. Finally the noise stopped. There was complete silence just before she heard, "Julia, come here."

Desperate to believe his call to her was for good news, she squeezed her eyes shut for a moment before slowly leaning back into the room, closing the door and securing the lock. There, in the darkened room, she could see his form clearly. He stood behind the desk, looking magnificent, powerful, and commanding, and holding a leather packet in his hand. Julia couldn't move. Was it over? Had her search come to an end? All of a sudden her heart lurched and she rushed over to him.

"Are there documents in it?" she asked breathlessly.

"I don't know. I thought you should be the one to open it."

She took it in her trembling hands and knelt down near the candlelight. Mr. Stockton knelt beside her and picked up the candle, holding it close so she could see better. She quickly untied the leather strings. Moving the flap aside, she opened it and saw perhaps thirty or forty sheets of letters and documents and a ledger. Giving no thought to the ledger, she laid it to the side and started leafing through the unbound pages, reading the title of each page. Halfway through the stack the Eubury-Broadwell Company seemed to jump out at her.

"This is it," Julia whispered, her hands trembling even more. She held it up for Mr. Stockton to see. "This is the company I heard him say he secretly owns. The one you said had an explosion. This document proves he owns it and he's not taking responsibility for it or caring for the families of those who were killed or injured in the explosion."

Mr. Stockton took the paper from her and glanced down. "This does seem to be a straightforward registered deed but it doesn't have the duke's name on it, Julia. It has Mr. Eubury's name on it. This only proves the duke has the deed in his possession. He could merely be keeping it safe for this man."

"What? No, no," she said irrationally, feeling close to losing her self-confidence. "You're wrong. You don't understand. I know it's the duke's company. I heard him say this man doesn't exist. The duke buys companies under made-up names so they can't be traced back to him."

Mr. Stockton's concerned gaze swept down her face. "I believe you, but this doesn't prove what you say, and it won't convince anyone."

His words rang true, but she didn't want to believe them. Determination not to let the duke defeat her rose up inside. "Maybe it's here in the ledger." She thrust the other documents aside and picked up the book, certain it would contain proof he owned the secret companies. But her eyes wouldn't focus on the first page. She turned to the second and it was the same. None of the letters or numbers made sense. It was gibberish. "I must be losing my mind," she said, despair in her tone. She looked over at Mr. Stockton. "I can't read it. It's—"

"Code," he answered tightly. "The ledger is written in a code. The alphabet and numbers are coded so no one can understand it. Each column probably represents something different. The company name, how much money it makes. Maybe the dates. There's no way of knowing."

Julia felt numb. She moved off her knees, sat on the floor, and leaned against the desk. Her hand tightened on the ledger. Frustration ate at her confidence. Outrage at the duke threatened to overwhelm her. What was she going to do?

"I can't let him win. I have to find a way to make sense of—"

"We will," Mr. Stockton said softly, moving to sit beside her. He pulled her close to his chest. "Don't give in to your doubts and fears. It's time to tell me everything you know about the duke and the properties that are here."

Julia wasn't sure she could talk. He kissed the top of her head and she melted against his warmth, his strength. She didn't know what she was going to do to escape the duke or to see that justice was done for the people he'd wronged. She had put all her faith in finding the hidden papers. She had nowhere else to turn, but then she felt Mr. Stockton's arms tighten around her. His hand rubbed her arm, her shoulder with slow rhythmic strokes that were meant to soothe her and let her know he wasn't going to leave her. She felt his breath in her hair, his lips moving softly just above her ear, and his heart beating strong and solid beneath her hand pressed against his chest.

A rush of deep longing filled her. From that afternoon in the tree, Julia had an undeniable trust in Mr. Stockton but it had been so hard to act on that feeling and allow him to help. She felt a reassuring sense of security whenever they were together. Now she wanted to place her complete faith in him.

The duke wasn't in this room. He had no control over her right now. Sitting in the pale glow of candlelight she was free to say, to do, and to be the person she wanted to be. Julia lifted her head from Mr. Stockton's chest. Their faces were close together. She stared into his eyes and saw disquiet and appreciated it, but she knew she wanted something else. It wasn't even comfort that she needed. There might be a time for that but not right now. She reached up and let her fingertips graze his cheek and follow the shape of his lips.

He took hold of her hand and kissed her fingers. "Your touch is like fire lighting a wick to me, Julia. This is not the time for—"

"Then when will be?" she asked, pulling her hand out of his and winding her arms around his neck. Her hands met at the back of his head and her fingers tangled in the richness of his hair.

"I don't want you in danger of being caught in here with me any longer than necessary," he said.

"I know what I am risking and I'm willing. The house is quiet. I don't know if I will ever be as free as I'm feeling right now. I have been attracted to you since the moment I saw you walking toward that tree. I don't want to pass on this opportunity to be with you."

His hand slid to the back of her neck, drawing her face closer to his. "I have wanted you," he whispered huskily.

"Then kiss me with all the desire you have for me."

"Yes," he murmured, and caught her up tighter against his chest as his lips came down on hers with glorious passion.

His kisses stole her breath. Julia responded with the same urgency. She ran her hands up and down the length of his muscular back, feeling power in his broad, firm shoulders. Their tongues swirled in each other's mouths as their bodies strained to get closer. His hand moved up her rib cage. He parted her thick velvet robe, pushed it off her shoulder and fondled her breast beneath the fine cotton of her dressing-gown.

At his touch, her breasts tingled and tightened. His hand cupped their fullness and his thumb aroused her nipples. "Yes," she whispered, giving him uninhibited access. Julia moaned softly and pressed into the bounty of his embrace, meeting his ardor with a fervency of her own, pressing closer and encouraging his every touch.

"You have no idea how I have ached for you," he whispered while kissing her nose, her cheeks, and down the column of her neck. "To touch you and kiss you like this."

"Yes, I do," she managed to respond between kisses. "I couldn't stop thinking about you and us being together like this."

Their kisses kept seeking, demanding, and savoring. Second after second, he was claiming her for his own, making sure she wanted him to continue. He had no need to worry. She was totally immersed in the welcoming, irrepressible sensations that kept thrilling her. She pulled on the tail of his shirt, tugging it from his trousers so she could feel his bare skin. He rewarded her with small gasps of pleasure.

Their kisses and touches didn't ebb. They were long, hard, and generous. Their breaths, moans, and sighs mingled into one passionate sound.

They were hungry, eager, and impatient. She felt his body tremble and his desire for her grow more desperate. Her gown was pushed up and his trousers pushed down. They came together in a quick single motion that was intense, powerful, and wild. It was mindless oblivion and far too fast. Moments after their bodies joined, pleasure like she'd never known sparked and flashed through her body like bolts of lightning shooting from the sky and piercing her. She clutched the back of his shirt in her hands. Her body shook as she savored the expanding essence of erotic fulfillment.

Moments later, Julia gathered her wits and realized that somehow they had managed to move to the softness of the rug. Garrett lay on top of her, his face pressed into the curve of her neck and shoulder. His breaths were gasping and shuddering.

"I waited for you," he whispered as his tense body started to relax. He lifted his head, kissed her lips softly, and then looked down into her eyes. "I don't know how I managed, but I haven't wanted anyone else since I met you."

Julia smiled, too. His husky words couldn't have pleased her more. "I've been waiting for you, too. You are the first man to touch me since Kitson died."

"I'm glad." He kissed her again. "I knew we would be together but I didn't expect it to happen tonight."

"Nor did I, but it seemed right," she said honestly.

"For me, too." With a long sigh, he rolled off her and they started straightening their clothing.

"Why don't you tell me everything you know about the duke's secret companies?"

"I've told you as much as I know. I overheard him and his solicitor talking about the secret companies and the solicitor suggested he destroy the documents on the Eubury Company. The duke holds himself up to Society as the epitome of a compassionate person and fair-minded to all mankind and righteous beyond all others. Yet, he hasn't come forward to say he owned the company or to help those who were injured in the blast. It seems I am the only one who has seen the bitter, controlling man he really is. He not only insists I live with him but also that I must live my life by his impossible standards. He is punishing me because I thwarted his plans and married Kitson. And because his son is dead and I am not. You saw support of my claim against him when he sent Mr. Pratt to tutor Chatwyn without consulting me."

He reached over and took hold of her hand and squeezed it gently. "I have never doubted anything you've said."

"Thank you for that. I know the duke's most prized possession is his standing in Society. He adores the accolades he receives, he is constantly reminding his family how everyone looks up to him for how they should live. I have to believe if I show him I have proof that he owns secret companies such as Eubury-Broadwell, he will give me my freedom rather than let all in London know of his treachery. I'm certain he doesn't want to be remembered as one of the most evil and uncaring men in history. I don't know of any way to ever be free of him other than confronting him. There's no way to challenge him in the courts because the laws are written for men. Not women."

"I know and understand all you say. But men like him are very hard to bring down, Julia." He picked up some of the loose sheets of foolscap and shuffled through them. "The Eubury-Broadwell was a gaming house. Why would such a pious man want to own a gaming house?"

She swallowed hard. "To make money I assume. I really don't know. He never gambles and speaks against it, saying it ruins families. He was a vicar before he inherited the title and doesn't believe in wagering on anything."

"You will continue to need my help."

Julia touched the side of his face. "I am grateful for whatever help you can give me."

He smiled and then reached over and kissed her lightly on the lips. "Do you know when the duke will arrive in London?"

"No, but in the letter Mr. Pratt brought, he told me the fever hasn't passed but he is feeling better. I know he will come as soon as he is strong enough to make the journey."

"It won't be safe for you to keep the duke's documents here with you," he said, and started gathering the scattered papers and stuffing them back into the leather packet. "I should take them with me."

A chill went up Julia's spine. "No." She grasped the packet from his hands and clutched it to her chest. "This is all I have. Now that I have it, I can't let go of it."

Tension crackled between them like a hot fire for a few seconds. His gaze stayed focused on hers. "You are no longer handling this alone. I'm going to help you, but I must have your trust, Julia."

"You do. I swear it, but I'm not sure you know how important this is to me. If this is what I think it is, it will change my life."

"I know," he said softly, and then continued to gather the sheets of paper from off the floor. "All of this is useless to you the way it is now."

Her hands tightened on the leather. "I will find someone to decipher the code. I'm certain the ledger will show the names of the companies, the names of the fake people who owned them, and that the duke is the one who has profited from them."

"Where will you hide it until you find someone?" he questioned. "If the duke returns and finds it missing, you will be the first person he suspects."

That was true, but the thought of giving up the evidence was terrifying. "I don't want to lose this chance, Garrett. I've waited for something to give me the opportunity to get away from the duke. I know I can convince him to allow me and my son to be free if I can prove he is not who he claims to be."

Garrett smiled and touched the side of her hair. "You won't lose it. I promise. Let me take care of it. There's a man in my office who is very good with numbers. His name is Mr. Urswick and he's my accountant. He may be able to make sense of the code."

Her spirits lifted and she swallowed down her misgivings. "Do you really think he can?"

"I don't know for certain, but I won't know until I try. Right now, he's the best shot we have unless you know of someone you can call on."

Julia shook her head. She had to trust him to help her. She handed over the packet.

Garrett stuffed the rest of the papers into the folder and retied the leather strings. "I'll have a list made of every company in here. When you confront the duke it's best you not have the real documents with you."

"What if the duke catches you with them in your possession? He could have you put in prison."

Garrett reached over and kissed her sweetly, earnestly, and then looked into her eyes. "I'm not afraid to go to prison, but I would be afraid for you to go. If we're both careful, I won't have to. Now, let's get the desk put back in its proper place and I'll get out of here. We don't want to give the housekeeper cause to suspect anyone ever touched it."

Julia grabbed hold of his arm and stopped him when he started to rise. "I want to know what you find out. I'll meet you at The Seafarer's School late tomorrow afternoon. There's a house in front of the school and a garden between the two. Can you meet me there?"

He smiled. "I'll meet you anywhere you want me to."

She squeezed his arm. "You must be careful not to be seen. A neighbor across the street has a spyglass and I'm told she's not shy about using it."

Chapter 10

Gray skies threatened rain as Garrett walked at a fast pace past shops and businesses on his way to the offices of Stockton Shipping Company, carrying the duke's documents in a satchel. The rare, humid heat that had settled upon London for a few days had lifted and was no longer scorching plants, animals, and human life. In its place were cool temperatures more common to late summer in London.

It was a short distance from Garrett's leased room at the prestigious Holcott-Fortney Inn to the business district of St. James, but the trek was invigorating. He could ride in a carriage from place to place as most proper gentlemen did, but Garrett walked. There'd been too many days onboard ships when he'd wished for land so he could walk as long as he wanted. When sailing, he often imagined himself on a horse, riding at full gallop across a wide expanse of English countryside. He intended to do that, but other things were more important right now.

He didn't have to look in the windows or open doorways to know what shops he passed. The scents told him all he needed to know. The tailor smelled of fabric, the bakery of fresh bread, and the apothecary of dried herbs and potent spices.

He hadn't gone to any of the clubs or the card room at the inn after he'd left Julia last night. All he'd wanted was a glass of brandy and the thought of her to lull him to sleep. The tension between them had been vibrant and hot since the moment they'd met. Every time he looked at her, he wanted her. And now that he'd been with her, he wanted her again. He had no doubt she felt the same. Making that happen wouldn't be so easy. She was right to be cautious in the duke's house.

Their coming together had been desperate, urgent and primitive but deeply satisfying. She'd been as passionate as he'd imagined, but what he was still trying to comprehend was how his feelings for her had grown so intensely so quickly. He hadn't been looking for a lady to capture his heart and soul. Garrett stopped. That thought took him by surprise. But, yes, he feared Julia might have done just that.

He started walking again. From the moment he saw her in the tree, he'd been enchanted by her. She'd had all his senses reeling and he hadn't been able to shake thoughts of her. Now, he didn't want to. She was beautiful, capable, and he admired her strength and tenacity in wanting to topple the duke from his domineering and self-righteous perch.

Garrett was going to help her. He nodded and smiled to a gentleman he passed, then chuckled under his breath.

Midday bustled with sounds of pedestrian chatter, horses' hooves clopping, and carriage wheels rumbling over hard-packed roads. Garrett tipped his hat to every lady he passed and nodded to every gentleman whether or not they were Society born. Now that he'd been all over the world, for the most part, anyway, he was beginning to think he was ready to spend more time in England once again. After ten years of traveling, London felt like home.

Lady Kitson Fairbright was the reason.

How could it have ever crossed his mind that a widow with a son of her own would be the lady of his dreams? Everything about her drew him. Her courage and her dedication impressed him. Her passion was real and strong whether she was protecting Chatwyn, going after the duke, or lying in his arms. She put all her strength into whatever she was doing.

Garrett's stomach tightened at the thought of her in his arms again. Much as he had ached to be with her, he would have never suggested they come together last night. Putting her in danger wasn't something he wanted to do. He wanted to protect her. If she hadn't made it clear that being with him was exactly what she wanted, he wouldn't have touched her.

"Damnation," he whispered to himself, aching to be with her again.

There was more between them than just words, glances, touches and kisses. More than just primal coming together. After last night, she had him thinking about giving up his life of the adventurer and living a settled life with a family, but would a lady like Julia take the chance that he wouldn't leave her and take to the sea again? He didn't even know the answer to that himself. Answers to that question would have to come later. For now, he'd concentrate on helping her with the duke.

He passed a perfumery, and the varied floral scents drifting onto the heavy air stirred his thoughts of how fresh Julia smelled. There wasn't a hint of rosewater, lavender, or any other fragrance on her skin. That made her different from any other woman he could remember being with. Her hair had been braided, and he would have liked nothing better than to free it from the tight coil and sink his fingers into its lush length while making her his. But there had been no time for slow strokes down the plane of her hip or kisses that went on forever. They'd been too desperate. But next time, he would touch, kiss and love her the way he wanted to.

A chuckle rumbled in Garrett's chest as he noticed a couple of street urchins eyeing him as he approached them. He knew they were looking him over, trying to decide if they could distract him long enough to lift his coin purse. It was a fairly common occurrence wherever he went, and Garrett never minded their attempts. It was a way of life for them.

The footpads caused Julia's little boy to come to mind. She had been horrified when he grabbed hold of Garrett's leg. If she only knew the many times he'd been rushed by a band of street urchins bent on pilfering his purse and dagger, or mobbed by a gang of gypsy children who'd been sent out by their parents to pick pockets clean of anything that might have value. They hadn't been particular about where they touched when robbing him. One little boy holding on to him wasn't going to disturb Garrett's disposition.

He reached into his pocket and pulled out a shilling.

He tossed it in the air toward the street urchins as he passed. They laughed with delight and shouted thank you.

Garrett inhaled the wet, earthy scent from the tobacco store next door as he walked up the three steps to the entrance of Stockton Shipping and entered the office. A stocky-built man with thinning gray hair jumped out of his chair from behind the simple desk and said, "Good-day to you, sir. Is there anything I can help you with this morning?"

Mr. Ashfield always asked the same question whenever Garrett was in the offices. "Yes, Mr. Ashfield, there is something."

Garrett took off his hat and placed it on a small table along with his umbrella. While removing his gloves, he looked around the spacious room, something he couldn't remember actually taking the time to do before. There was never any reason to. He spent so little time at the offices of his shipping company. It was the first time he realized there was very little furniture sitting about and absolutely nothing hung on the walls. No framed writings, etchings, or drawings. No paintings of ships, landscapes, or fruit and flowers. There wasn't a candlestick holder on either side of the room or a clock standing in one of the corners.

It was odd that today he was aware of how barren the room was. It had nothing to give it the liveliness of being occupied. Garrett had never set up an office for himself in his own building. There was no purpose, he'd always told himself. He was seldom in London, and when he was, he spent most of his time in Mr. Urswick's office.

But today, for reasons Garrett didn't want to ponder too closely, he was being more honest with his thoughts. If he set up an office for himself in the shipping company, the old guard in the ton could legitimately say he no longer simply owned ships and traveled about the world as a sojourner, and that he'd gone into trade. But now that he'd met Julia, Garrett was glad he hadn't made the final commitment to give up his link with Polite Society.

He walked over to Mr. Ashfield and pulled a leather bag not much larger than a man's coin purse out of his pocket. He looked down at Ashfield's hands. They were definitely worse than the last time he saw the man. His knuckles were large and knobby.

"How are the joints moving these days?"

"Difficult, to be sure, but I can still grip a quill and turn a page as quickly as any man."

"I've never doubted that." Garrett laid the bag on his desk. "I finally got around to having my trunks delivered from the ship to the inn. I brought this back for you. Try it and see if it helps. Mix a level spoon of it in a little water every morning and drink it."

Ashfield picked up the little sack and spread it open. A damp, putrid smell permeated the air around them. He grimaced and turned his head away from the foul odor.

"I know," Garrett offered before the man said a word. "It doesn't smell good and it probably tastes even worse, but I'm told it will diminish the pain you have and give you more movement in your fingers. It might make the knees feel a little better, too."

Ashfield looked doubtful. "Where did it come from?"

"India. Don't ask me what's in it because I don't know. I can't swear it will help your joints but I'd trust the man who gave it to me with my life, and he said it would. This isn't like laudanum. You won't feel better in a few minutes and probably not for a few days. This works over time and you have to take it every day. I promise it's not poisonous. It's ground plant roots and herbs and maybe a spice or two. Try it. I brought a couple of barrels back with me. If it helps you, I'm going to see if any of the apothecaries in London are interested in selling it."

"Thank you, Mr. Stockton. A spoonful every morning. Don't you worry, I'll get it down."

Garrett then pulled the stack of documents from the duke's office out of the leather package and placed them on Mr. Ashfield's desk. "I need you to copy each of these documents as accurately as possible."

The secretary's eyes widened as he began looking through the stack. "There are many pages here, sir. This will take some time, but I'll do my best to get them done as quickly as I can."

As Ashfield glanced through the papers, something caught Garrett's eye. "Wait," he said. "Let me see that one." He reached over and pulled one of the documents from his assistant's hand. "I don't believe this." Garrett stared at the name on the deed. Mr. Peter Moorshavan was listed as owner of the house on Poppinbrook. What the devil was the duke doing with papers on that house? But then pieces of the puzzle started falling into place for Garrett. Wiley had said no one knew Mr. Moorshavan before he arrived in London and no one had heard from him since the discovery that the house had been turned into a hidden brothel. Julia said the duke was using fake names to buy property and he was obviously hiring men to pose as the fake owners.

What were the odds that in trying to help Julia he'd find the man he was looking for? Or at least the name of the man. He'd believed Julia when she said the duke was an unjust man, and was controlling her life and Chatwyn's. He wasn't so sure he'd been convinced the duke owned secret companies, but he had no doubts now. But why would someone as wealthy as the duke engage in such practices? It didn't make sense that he would do it just for the money. But what else could it be? And none of this matched with the fact Julia insisted the duke was a pious, straight-as-an-arrow man. Garrett didn't know the answers, but he intended to find out. He hoped the coded ledger had the answers. And that his manager could unravel the code.

"Yes, Mr. Ashfield, this is a priority. Start with these two." He gave the Poppinbrook and Eubury-Broadwell deeds back to Ashfield. "And keep all of these in the iron chest when you're not working on them."

"You can be sure I will. I'll get right on them."

Garrett nodded, walked over to Mr. Urswick's door, and lifted his hand to knock, but stopped and turned back to the secretary. "After the pages are copied, see to it some paintings are put on the walls in here. Your choice, but I'd like to see some ships sailing waters."

The man's chest, shoulders, and chin lifted all at once and his hand squeezed around the little sack. "Yes, Mr. Stockton. I'd be most pleased to do that for you."

Garrett then knocked on the door and waited for the response to enter. His manager was standing and bent over a very large book that rested on a pedestal. He didn't bother to look up from his quizzing glass, but said in a muffled tone, "Put the papers on my desk, Mr. Ashfield, and I'll get to them in a few minutes."

Mr. Miles Urswick was the most intelligent man Garrett had ever met and an expert with numbers. His mind absorbed and held almost everything he'd ever heard or read. Strangely enough, Garrett had met the young man late one night in a gaming hall on the east side of Bond Street.

Urswick was a tall, heavyset fellow with the thickest red hair Garrett had ever seen. One of the players at the table that night hadn't taken kindly to the husky man's stack of winnings. He started, politely enough in the beginning, making references about Urswick looking Irish. To his credit, Urswick brushed off the oaf's needling at first, swearing there wasn't a drop of Irish blood in him, but after a time, proceeded to tell the discontented player where he could stuff his assumptions. That wasn't a good idea for someone who didn't know how to fight a man with a knife.

Before the game was over, it was clear that Urswick was better at remembering what cards had been played than he was at defending himself. Urswick was getting sliced swipe after swipe because he didn't know how to dodge and maneuver away from his opponent.

Garrett found it difficult to watch the bear of a man getting cut up over something he didn't start, and he certainly didn't want Urswick getting killed. If it had been an even fight, Garrett would have stayed out of it and let the best man win. But it wasn't, so without thinking twice, he pulled his dagger out of his boot, pushed the big guy out of his way, and took over. Once the troublemaker realized Garrett was as good with a knife as he was, he sensibly backed away, leaving his cards and his blunt on the table.

Urswick thanked Garrett for saving his life and swore off gambling for good that night. Garrett had been looking for a man he could trust to manage his business in London while he traveled. He'd asked Urswick to be that man and he'd never regretted it. Urswick kept flawless account books with every shilling and pence accounted for. His records of every ship, its assignments as to cargo and points of origins and destinations were always impeccable.

"I have no papers for you today," Garrett said, entering the room and closing the door behind him. "But I do have a ledger I want you to take a look at for me."

"Oh, Mr. Stockton," Urswick said, removing his spectacles and walking around to shake Garrett's hand. "My apologies for being so inconsiderate and not looking up to greet you."

"Am I interrupting anything important?"

"I consider everything I do for you important." Urswick closed the book he'd been looking at. "I can finish these columns later. From the records I received from the ship after you docked and while you were away, your journey appears to have been most prosperous."

"It was." Garrett lifted the duke's ledger from his satchel and handed it to his accountant. "Have you ever seen anything like this?"

Mr. Urswick thumbed through the book. "Hmm. Someone has gone to great trouble and length to keep anyone from knowing what this says."

"That's what I was thinking. Do you think you can break the code and unravel what it says?"

The manager looked as wide-eyed as Mr. Ashfield at seeing the deeds. "I—I don't know. The pattern could be anything." Mr. Urswick shook his head. "I've never tried to do anything like this."

"Do you know of anyone who can?"

"Never had a reason to even think about it. But

I would assume that people who can do this kind of work wouldn't go around talking about it."

Garrett pondered that. "You're right. And they would probably serve in the military where their expertise would be needed."

"I can ask around if you would like?"

"No," Garrett said. The last thing he needed was word somehow getting back to the duke someone wanted to decipher a ledger. He couldn't take that chance.

"I can work on it and see what I can do."

"That's all I'm asking. Everything else you are currently working on can wait. I need to know what is written in here. I need you to keep this safe and private."

"I'll make sure it's in the iron chest when I'm not working on it."

Garrett nodded.

"And while you are here, I do need to mention something you might consider important." He opened a drawer on his desk and removed a letter. "I had a note from the Prince's emissary, Mr. Brownley saying he heard you're in London. He wants me to set up an appointment for you to see him."

Lady Kitson came immediately to Garrett's mind. She'd left him no doubt she didn't approve of the King's son and his mindless penchant for indulging his every whim. Garrett had to admit he'd never given much thought to the Prince's lavish spending on his homes until she'd mentioned it. Most everyone in Society indulged in whatever luxury they desired and could afford. The Prince wasn't the only one who had extravagant and unnecessary purchases. What someone else did wasn't Garrett's business unless they were doing what the duke was doing—shielding his companies so he had no responsibilities when accidents happened.

Nonetheless, Garrett had to see what the Regent wanted him to do this time. He'd taken a chance on Garrett and given him much-needed exposure and credibility in the shipping industry when he was young, impetuous, and trying to find a way to build his empire. Being able to say he'd sailed for the Prince gave him leverage other small companies didn't have. Garrett had used that connection to secure business from around the world, and it had paid off in spades. He had no idea what Mr. Brownley wanted now. Probably to ferry more unearthed priceless treasures from Egypt, Turkey, or other countries for far less than their true value to history.

Garrett had never pried into the Prince's dealings and he wasn't going to start. The only problem was that right now Garrett had no desire to set sail and oversee the project. He wanted to be exactly where he was and helping Julia. Doing that would also help him discover the true owner of Poppinbrook.

"Set up an appointment for me to see him here."

"I'll send over Mr. Brownley's answer to you as soon as I receive it. And you may want to know the *Enchanted Siren* has arrived from Singapore."

"Remind me what the ship is carrying, Mr. Urswick."

"The bulk of the cargo is rice and tea. There was also mention of an unknown quantity of fabrics, threads, beads, buttons, and feathers. The origins of the feathers weren't specified."

Good, Garrett thought. "I have one other thing I want you to do."

Chapter 11

Julia waited restlessly in the garden of the house that stood in front of The Seafarer's School for Girls. She would often visit the school when she was in London. She'd explained to the housekeeper that she'd be receiving a visitor in the garden, and knew she could count on the woman to be discreet and not mention it to anyone. The minutes passed and Julia looked at every flower and shrub from the back gate to the front lawn and back again. No exact time had been set for Garrett to come, but she'd been eager not to miss him, so she'd already waited more than an hour.

Garrett. She smiled just thinking about him.

She didn't know exactly why she'd started calling him by his first name. Perhaps because that's how she thought of him now. Surely, especially after last night, Mr. Stockton was far too formal between them. Except, of course, when they were around other people. She liked the idea of him calling her Julia. Lady Kitson was the title she'd received by marrying the duke's youngest son. She would never forget Kitson because of their son, but it was time she moved on with her life. Being with Garrett last night made her realize all the more how restricted her life had become and how desperately she wanted to be free to make her own decisions.

There was a moist chill in the air but Julia's long-sleeved, lightweight wool dress kept her comfortable. The grass in the garden was still damp from a long morning shower. She knew the cooler temperatures would do away with the lush greenery of summer and give way to the more somber colors of autumn. Julia lifted her face up to the slice of sun that had appeared from behind a gray wispy cloud and closed her eyes. Thinking about Garrett was far too easy for her to do.

Her time in his arms had been glorious but far too short. If they could have had more time together, if she could have lingered in his arms, maybe she wouldn't be so eager to repeat their coming together. Being with Kitson hadn't prepared her for the all-consuming desire that had seeped into her soul, satisfying her so intimately she ached for the breathtaking feelings to never end. If not for Mr. Stockton, how could she have ever known that such stirring sensations existed inside the body, waiting to be brought so vividly to life? And even now that hunger to be with him and feel them again was relentless.

All day she'd kept thinking, *I want to touch his bare skin again and feel his lips on mine. I want to hear him whisper my name in passion again. I want his body*

joined with mine and that soul-shattering pinnacle of
desire to wash through me and leave me breathless
and wanting more.

A bird chirped and Julia opened her eyes and looked
around the garden. No sign of Garrett yet. She was
eager to hear what he had found about decoding the
ledger, but there was so much more to what she was
feeling inside. Which was highly dangerous. At the
time she hadn't thought about the possibility of getting
in the family way. She hadn't thought of anything past
her desire for him. Now she had to consider that and
realize nothing could be worse for her at this time than
a secret affair with the rogue. No matter that was exactly what she wanted.

Even meeting Garrett so near the school was a great
risk. Mrs. Feversham across the street wouldn't blink
an eye at seeing Julia at the house. She was one of the
owners and had been there many times. But the nosy
neighbor would question seeing a handsome young
man, and that would give her reason to talk. Which
was why Julia had to be very careful.

Julia walked over to the trellised archway that
served as an entry to the school grounds and led
straight to the main door of the building that housed
The Seafarer's School for Girls. It was situated at the
rear of the property. At one time, the plain white three-
story building was a residence for the servants of the
main house. Julia, Brina, and Adeline had purchased
the property almost a year after their husbands had
been killed in the sinking of the *Salty Dove*.

It was daunting for the three widows to even attempt
to start such an establishment and then to place it in
the middle of a valuable street of houses, but all agreed
it was the ideal place. Their solicitor had managed

everything for them and had been invaluable in all aspects of starting the school—since Society deemed ladies should never concern themselves with anything that might have to do with conducting any type of business or having a responsibility that involved money. No matter how capable the lady might be.

At the time, the three friends had agreed Adeline would live in the main house, since Julia was more or less forced to live permanently with the duke because of her son, and Brina, having been married only three months when her husband died, had returned to her parents' home to live. What the young widows couldn't have known when they acquired the property was Adeline falling in love with the earl next door and marrying him. That had left the beautiful main house unoccupied except for the housekeeper and her occasional helpers.

Julia had wanted to move into the house when Adeline married. The duke had told her he'd be happy for her to do so. But she wouldn't be taking her son. Chatwyn was staying with him and would be raised as the grandson of a duke should be. Therefore, Julia had resigned herself to living with the duke. She couldn't live in the house at the school, but it would be the perfect place to meet with Garrett.

Julia leaned against the trellis and thought back to the day she'd met Adeline and renewed her acquaintance with Brina. It wasn't an ideal setting for anyone to meet—the designated place to collect your husband's last possessions. Items that had slowly washed ashore from the ill-fated ship that took their husbands' lives. None of the widows were there because they wanted to be but because it would have seemed callous of them if they hadn't respected the efforts of the ones who'd found and collected the articles to return to the appropriate families.

That was the day the idea of starting a charitable boarding school for the daughters and sisters of the workers on the ship was born. Polite Society and the ton would take care of their own, but who would take care of the families of the men who perished with the ship? Julia, Adeline, and Brina decided they would.

At first the task to educate and teach the girls a trade seemed impossible. It hadn't been easy to find the right property, nor to convince the girls' relatives to allow them to leave their homes and live at the school. Boarding schools for boys were common but not so for girls. Some families had to get used to the idea. But after more than a year, all the girls had adjusted and were doing well in their lessons and in their sewing. Julia, Brina, and Adeline had reason to be pleased.

"What are you looking at, Lady Kitson?"

The sound of a girl's voice startled Julia. She turned to see Fanny standing behind her. The red-haired girl had her hands behind her back and was staring at Julia. It shouldn't have surprised her to see the freckle-faced miss. She was known for slipping out of the schoolhouse but thankfully she'd never been caught wandering off the property. At eleven years of age, she seemed to value independence. Perhaps she was much like Chatwyn and simply didn't want to obey the rules. Or it could be that Fanny was more like her and wanted to be by herself without anyone's watchful eyes.

"Good afternoon, Fanny," Julia said. "How are

things at the school today? Have there been any problems?"

The girl curtseyed and smiled. "Not from me, my lady. I'm through being bad. I've been a good girl just like Mum wants me to be."

Julia smiled. "That's good to hear. Is everyone happy?"

"I am. Nora doesn't cry anymore so I guess she's happy, too."

"I'm glad. So tell me, does Mrs. Tallon know you're out here?"

She nodded and the long curls on her shoulders bounced. "I saw you standing under the trellis from the window. I told Mrs. Tallon and she thought you might be on your way over to the school. I said I could come ask you."

"That was nice of you but no. I won't be going to the schoolhouse today."

"I'll tell her. Mrs. Tallon thinks I'm very intelligent. But don't tell her I told you. She doesn't know I heard her speaking to Miss Hinson. She wouldn't like it if she knew I was listening to her conversations."

"I'm sure you're right about that." Julia started to tell her that no one would appreciate anyone eavesdropping on their conversation but decided she didn't have the heart to reprimand her. She'd let Mrs. Tallon do that.

"That's a very pretty dress you are wearing, my lady."

Julia looked down at her skirt. There were no flounces, or gathers on it. No ribbons, lace, or bows. The blue was so deep it was almost black. She wondered how anyone could think it pretty. She was twenty-five years old and dressed as if she were a much older woman.

"Thank you, Fanny," she said.

"If I had made it for you I would have sewn some ruffles on it and made you some satin bows for the skirt."

"I know you will make beautiful dresses and gowns when you are finished with your education."

"Yes, my lady. I don't have any trim on my dress either and it looks just like all the other girls' dresses. When I get older and start making my own clothing I'm going to have all the bows and ruffles I want."

Julia laughed. "I'm sure you will. Now, you best get back to the school. Tell Mrs. Tallon I'll let her know when I'll be stopping over."

"All right," Fanny said cheerfully. "I'm glad I saw you today." She then turned and skipped back toward the school.

Julia headed back to the garden. Talking to Fanny had made Julia relax. Mrs. Tallon said the girls had adjusted and were doing well, but it was heartening to hear the same report from one of the girls.

A hinge creaked. She looked around and saw Garrett standing in front of the back gate. All the wondrous things he made her feel came rushing back—every touch, every kiss, and every sigh of pleasure they made. She wanted to run and throw herself into his arms. She wanted to hold him tightly and kiss him madly. Instead, she kept her composure and said, "I've been anxious for you to arrive."

He smiled as he took off his hat and laid it on the gatepost. He started walking toward her. "I've wanted to see you, too."

"Let's sit on the bench that's against the back wall of the house." She pointed to the seat. "It's more sheltered there, and it will be difficult for anyone from neighboring houses to see us."

As soon as they'd settled themselves on the bench, she moistened her lips and asked what was most on her mind. "Did you find someone who can read the code?"

He smiled. "First tell me about Chatwyn. How is he doing today?"

"Frightened. Even when I told him Miss Periwinkle could take him to the park he wanted to cling to me and not let go. I know he doesn't want Mr. Pratt to return."

His gaze caressed her face with concern. "You should have brought him with you. He could have played while we talk."

Julia's heart softened, knowing he meant what he said. She was pleased he didn't mind her son being with them. "Thank you, but it was best he not come this afternoon.

"Perhaps the duke has received your letter and has already dispatched someone to take care of Mr. Pratt."

"That would be wonderful, but I'm certain it's not true. I kept looking behind me, fearful that Mr. Pratt was following me."

"So you think he might be a spy, too?"

"I wouldn't put it past the duke to watch my every step. I've always thought he does anyway. I know he did when I was married to Kitson. He always thought he was going to find me being unfaithful. I would never have done that."

"I know," he said with conviction. "Do you know why the duke would be so distrusting?"

"Not for sure, no. I mean I haven't discussed it with him. I do know from gossip and Kitson that the duke's second wife, a beautiful lady, left him for a man much younger than the duke. Apparently she couldn't abide by the duke's iron rules. The man she ran away with was a known charmer and gambler who'd somehow wormed his way into Society. That happened when Kitson was still a little boy so he didn't know much about his father's second wife or the man she ran away with. I've never heard the duke speak about her and it's certainly not something anyone would ever ask him about."

"I can see why. Was his wife ever heard from again?"

"I guess it's possible, but not that I heard. Now, tell me do you think the man you had in mind can figure out what is written in the ledger?"

"He's not sure yet. All Mr. Urswick can do is try. He's very good with figuring out discrepancies in shipping logs and remembering what ship is carrying what cargo. I have hope he can find the pattern that was used. Once he knows that, he should be able to read it. Mr. Ashfield has already started copying the documents so the duke will know for sure you have the originals. I have no idea how long that will take him. All of it will be kept in an iron chest I have in my office. It would not be easy for anyone to break into it even if they should somehow learn the deeds were in there. But I do have some more information you might like to hear."

"Yes, anything," she said, scooting closer to him.

"I found more proof that you were right and the duke has secret companies bought in the names of men who don't really exist."

Hope rose inside her and she leaned toward him. "That's wonderful, Garrett. What did you find? How did you discover it?"

"You and I didn't take time last night to examine all the documents that were in that hidden packet under the desk. I didn't even look at them when I returned to the inn last night. Today, when Mr. Ashfield was thumbing through them, I recognized a name on one of the documents."

"What company was it?"

"Not a company. It was a deed for transfer for the house where I grew up. The house I want to buy. The man whose name is registered on the deed is Mr. Peter Moorshavan. When I asked my friend Wiley about the property, he told me the owner had all but vanished. No one seems to know where Mr. Moorshavan went. I have a feeling he hasn't been found because there is no such man, and we'll find proof he's as fictitious as Mr. Eubury."

Julia tried to tamp down the excitement that made her stomach jump. "That's welcome news, Garrett. Now you believe me that the duke has secret companies and obviously secret homes, too." She stopped and gave him a curious look. "I can understand why the duke might want to keep his ownership in suspect companies a secret, but why would he need a secret home?"

Garrett's mouth narrowed and he gave her a short, whispered laugh. "First, I have never doubted you, Julia. And the house I want to buy wasn't a home for anyone. It was a business. He had turned it into a hidden brothel."

"Oh," she whispered, unable to think of anything else to say immediately. She knew about such places but had never had a reason to talk about one. That subject was as off-limits for a lady to discuss with a gentleman as was money. "The duke is so morally rigid I find it hard to believe he'd have anything to do with a brothel or a gaming house. It simply doesn't fit with the man I know."

"Chances are more of the companies and properties he owns will turn out to be places like this and places that illegally store hordes of gunpowder in stores on busy streets."

"But I'm still left wondering why would he do this?"

Garrett shrugged. "Men usually do things for either power, money, revenge, or love. I'm hoping we'll find some answers in the ledger."

"Sometimes I think people do things simply because they are miserable," Julia offered. "He seems a very unhappy and trite man. Especially when no one other than me is around. Chatwyn is the only one who can bring a natural smile to his face, and I do think it's because he wants to believe Chatwyn makes him think that Kitson is still alive."

"That's probably why he has such fear of losing Chatwyn. Tell me, did you find anything else in your search of his office that might have bearing on the secret companies?"

"No." She looked out over the garden, suddenly feeling pensive. "All the other papers in his office were correspondence-type letters, invitations to various events, or of a political nature. I had thought to search his bedchamber and dressing rooms if nothing was found under his desk. He could have a secret compartment under his bed or chest."

"I can see the idea of doing that doesn't appeal to you and I don't think it's necessary at this point." He reached over and skimmed the back of his fingers over her jawline to behind her ear, where he lightly caressed the soft skin. There was soothing warmth in his touch. "We may need to do that, but why don't we see what Mr. Urswick is capable of doing with the ledger first."

Julia gazed into Garrett's searching eyes. The sun was warm on her back, but a light breeze had kicked up and was cooling down the air even more. "I don't know how much time we have. I told you in the letter Mr. Pratt brought me that he was feeling stronger. At least strong enough to engage the tutor for Chatwyn. I know he will come to London as soon as he's able to travel. He wants to see a new physician that he's heard about and a new apothecary in hopes of finding a tonic that will help him feel young again."

"Don't worry," he said. "We will find a way to prove what the duke is doing and confront him about his wrongdoing concerning the explosion in Manchester. In the meantime, this is a safe place for us to meet."

Her gaze swept down his face to his lips. "Yes," she said hopefully. Talking to him made it easy for her to believe they might actually pull this off and bring down the duke.

He picked up her hand and squeezed her fingers. His were warm, and his expression was gentle. "Do you want to talk about last night?"

There was a shudder of delight at his mention of their coming together. Her breath seemed to skip. "What is there to say? It was something we both wanted to happen."

"But I didn't want it to be so rushed. I didn't want it to be the place where we were. You should be treated like a lady."

"No," she whispered softly. "I had a husband who treated me like a lady—fearful of touching me more than necessary for fear of disturbing my sensibilities. He was determined not to show me passion and expected none from me in return, as though ladies shouldn't indulge in such intimacies as enjoying the marriage bed with their husbands. I was happy you didn't treat me like a flower too delicate to fondle. You made me feel passion in a way I knew was possible but had never felt."

"I hope I always do."

She smiled shyly as she slipped a strand of hair behind her ear. She hoped so, too. "I suppose I shouldn't confide something so private to you."

"You're still not sure you can trust me, are you?"

"I believe I do." Julia swallowed hard. "It's just that I've always been at the mercy of what the men in my life want for me. I went from my uncle to my husband dictating my life. I thought that after Kitson died I'd finally be on my own. A widow. Free. Strong and capable of making decisions for myself and my son. But I'm not. My father-in-law rules my life."

"We are closer in heart than you think, Julia. I understand your feelings. They are the same ones that urged me to leave London and work to make the life I wanted."

"But you were allowed to do so. I am not. Society has bound a lady's hands so that everything she has is directed by a man."

His hand slid around her to the back of her neck and he grasped her nape. "You are free to make your own decisions with me. Tell me, do you want me to kiss you right now? Here in the back garden where passion should be held in check because of the possibility that nosy neighbors might wander over, or the housekeeper might open the back door? Do you want to take the chance on a kiss?"

"Yes," she whispered.

"So do I."

Garrett moved close to her on the seat. He lowered his head to hers and let his lips fall softly against hers. The contact was undemanding as his lips gently grazed over hers. His kiss felt as wonderful as she'd remembered.

It was a welcoming feeling. His hand moved slowly down her back, around her waist, and up her midriff to her breast. A prickle of shivery warmth tightened her most womanly part, making her ache to be even closer to him. She deepened the kiss, slanting her lips against his and adding pressure. Her hands roved freely over his strong back and shoulders.

Their kisses were deep, and lingering. His caresses were firm and deliberate, causing spirals of delight to shoot through her. Their breaths and sighs of pleasure mingled together. Waves of desire surged inside her.

Time seemed to stand still as they kissed, until suddenly the sound of a door banging open and the shrill squeal of children laughing, yelling, and running down steps broke them apart and they rose. It sounded as if the girls were going to run straight into the garden where Julia and Garrett stood. A moment later, she realized the girls were heading to their own play area on the side of the school.

After catching her breath, Julia said, "I forgot we were so close to the school. You are not good for me, Mr. Stockton. You make me forget myself and what's at risk. I take too many chances whenever you are around. I think you should go now."

"When can I see you again?"

"Soon, I hope. You will let me know if Mr. Urswick makes progress?"

"You don't have to ask that."

"I can't leave tomorrow. Mr. Pratt promised he'll return. I fear what he may do if I'm not there."

"Take care of your son, Julia, but know I want to be with you."

Julia swallowed hard and nodded. She wanted that too, but she had to be sensible about what was at stake. She couldn't let her desire for the rogue overrule what was best for Chatwyn.

Garrett turned to go, but suddenly spun around. Without warning, he took the steps that separated them, caught her up into his powerful arms, and gave her a hard, quick kiss.

"I will help you, Julia," he whispered. "With whatever you need."

He then kissed her forehead, let go of her, and walked out the back gate.

Chapter 12

Julia looked into the mirror hanging over the side table in the vestibule as she fitted the short-brimmed dark gray bonnet onto her head. "Do you know if the wind has been strong today, Mrs. Desford?"

"I don't think there's a stir about today, my lady," the housekeeper informed her.

"Good. That means I can tie a loose ribbon under my chin."

It was late enough in the day that Mr. Pratt had already left and Julia felt comfortable leaving Chatwyn with Miss Periwinkle so she could join Brina at the girls' school. A few minutes ago, she'd received a note from Brina stating that Mrs. Tallon wanted to see them as soon as possible about a problem.

The day with the tutor had been as unpleasant as all the others. Mr. Pratt kept insisting Julia leave the room but she never would. His tone and expressions were so stern and angry, at times she feared he might strike Chatwyn.

She kept hoping she would receive a letter from the duke stating the dismissal of Mr. Pratt, or that the man would realize Chatwyn wasn't old enough to be a student and not want to put up with another day of a little boy crying and having tantrums. No matter what the duke or Mr. Pratt said, she would never leave her son alone with him.

A knock sounded from the door and Julia tensed. For a moment she thought it might be the horrible man she was just thinking about returning. She squeezed her eyes shut tightly for a moment and took three deep breaths, but then Julia heard Mrs. Desford say, "Yes, I'll see she gets it," to someone, and then she immediately closed the door.

"It's a note for you, my lady," the housekeeper said.

Hoping it was news from Garrett, Julia's heart raced. It had been three days since they'd met at the school, and there hadn't been one word from him.

"Thank you." She calmly took the note, but when she looked down at it her heart sank. The letter wasn't from Garrett. She recognized the handwriting as the duke's secretary's writing. Disappointment quickly overwhelmed her other emotions. But almost as quickly, she thought perhaps the duke was sending word that he'd dismissed that vile Mr. Pratt. She broke the duke's seal and scanned the page.

Lady Kitson,
I grow stronger each day and am assured I will feel up to traveling soon. I will continue to allow Mr. Pratt to instruct Chatwyn until I ar-

*rive in London and personally assess the man's
instruction abilities.*

Duke

"No," she whispered, as anger tightened her chest.
Mr. Pratt was allowed to continue and the duke getting better. That was her greatest fear. What was she
going to do? She needed more time. Mr. Urswick obviously needed more time.

"Did you receive bad news, my lady?"

Julia looked over to the housekeeper. "No, not really.
I mean, good news, that the duke is recovering and
says he'll soon be strong enough to travel." Julia just
didn't know what *soon* meant. Two days? Three? A
week or two? "It's just that he wants to wait to make
a judgment about Mr. Pratt until he can personally
assess the situation. That means the man will return
tomorrow. I've written the duke two letters complain-
ing about Mr. Pratt's harshness and was hoping the
duke would tell him not to return."

"Master Chatwyn hasn't been himself since he
started lessons with Mr. Pratt."

"No, he hasn't. I'll write the duke again," she said
more to herself than the housekeeper. Julia couldn't
consider her efforts futile. She had to have hope the
duke would understand what he was doing to her little
boy by putting him through lessons with that man.

"I'll work on getting the duke's rooms ready."

"Yes, that will probably be a good idea. Would you
put this on my desk?" She gave the letter back to
Mrs. Desford. "I'll answer it in the morning. I'm going
to wait out by the street for Mrs. Feld."

Julia picked up her dark blue velvet reticule, match-
ing lightweight wool shawl, and gloves, and walked

out into the chilly air. Her shoes felt as if they were
filled with boulders as she made her way down the
stone path to the street. The sky was a smoky shade of
light gray. Julia felt as if there were a cloud envelop-
ing her, too. She stared at the row of houses in front of
her. Some had fancy iron gates at the entrance and two
had stone arches, but most had only a simple wooden
door.

The street was quiet. No sounds of children playing, birds chirping, or even the approach of carriage
wheels in the distance. Nothing to cheer her. The duke
was better, Mr. Pratt hadn't been dismissed, and she
hadn't heard from Garrett. If he had any news he would
have contacted her.

Trying to shake off the gloom of her troubles, she
lifted her chin and her shoulders. There was still time
before the duke arrived. How much, she didn't know.
When she got to the school she would write Garrett
about the duke and ask Mrs. Tallon to see that her note
was delivered to him at the Holcott-Fortney Inn. In the
meantime, she had to think about what she was going to
do if the duke returned before the ledger could be read
and the documents copied. She didn't know if she had
it in her to bluff the duke into thinking she'd found
someone to decipher the code.

Julia heard the clip-clop of horses and looked up.
She recognized Brina's carriage and was suddenly
reminded of what her friend wanted to do. If Brina
was strong enough to consider joining a convent, Julia
was strong enough to handle the duke. She thought of
the wondrous things Garrett made her feel when he
looked at her, when he touched and kissed her. She
didn't want to give that up. There was a way to free
herself. She just hadn't found it yet.

It was a short drive to the school. On the way, Julia had filled Brina in on the duke's letter concerning the tutor and finding the deeds with Garrett's help. She also told her that she was still waiting to hear from Garrett again. Brina shared her news that she'd decided to make an appointment for them to go visit with one of the sisters at Pilwillow Crossings.

When they entered the large front room of the schoolhouse, the girls were seated at a long table with slates and chalk in front of them. They all stood up and bowed. Fanny raised her hand just a little and gave Julia a wave. Off to the side, Mrs. Tallon was standing in front of several large crates and two wooden barrels.

Julia and Brina greeted the girls, taking time to ask them a few questions about their studies and sewing work. The mistress wore a grim, perplexed expression on her face and waited until they walked over to greet her.

"Good afternoon, Lady Kitson, Mrs. Feld. Thank you for coming over right away. I don't know what to do."

Concerned because she didn't see anything askance, Julia asked, "Tell us the problem and together we'll find an answer."

Mrs. Tallon pointed to the crates. "These are the problem. I have no idea why they were delivered to the school. I didn't order any of this, and I don't believe Lady Lyonwood ordered it. We talked about supplies the day before she left on her journey and decided we had enough of everything and would wait until she returned to resupply the sewing room."

From where Julia was standing she could see that the crates had been opened and were filled with bolts of fabric, spools of threads, ribbons, and lace.

Julia looked at the innocuous items before her. "I'm not clear what the problem is. Do you think these were delivered to the wrong address?"

"They must have been. The man in charge of this delivery said he was positive he had the correct place. The Seafarer's School for Girls. He insisted he had no idea who this came from. His only job was to bring it here. I had him take the tops off the crates before he left so I would know what they were leaving."

"Maybe Lady Lyonwood ordered it while she's away?" Brina offered as a way of explanation.

"I don't think so. Look at what is inside these crates, Mrs. Feld," Mrs. Tallon said, her brows pinching together. "These girls are still learning to make their stitches, use scissors correctly, and make their buttons tight. They aren't ready to work on such fine fabrics as these. This—this isn't for students. Some of these items belong in the finest modiste shops in London. Who would send this quality to a school?"

Puzzled by what the mistress was saying, Julia and Brina walked closer and looked into the opened crates.

One box was overflowing with lace, and still another contained large spools of colorful sewing and embroidery threads. Julia laid her reticule, gloves, and shawl aside and pulled open the drawstrings of one of the bags from a barrel. It was filled with high-quality white glass beads. Opening another bag, she found more expensive beads. Another contained beautiful ostrich and pheasant feathers.

Julia was stunned. "Yes, of course, you're right, Mrs. Tallon. Some of these things aren't appropriate for our students to work with. Are you sure he said these were to come to the school?"

"Positive. I had him show me the note he'd been given with the name of the school and the address."

Julia's and Brina's gazes connected once again. Suddenly Julia had a feeling she knew where the gifts had come from, and she murmured, "Perhaps a pirate sent them over."

Brina pursed her lips and then smiled. "That's the same thought I had. You don't suppose he—he?"

"No. No, of course not," Julia said, but wasn't convinced that Mr. Stockton hadn't somehow absconded with someone else's shipment and given it to the girls.

"I need to know what I'm to do with this," Mrs. Tallon said, showing her frustration in a tight, determined expression. "I'm sure we can use much of what's here, if not now, then later as the girls progress," Mrs. Tallon continued. "I haven't been through all the crates, but some of these fabrics are simply too delicate, and the girls aren't anywhere near ready for beading and feather work."

Julia turned to Mrs. Tallon. "We won't worry about that right now. I have reason to believe these were delivered to the correct address. I'll leave it to you to decide what you can use and how best to use it. Re-crate the rest and let me know when it's ready. In the meantime, Brina and I will think of something to do with what's left over. And please let the girls look over all the fabrics and beading. It will be good for them to know the difference in the textures of the fabrics and what needle works best with each one. I'm sure I don't need to tell you these things so I'll leave it all to you."

"I'll make it part of their lessons."

"Now, if you don't mind, Mrs. Tallon," Julia said. "I'd like to use a quill and a sheet of vellum or foolscap—whatever you have nearby. I need to write a note. If you could have one of your helpers deliver it to the Holcott-Fortney Inn, I'd be most grateful."

"Of course," she said, seeming pleased she could do something for Julia. "I'll see that it's done."

"Thank you."

After the letter to Garrett was sealed and goodbyes were said, Julia and Brina headed toward the street where the carriage waited.

"It must have been Mr. Stockton who sent the boxes over," Brina said as soon as they were away from the school.

"Of course he did," Julia answered tightly. "He is the only pirate we've ever met. Who else would have access to such expensive cloth and beads to give away? What I want to know is where did he get it and why did he give it to the school?"

"I think that is simple enough to understand. He wanted to do something nice for the school and help the girls."

"Does he think we can't take care of the school we started?" Julia asked, not really knowing why she was irritated about his extravagant donation. Perhaps it was because he hadn't been in touch for three days. Didn't he know she was anxious to hear from him? Even if it was only to see and talk to him.

"That's nonsense. I think we've proven to everyone we can take care of the girls," Brina answered. "To me it says he's a kind and generous man."

They stopped in front of the open carriage door. Julia looked at the driver and said, "Don't drive too fast. We don't want to tire the horses."

"Really, Julia," Brina protested in earnest. "Can't we go at a normal pace this time?"

"Animals need to be taken care of just like people.

We wouldn't run anywhere unless there was an emergency, and neither should the horses."

"All right," Brina said, her expression softening. "Since it's only a short drive to Pilwillow Crossings from here, do you mind if we go there? Not for a visit. That hasn't been arranged. Just to look. It's one of the days they serve food."

The duke would be returning any day now, and there was no sign of help from Garrett or his accountant, Mr. Urswick. Mr. Pratt was a beast, and thoughts of Garrett's touch were never far from her mind. Yet with all that to worry about, she couldn't deny Brina's request.

"Yes. Let's go," Julia said after taking in a deep breath. "We have the rest of the afternoon. We might as well put it to use."

After they boarded the coach and the ride was underway, Brina said, "I'm assuming the note you wrote was to thank Mr. Stockton on behalf of the school."

Julia turned to look out the window as the carriage rolled along.

That thought hadn't even entered Julia's mind. She had told him only that the duke was better and hoped to travel to London soon. Perhaps he'd be on his way by the end of the week. She then asked if there had been any progress made on the code.

"You can't ignore me when I'm sitting right across from you," Brina said, breaking into her bleak thoughts.

"What? No, I'm not trying to ignore you. It's just—"

"If you've decided you aren't attracted to Mr. Stockton, tell me, and I'll leave you alone about him and never mention him again. It's just—the way you two looked at each other when you were standing together at Lady Hallbury's party had me feeling you belonged together."

"Brina," Julia whispered softly.

"It's true. You were so engrossed with each other it was as if you didn't know there was anyone else in the room."

That's how she'd felt. "I've already admitted that something stirs inside me whenever I look at him. Feelings I've never felt before shudder through me. Magnificent sensations I'd like to pursue more deeply, but you know I can't. Not until I put an end to the prison I am living in."

"What can I do to help you? I keep asking and you don't let me help you in any way."

"But you are. By doing exactly what you are doing now. Giving me something to think about other than myself and my problems. I know what you decide to do about your future is as important as what happens to mine."

"Yes. I suppose it's as if we are both caught in our own separate whirlpools and we're simply swirling in circles and making no progress of going forward."

"That is exactly how I feel, Brina."

The carriage rumbled to a stop and let them out at the corner two streets over from the abbey. After telling the driver to wait for them, Julia and Brina walked to where a large, three-story building stood among much smaller dwellings on each side of it. In front of the abbey was a long line of poorly clothed men, women, and children. Orderly and in single file, they passed by a table where a sister dipped into a large pot and filled the bowls and cups they held out. Each one nodded their thanks and moved on to where another sister handed them a piece of bread.

Off to the side at another table stood two sisters handing out rolled bandages and what Julia assumed were little bags of herbs or tea. The longer she watched, the heavier her chest felt. The trail of people was somber as they walked away.

"Look at the little girl with long blond hair," Brina said softly. "And the little boy who's not wearing shoes. It's going to get cold soon. I hope he has some at home. And there's a woman carrying a baby."

Julia saw everything that Brina saw. "Like you, Brina, I'm overcome with compassion for these people and for the sisters and the selfless work they're doing."

"It made me feel wonderful when I saw this for the first time. To know there are such good-hearted, strong women who do kind things like this for people they don't know. They rise in the mornings and say, 'How many people can I help today?' I rise in the mornings and say, 'What dress should I wear to visit with Julia?'"

"I take nothing from these selfless-hearted women who are so generous to give up their lives to do this for other people, but you don't give yourself enough credit for how good you are to others already. Remember you helped start the school."

"I know what my life is, Julia. I live it."

"Yes, of course you do, but I believe it takes a person with a different kind of strength to do this kind of compassionate work."

"Is it that you don't think I have that special kind of strength or heart? Or that I can't learn how to make bread or roll a bandage?"

Tears pooled in Brina's eyes.

"Certainly not. You are the kindest person I know. You are more than capable of doing whatever you wish.

It's just that I think some people help best with actually doing the work of caring for others, as we have Mrs. Tallon and her helpers at the school to teach the girls. Other people are better at helping to fund projects, as we do for the school. It takes both to make a charitable house work."

"I believe I have the heart and the strength to do the kind of work these women do."

"Good." Julia touched Brina's gloved hand with affection. "You are very brave to even consider this. That makes you stronger than most of us, because I know I am not suited. You must make sure this is what you want to do for the rest of your life. I don't think there would ever be any going back."

Brina turned back toward the sisters. "I know. And that is a worry. I'm waiting to talk to Sister Francine. I'll know more after I talk to her."

They turned and started walking back to the carriage. "I just had a thought," Julia said, feeling inspired. "Why don't we donate the leftover fabrics, beads, and feathers to the convent? They can sell the supplies and use the money for more food, herbs, cloth for bandages, or for whatever they need."

Brina's eyes brightened. "That's an excellent idea. I'm sure they would love to have a donation like that. We can talk to Sister Francine about it when we visit. But—" Brina paused and looked at Julia curiously.

"But what?"

"We should make absolutely sure it came from Mr. Stockton before we start giving it away."

Julia's heartbeat raced at the thought of seeing him again.

Chapter 13

"The clientele who frequented the Holcott-Fortney Inn were as prestigious as those who visited the Prince's homes. Its stately stone and Corinthian column front as well as the grandeur of the Rococo décor inside were noted with superb detail all over England. It was considered the place to overnight or stay for months, if necessary, when in London. Dignitaries from all over the world had been welcomed beneath the roof for over fifty years.

Suites in the expensively ornamented inn weren't spacious but Garrett had never found lodgings that were. It had never mattered. He never looked at where he was staying the night as home. Until now.

Julia had him thinking about dinner around a dining table, a game of chess in front of the fire, and waking up in the mornings beside a woman—a lady he cared for.

Garrett bypassed the dining area and walked into the card room. Wiley rose from the table where he was seated near an unlit fireplace. The room smelled of food, oil lamps, and freshly poured ale.

"It's about time you showed up," he offered with his usual good-natured smile.

"I'm lucky to have made it at all. I received word there was a problem with one of my ships in Southampton. Three of the men had come down with a fever. The captain was worried it might be something serious and infect the entire crew. I rode over there to check on them. Thankfully they were already getting better by the time I arrived, so I didn't stay long."

Wiley leaned back in his chair. "But you're sure they don't have anything contagious, right?"

"Claret," Garrett said to the attendant who appeared at his side, and then looked back to Wiley. "I'm sure they do, but it's not something that's going to kill anyone. And don't worry. I never boarded the ship."

"Oh, well, that's good."

Garrett chuckled. "Tell me about Moorshavan—did you find out any more about him?"

"I found out it's as if the man never existed. I checked the legal records and the house is registered to Mr. Moorshavan but he must have hightailed it back to Boston—where he said he was from, because no one in London has seen or heard from him since someone from the Lord Mayor's office paid him a visit. I'm still waiting to hear from some of the men I talked to but I don't know of any way to find Mr. Moorshavan other than hire someone to sail to Boston and look for him there."

And that's exactly what Garrett would do if it turned out the duke didn't own the property. He intended to buy that house and tear it down because of what it represented to him—a life of never owning anything, never working for what you wanted, and always being beholden to family for every penny of your existence. He was going to build his new house there where he would live as a gentleman and a tradesman.

Garrett took a sip from the wine the attendant put in front of him. "Tell me about Miss Osborne. Has she arrived?"

Wiley looked down at his glass for a moment. "Not yet, but I'm hopeful it will be soon." He huffed. "Imagine me waiting around for a lady to arrive and hoping the days will pass quickly until she does. Did you ever think you'd see the day?"

"I can't say I did." But Garrett knew exactly how his friend felt. He was anxious to see Julia. "Do you have a shilling in your pocket?"

Wiley shrugged. "A few."

"I only want one."

Wiley dug into his coat pocket for the coin and laid it on the table in front of Garrett.

Garrett placed a small box on the table and slid it toward Wiley. "It's for you to give to your bride. It came from Africa. It's made from ebony, their finest wood, and inlaid with gold and ivory. You told me if you ever married I'd have to pick out a gift for you from another country to give to your bride."

"I remember but I didn't expect you to." Wiley picked up the box and examined it. "This is extraordinary workmanship and there's no small amount of gold on this. It's worth more than a shilling."

"Its only worth will be in how much Miss Osborne treasures it."

"Mr. Stockton," an attendant said. "I have a note for you that's just arrived."

Garrett thanked the man, took the note and opened it. Julia wanted to see him. He looked around to the clock that stood in a corner. He had just enough time to go by and see Mr. Urswick before meeting Julia.

"Wiley, I'm going to have to cut short our meeting."

"More problems with your ship?"

"No," he said rising. "I need to call on Lady Kitson."

"So you've gotten to know her," Wiley said with a quirk of a smile.

"Quite well and I'm hoping to get to know her even better."

After a frustrating visit with Mr. Urswick, Garrett found himself in the drawing room at the duke's house. His manager had been diligent in going over the lettering and numbering in the book, and while Urswick was a genius when it came to adding long columns of numbers in his head, he wasn't good at figuring out coded writing. He'd told the man to go home and rest. They would start fresh in the morning.

Garrett needed to do that, too. He'd spent the better part of three days in the saddle, but he had to see Julia.

He heard a door open and shut. His gaze zeroed in on the doorway to the drawing room as he heard light footsteps hurrying down the corridor. When she entered, Garrett took a step forward, but then stopped. She was flushed and out of breath. Her long-sleeved, cheerless widow's garb was gone. She wore a dress of crisp, light blue muslin embellished with narrow bands of white satin ribbon at the waistline and hem.

The low, rounded neckline showed the pillow-soft rise of her breasts. Capped sleeves showed her beautifully trim arms. Her shiny chestnut-colored hair was pulled up at the sides and hung down the back of her shoulders.

She'd never looked more beautiful. He wanted to pull her into his arms and kiss her for as long as he wanted. If she'd been any other widow he could have. Just his being there for the second time could put her at risk—would put her at risk. That's why Urswick had to find a way to make sense of the ledger.

"Lady Kitson," he said with a nod of his head.

"Mr. Stockton." She walked farther into the room and stopped on the far side of the fireplace. "I was outside with Chatwyn. I take it you received my note."

Garrett grimaced. "Yes. I came straight here from my office." He walked over to stand closer to her. "Did you have information for me?"

She glanced at the doorway and then returned softly, "Yes. The duke is better. I fear he'll be up to traveling by the end of the week."

"Time is short."

"Yes."

Garrett sensed movement in the corridor and it wasn't York. It had to be the housekeeper. "I'm sorry to report that your butterfly net hasn't been repaired yet. The man I left it with didn't realize it was the duke's, and he hasn't put any time into it."

He motioned toward the doorway with his head. Julia acknowledged him with a deep breath.

"It's kind of you to stop by and let me know about it. Just today I heard the duke should be traveling to London soon." She spoke calmly and moved away from him and more toward the farthest side of the room. "I'm sorry to hear it's not ready. However, there's another reason I'm glad you stopped by."

He followed her, but didn't take his eyes off the doorway. "What's that?"

"Someone made a gift of fabrics and sewing supplies to the girls' school. I was wondering if that might have been you?"

"Yes," he answered. "I hope it was all right."

"It was an enormously extravagant donation for the school, Mr. Stockton."

"You have a sewing school. It was cloth and thread. How can that be extravagant?"

"It was more than that, really," she said, a little tersely. "I can't imagine what you were thinking."

He lowered his gaze to her lips and thought how much he wanted to kiss them. It didn't bother him at all that she was a little miffed at him for his gift. It made her all the more delightful. "My pardon for doing something charitable for a charitable school."

She stared at him sternly, and whispered, "It's not the gift, but did you pay for it or did you find it adrift at sea?"

Garrett had to admit that the question surprised him. "You think I stole the things I gave to the girls?"

"I don't know," she stated, clearly unsure of her condemning question. "However, I must admit it crossed my mind that you might have. You can't make the school a party to your ill-gotten gains."

Garrett and his men had risked their lives to take the grain off a foundering ship. They could have gone to the bottom of the ocean with it or caught the fever that had killed all who were onboard. And they didn't take a penny for their efforts but gave it all away.

"The answer is no." Garrett slowly scoffed out a laugh as he looked around the room, finding it hard to believe the woman he desired like no other thought he was a real pirate. Taking from the wealthy to give to the unfortunate. York woofed and Garrett looked back to the doorway. He sensed that whoever was there had walked away.

The truth was that Julia wasn't all wrong about him. There were things he'd done that he wasn't proud of, and his gentleman father wouldn't have approved of. Life was a series of choices and he'd never met a man who always chose the right one.

"You really think I'm a pirate, don't you?"

He watched her shoulders relax a little. "No. Maybe. Sometimes, I suppose. You are dangerous. I really don't know what to think about you other than I can't stop thinking about you." She walked closer to him and lifted her hand as if to touch him, but thinking better of it, she lowered her arm. "But even if you did—"

"No, Julia," he interrupted her quickly. "There is no *if*. I didn't. I paid for every needle I sent to the school."

"I believe you," she whispered.

"You can relax a little," he said. "Whoever was lingering at the door has left."

She nodded. "But that doesn't change the fact that we can't use some of the fabrics. Only the highest paid modistes in London and Paris work with some of the fabrics and beading you sent over. The girls can't use some of what you sent until much further along in their sewing skills. They've hardly learned to properly sew on a button. Most of the fabrics are much too delicate for them to work with."

Garrett smiled. He was enjoying the banter with her. "The school is over a year old now. How long does it take to learn how to sew a dress or put a bow on a hat?"

"They are also learning to read, write, and add and subtract numbers. All these things combined takes time. A few lengths of muslin and broadcloth would have been much better."

He bent his head forward, almost touching his nose to hers. "Are you going to give it back?"

"Of course not," she answered breathlessly.

That's what he wanted to hear. The tension that had built inside him ebbed away. "Then why are we arguing?" he said, his tone softening considerably.

"I don't know."

"Neither do I, Julia. I don't want—"

One moment he was talking and the next he was silenced by the eager touch of her lips on his. His instinct was quick and impatient. He slid his arms around her narrow waist and brought her slender body against his. She leaned into his chest and a shock of pleasure ripped through him. The taste of her mouth was euphoric, inciting him to unleash all the stored-up desire he had for her in this one arousing kiss.

This was no dream. She was in his arms.

Garrett accepted the unexpected kiss with urgency and took control. Her lips softened and surrendered beneath his as they kissed over and over again. Her arms circled his neck and she traced the breadth of his shoulders and cupped his neck before her hands settled in the center of his back, holding him fiercely, possessively. His body stirred with wanting.

Whispered moans of hectic pleasure wafted past her sweet lips. Garrett caught each in his mouth and savored and swallowed each one. With an intensity initiated by her, he kissed down the length of her neck, across the swell of her breasts, and back up to her lips again and again as if he were a desperate, thirsty man drawing cool water from a well. She welcomed and participated in his greedy assault.

Their kissing was impatient and unrelenting in its fervor. Her body was warm, soft, enticing. His hands caught and tangled in her long hair falling against her shoulders. He crushed its softness between his fingers before moving his hands up and down her back, around her waist again, and past the flare of her slim hips. He wanted to touch every inch of her.

Much too soon she pulled back from him, gasping with little short breaths that caused her chest to heave seductively. Her moist lips hovered close to his. They were lush and tempting him to capture them beneath his once again.

Her bright violet eyes searched his, but for what, he wasn't sure. Hadn't his response to her unprovoked kiss told her everything she needed to know about what he was feeling and how much he wanted her? He'd wanted a sign that she was as thoroughly, madly hungry for him as he was for her.

Just in case she didn't know what she had started, he pulled her up closer and tighter to his chest, pressing her soft breasts against him so there would be no doubt that at this moment he considered her his. Yet she continued to stay silent.

With a hint of a smile and in a huskily whispered voice, he said, "You shouldn't have done that."

"I know," she said with uncertainty in her tone, as a tremor shook her. "It was dangerous and very forward of me."

"No." His smile grew wider. "It was what I wanted, but one kiss from you is not enough to satisfy me. I need more."

A smile eased across her beautiful, full lips, and she whispered, "Then don't let me stop you."

He lightly, briefly brushed his lips across hers and then looked into her eyes once again. "You're beautiful, Julia," he whispered, and then reached over and kissed along the bare skin of her upper arm. He smiled again when he saw goose bumps pebble her smooth skin.

Garrett placed his lips on hers, giving her a slow, yearning kiss. He didn't want them to rush and devour this kiss as they had their first kisses. This time they would linger, revel, and explore all the sensations blossoming inside them.

Julia tempted him with her excitement and willingness to be an equal partner in their embrace. He explored her body and she explored his with equal desire and respect. Their kisses were searching and desiring. Each kiss melted into the next and all he could think of was how good and desirable she felt cuddled in the circle of his arms.

Long ago he'd learned how to control his sexual emotions, as most seafaring men had. And it usually didn't take him long to find his way into the arms of a willing woman shortly after setting his feet on land, but this time had been different. Somehow he knew he was waiting for someone special.

Something hard thumped Garret in the middle of his back. Fearing they'd been caught, he instinctively swung around and shielded Julia behind him, ready to do battle with whomever was challenging him. No one was there. His chest tightened, his heart thumped. A boyish giggle sounded down the corridor. A leather ball lay at his feet.

"Chatwyn," Julia whispered, breathlessly.

Garrett's tension eased and he chuckled. "The mischievous little imp threw the ball at me."

"He—he saw me. Saw us kissing. I should have been more careful, but you make me lose all sanity."

She seemed horrified by the possibility. "Don't worry about him," Garrett offered, wanting to calm her. "He obviously didn't know what we were doing. He was laughing."

"But I should have remembered he was in the house. The housekeeper was lingering outside the door. I was so caught up in how I was feeling that I—"

"Julia, it's all right. We were just kissing. He's fine." Garrett reached for her, but she turned away. "I was certain that Mrs. Desford had left or I'd never have kissed you."

"But I'm not." She breathed in deeply. "I shouldn't have forgotten myself, but it's just that you—"

Chatwyn appeared in the doorway and looked directly at Garrett. "You get the ball," he stated, his bright blue eyes sparkling. "It's your turn to chase after me."

"All right," Garrett said. "You'd better start running."

"You've got to catch me first," Chatwyn said, then turned and bumped right into Miss Periwinkle, who took a firm hold of his hand.

"Begging your pardon, Lady Kitson," the governess said. "He was thirsty and I brought him in for a sip of water. He slipped away from me while I was pouring it. I hope he didn't disturb you. I'll take him back outside."

"Wait." Julia walked over to Chatwyn and looked down at him with a glaring stare. "I want your attention right now, young man."

His smile faded and he fixed his gaze on his mother's perturbed face. "Yes, Mama."

"What have I told you about a ball in the house?"

He didn't move his head but shrugged and rolled his eyes to look up at Garrett, as if he'd been his partner in this offense. There was no doubt he knew he'd done something his mother didn't like.

"Chatwyn, this is not a time to be amused," she said sternly. "Look at me and answer."

His smile faded again and he said, "Don't throw a ball in the house."

"That's right. There will be no more outside play for you today. You must go to your room and sit in the corner with nothing to occupy your hands but your fingers. It should be a good time for you to practice counting." She looked at the governess. "If he gets up, Miss Periwinkle, you are to scold him and put him back in the corner. He must stay there a full hour. After that, he's not to come belowstairs the rest of the day. Do I make myself clear?"

"Yes, my lady," she said timidly.

"Go."

Garrett reached down, picked up the ball, and threw it up in the air a couple of times before saying, "Don't you think that was a little harsh? He didn't hurt me when he threw the ball."

"It's not that he hit you," she said, with a twitch of a little smile. "I wouldn't have minded if he'd hit you a little harder."

Garrett chuckled. He loved her spitfire attitude. "You are always full of surprises."

She accepted his praise with a nod. "I hate to admit it, but I do realize Chatwyn has a discipline problem. He knows better than to throw a ball or anything in the house. We've had more than one broken vase to contend with because of his wild pitches, but broken porcelain is easy to clean up. He recently threw a ball and overturned a lamp that caught a rug on fire. It could have burned the house down if the duke and I hadn't been in the room and put it out quickly. So I would thank you not to tell me how to discipline him."

That put Garrett in his place rather quickly. The only thing he could say was, "I'll be more careful in the future."

Julia clasped her hands together behind her back and lifted her chin and shoulders. "I was attracted to you the moment I saw you, Mr. Stockton. I should have never given in to our first kiss. It's so much harder now to deny myself."

"Passionately? I will never be sorry about that, Julia."

Garrett's stomach tightened and he strode up next to her. She remained still and calm. "We aren't bound by vows to anyone else. What we do together will hurt no one. We are both free to do as we choose."

Her gaze swept down his face, and he couldn't have been more convinced that he wanted her more than he'd ever wanted any other woman.

She turned away and murmured, "No, I'm not free. My first duty is to my son. Right now, he should be the only man in my life. I'll walk you to the door."

He started to grab her arm to stop her, but remembered how headstrong she was and knew he had to be patient with her. She wasn't a woman to be rushed into anything. He must take his time and save this fight for another day.

"Before you go," she said, handing his hat and gloves to him, "I wanted to ask you if we might share the good fortune your donation brought to the school with others. We can't possibly use all the things you sent over. Do you mind if we donate some of it to another charitable organization?"

Her request didn't surprise him. "Are there more children or dogs you want to help?"

"No," she laughed softly. "It's for the Sisters of Pilwillow Crossings. They can sell the excess of what we can't use. The money will help them with their charitable work. They feed the poor three days a week and also help supply bandages and other things for those in need."

"Do with it as you wish, Julia. Share it all if you wish. There were no strings attached to it."

"Thank you. I've been thinking on this all day and before I have it packed, I've decided to let each girl pick a fabric, thread, and adornment for trim to have as her own. Since it was a gift to them. That way, when they are skilled and ready to sew on their own, they can make a dress of their choosing."

An unfamiliar feeling stole over Garrett. He had endangered his life countless times on the seas and in gaming hells all over the world, but this was the first time his heart had ever been at risk. That was startling. But he had no doubt this lady was worth any price.

"That's a considerate gesture. You are very caring of others, Julia."

"One of the girls at the school gave me the idea. I remembered that she said when she makes her own dresses, she's going to put many bows on them. I want her first dress to be special."

Garrett smiled. "It will be."

"I hope to hear you have good news soon, Mr. Stockton. Time is running out."

Chapter 14

Julia and Brina sat quietly in straight-backed chairs in a dark corridor of the abbey, waiting to see Sister Francine. There were the occasional sounds of voices and footsteps, but otherwise the big, cavernous building was quiet and oddly cold for a place that was known for giving out compassion and expecting nothing in return. Brina seemed calm and patient. Julia, on the other hand, was anything but.

She would cross her feet at her ankles and then thirty seconds later she would uncross them. For a time, she'd studied the braided fringe on the bottom of her velvet reticule. She'd smoothed her gloves more than once, brushed her dress often, and touched her bonnet countless times. None of her twitching seemed to bother Brina, who was, somehow, managing not to move a muscle.

The quietness was giving Julia too much time to

think. Which wasn't a good thing. If she wasn't doing something to keep her busy, she was thinking about Garrett and how she yearned to be with him again. Dreaming about his kisses, caresses, and how desperately she wanted to be with him again but realizing the dangers of doing so. The only thing it accomplished was creating frustration inside her.

She supposed it was bound to happen one day. That there would come a man who would awaken all her feminine senses and make her desire him beyond all others and continue to take chances to be with him. She had certainly thought on that the past couple of days. But she always came to the same conclusion: the risks were too great that the duke would find out and make good on his promise.

And there was the intolerable Mr. Pratt. She didn't know why but he hadn't come to give lessons yesterday or today. It had been a blessing. She prayed the duke had finally listened to her pleadings in her letters and realized the error of his decision and dismissed the man.

The door to their left opened suddenly, startling Julia from her pensive thoughts. She immediately rose, expecting it to be her and Brina's time to go inside, but three sisters walked out and politely closed the door behind them. They all smiled at Brina and Julia as they passed, but hurried on without speaking.

"I hope they were in the meeting with Sister Francine and she will now be free to see us," Julia said as the sisters disappeared around a corner. "We don't want to be so late returning that your driver becomes concerned about us."

Brina looked up at her and smiled. "My driver will not worry about us, but I'm concerned about you. Why are you acting like you have ants crawling under your skirts? It's so unlike you."

"I know. I can only explain it by saying I'm quite anxious about this for you. It's difficult to remain objective in this journey you're on because of my misgivings about it."

"Don't be anxious about this. I'm not. I'm quite calm about it. I know I'll make the right decision."

That's what bothered Julia. Trying to decide if you wanted to join an order should make you restless. Brina was too peaceful. However, Julia returned to her seat and had hardly crossed her ankles when the door opened again and another nun walked out and smiled at them.

"Sister Francine will see you now," she said.

Julia and Brina followed her past one office and into an inner room where a tall, robust woman rose from the chair at her desk and laced her fingers and hands together just above her waist. She gave them a generous, friendly smile. Julia liked her immediately. The nun's light green eyes were small but bright, with a contentment so many of the people Julia knew didn't have, including herself. A few softened wrinkles lined her forehead and around her mouth. The fabric of her black tunic was faded and her headdress was no longer a pristine white but both were perfectly starched and pressed.

"Good afternoon, ladies," she said. "Welcome to the Sisters of Pilwillow Crossings."

"Thank you for agreeing to see us," Brina said.

"Why wouldn't I?" she asked in a jovial tone. "I'm happy you are here. As you can imagine, we don't get many visitors here. I was delighted when Sister Helen told me someone was waiting to meet with me. Please sit down."

They seated themselves in the two straight-backed, cushionless chairs in front of the simple desk. Brina glanced at Julia and took a deep breath before looking back to Sister Francine and saying, "I want to join the sisters here. I'm sorry, I'm a bit nervous. That is to say, I think I do. I haven't made up my mind completely yet. There are a few hesitations I have, but I felt the only way to put them to rest and know for sure was to come and talk to you."

The nun nodded to Julia and questioned, "Are both of you contemplating joining us?"

Julia shook her head. The way she felt when Mr. Stockton was kissing her immediately popped into her mind and she stated, "No, no, not me. I'm here only as Brina's companion."

"I see." The sister's gaze fell to Brina's white-gloved hands lying so properly and beautifully in her lap, with the ribbons of her satin reticule wrapped perfectly around her small wrist. Her gaze then moved to her own dry, pale hands with short, work-hardened nails and deep blue veins showing beneath her aged skin. "You think you might be suited to the secluded life we live here, Mrs. Feld?"

"Yes. I believe so."

"Would you like to tell me why?" Sister Francine asked with no condescension in her tone.

"I've seen what you do here. I've stood across the street and watched how you help people. You have good women here. Women I would be proud to join." Brina's chin lifted. "You are selfless in all you do and you have genuine purpose to your life. A kind and compassionate purpose. You take care of the unfortunate of our Society. You must get immense satisfaction from all you do for others."

"We do," she said quietly and without a hint of pride. "Everyone here does. But for you, Mrs. Feld, you would be starting from a different perspective than all the rest of us. For many reasons, coming here has made a better life for most of us."

"That's what I want," Brina said anxiously, leaning forward. "A more fulfilled life. A life where I do good things for others rather than myself. I've watched you feed the children and elderly people who can hardly walk without aid from someone." Brina placed her hand to her chest. "My heart aches for them and I want to help them, too."

"We all do what we can for those in need. I've found that most people are good-hearted and want to help others. I'm not sure you understand exactly what a life of servitude is, Mrs. Feld. I don't doubt in your heart you want to find peace in your life and do something rewarding for others, but I would have concerns that you can physically, mentally, and emotionally do what would be required of you to live here with us."

"I don't know what you mean," Brina said quickly and defensively. "I'm strong and healthy. My mind and reasoning capabilities are sound, and I understand all the consequences to myself and my family for what I'm considering."

Sister Francine only smiled at her and then continued in her straightforward tone. "What we do is difficult, Mrs. Feld. I'm not talking only about the physical work we do. That can be learned by anyone. It's that some women find they can't cope with all the hardship and suffering they see others enduring. They take each person, each wound, and each sorrow as if it were their own, and when they do, the burden becomes too great to carry. That can't be done here. You must be able to put aside all your emotions and concentrate only on the effort of what is required of you."

"I can do that."

"Can you?" The sister sighed. "I suggest you return home and think about the magnitude of this endeavor. You would encounter a world you know nothing about and I'm not sure you fully understand. Consider it carefully and then come back and we'll talk again."

Julia knew Brina hadn't convinced the sister of anything, but Brina's countenance hadn't changed. Her eyes had narrowed just enough for Julia to know she wasn't happy that Sister Francine had all but dismissed her as a weakling.

"Thank you, Sister Francine," Julia answered, understanding exactly what the woman said, whether or not Brina did. "Mrs. Feld will continue to search her heart concerning this matter. I do believe she knows the impact this would make in her life as well as her loved ones' lives. She will consider it more. For now, there is a different subject I'd like to discuss with you, if you have the time."

"I'd be happy to," Sister Francine answered, seemingly not bothered at all by how her comments affected Brina and the quiet aura that had settled over her.

"Mrs. Feld and I, along with another friend, started a benevolent school for girls where they are taught the trade of seamstresses so they can earn a wage one day—when they are older. The school was recently the beneficiary of more fabrics, threads, and such than we can use. We thought perhaps we could share some of it with you. It's not the kind of fabrics and materials the sisters would use for themselves but we thought perhaps you might sell the items and utilize the money to then buy whatever you may need."

"We gratefully take donations, Lady Kitson, and I don't want to seem unappreciative of you for thinking about us, but none of us here would know how or where to go about selling merchandise."

"Oh," Julia said. "Yes, I should have realized that and do understand exactly what you mean." In truth, she and Brina were in the same predicament. Entering a seamstress or modiste shop and asking them to buy ostrich plumes and beads for ball gowns wasn't something a lady of Society would ever do.

Sister Francine rose. "If you have black or white thread or fabric we can make use of it. Otherwise, I have to decline your generous offer."

"Yes, of course. We'll find a way to sell it ourselves and bring our donations back to you at another time."

"In that case, we'd be pleased to accept. And I'll be happy to talk with you another time about your aspirations to serve, Mrs. Feld."

"Thank you, Sister," Brina said tightly.

Julia and Brina remained quiet until they made it out of the building and down onto the pavement.

"I can't believe it!" Brina exclaimed. "She doesn't think I'm physically or mentally strong enough to feed people."

Brina started marching down the street at a fast pace.

Julia rushed after her. "That's not what she said."

"Yes, it is," Brina argued, not bothering to look at Julia. "How could she possibly know what I'm capable of doing from one meeting? Look at me. I am strong and healthy. I'm only twenty-three years old. I could be of service to them for many years to come."

"Yes, Brina, look at you," Julia answered. "Look at yourself and tell me what you see."

Brina stopped abruptly and faced Julia. "You agree with her," she accused her with a huff of breath. "You don't think I'm capable of doing this for others either."

"No," Julia defended earnestly. "I'm not saying that. Not exactly, but I see what she is seeing. You've had an easy life. Look at how you're dressed. You change your wardrobe from year to year. Her habit was old and worn. You're young and beautiful. You're small-boned and have delicate features. You look fragile."

"I'm not fragile!" she exclaimed, raising her voice and jerking her hands to her hips in anger. "How can you say that about me? You know me. I'm not a weak-kneed simpleton. I know what I want to do. I want to help people in need. And I don't appreciate Sister Francine all but patting me on the head and telling me to go home and enjoy the life I have."

Julia hadn't often seen Brina angry. In fact, she had never seen her in such a tizzy. And Brina was miffed at her, too.

"I'll go to a different abbey." Brina stomped off again. "That's what I'll do. If they don't want my help at Pilwillow Crossings, fine. I'll find one that does."

Julia caught back up to her again. "That will do no good. They will all see the same person Sister Francine saw."

"Then I'll buy some old clothing. Or I'll start my own house for the poor."

"That won't change who you are. Someone who's never made her own bed or a loaf of bread."

"Just because I don't have to make a bed doesn't mean I can't do it. And I can learn how to bake bread."

Julia thought about Brina's words for a few steps.

Of course, Julia could make a bed, too. Not that she'd ever had to, but she was sure she could manage to tuck the sheets and put all the covers and pillows in the right places. But could she make bread? If she had to in order to feed Chatwyn, could she do it?

"I have an idea," Julia said, keeping up with Brina's fast, irritable pace.

"I probably won't like your idea any better than I liked Sister Francine's."

Julia couldn't help but smile. Brina wasn't ready to forgive either one of them. "Maybe you won't, but listen to me anyway."

"I have nothing else to do while we walk to the carriage," she said tightly.

"Let's you and I bake bread one day."

Brina stopped again and looked at Julia with interest but remained silent.

"I'm serious about this," Julia said. "I'll arrange to have Mrs. Lawton be away from the house at the school for an entire day so we can be there by ourselves." How Julia would manage that right now, she didn't know. "You and I will go into the kitchen and we will bake bread and make a pot of soup."

Brina folded her arms across her chest and breathed in deeply before asking. "Do you know how?"

"I have no idea," Julia admitted honestly. "But it can't be that difficult, can it? You mix yeast and flour with water and put it into a pan and bake it. I know that much. After we finish, we can take the food to the school for the girls to enjoy and we'll clean up before Mrs. Lawton returns. No one else need ever know."

"I think I like this idea, Julia. That way I can tell Sister Francine that I might look delicate but I'm not. I know how to work and will be able to do my share."

"Yes," Julia agreed, feeling quite pleased with herself for coming up with such a good plan. "You can tell Sister Francine that you have actually baked bread and cooked soup."

"Yes," Brina said, sounding more excited than ever. "We'll make chicken soup. That will be delicious for the girls and it must be easy. You just drop a chicken in water and boil it and add some potatoes. Right?"

Julia's stomach roiled. She cared too much for animals to think about eating meat or fowl of any kind. Occasionally, she would indulge in fish or other delicacies that came from the sea. The thought of cooking a chicken—well—no—not even for her friend.

Brina must have realized Julia's hesitation. "I forgot that you don't eat—never mind about the chicken. I don't know where we would get one anyway. We'll make vegetable and root soup. We should find plenty of those in the kitchen's cupboard and larder."

"Yes," Julia said, thankful that was settled. "Vegetable soup sounds much better."

Brina's smile returned. "Thank you, Julia. You are the dearest friend. This is the perfect solution to my problem."

"We'll make sure you can do this before you go back for another meeting with Sister Francine. I want you to make the best decision for you."

The two fell silent as they walked. There was much for both of them to think about. Julia wasn't immune to the struggles of Brina's dilemma. It was as real as Julia's with the duke, Mr. Pratt, and Garrett.

Garrett.

Her breaths quickened. She remembered in detail every touch, every taste, and every sound they'd made when he held her so tightly and they kissed so passionately. He'd made her ravenous for his touch. When she was in his arms she felt as if he couldn't bear the thought of letting her go.

Suddenly Julia blinked against the dry air. She used to think of *a man's touch*, but now she thought of *Garrett's* touch.

Chapter 15

"Good afternoon, Mr. Ashfield." Garrett took off his hat and gloves and laid them on the table. The first thing he noticed upon entering was that Urswick's assistant had added a painting to one of the walls, just as Garrett had asked. It was a ship with full sails gliding on calm waters, the beautiful and peaceful colors of early morning sunrise breaking across the sky behind it.

"And good day to you, Mr. Stockton," Ashfield said excitedly, coming from behind his desk. "May I show you something, sir?"

"Certainly," Garrett said, assuming the man wanted to make sure he saw the painting on the wall. Instead, the secretary held out his hands before Garrett and made tight fists and then opened and spread his fingers wide. "The grip in my hands has improved greatly." He repeated the action a couple more times. "And it's not just the movements of my hands, sir. All my joints, hips, knees and shoulders feel better than they have in years. Even my wife has noticed I have more of a happy bounce to my step."

"Well, if the wife has noticed then it is good news." Ashfield beamed.

"Do you think it's the powder I gave you that's made the difference in your movements?" asked Garrett.

"It has to be," Ashfield said without equivocating. "It's the only thing I've done differently. And I've not had any ill effects from the mixture, though I have to admit, the first few mornings I didn't know if it would stay down after I managed to swallow it. I've found strong coffee or a nip of brandy helps hide the taste."

Garrett chuckled. "That's good to know."

"Yes, sir. I hope I will continue to get even better, but if I don't, it's worth the relief I already have. I have about half of the documents you wanted copied. Would you like for me to go ahead and return those to you today?"

"I'm glad to hear that, and no. It's best we keep them all together."

"Thank you, sir. I'll do that. Mr. Urswick and Mr. Brownley are waiting for you."

Garrett walked over and knocked on Urswick's door, and then looked back to Ashfield and said, "Well done on the ship."

Ashfield beamed again.

"Mr. Stockton," Urswick greeted as he opened the door wide for Garrett to enter.

Garrett nodded to him and then toward Mr. Brownley, who was rising from his chair. The Prince's emissary was a man of average build, height, and girth. What set him apart from most other average men was his haughty attitude in most things. Garrett had never met a man who wore his collar points higher, and Brownley wore his position of being in the Prince's inner circle just as lofty.

"Good day, Mr. Stockton," he said, with his chin held high. "I trust your stay in London has been advantageous so far."

Garrett shook the man's hand. "Pleasant. How's the Prince?"

"He's well. It appears you are, too."

Urswick looked at Garrett and said, "If you'll excuse me, I'll step outside for a few minutes and handle some other things. You can let me know if you need anything."

Garrett nodded to his manager, who closed the door as he left the office.

"The Prince was glad to hear you're back in Town, Mr. Stockton. He will soon have need of your fast ship and your temperament."

Garrett frowned. "Will another country's ships be chasing me, as happened when I sailed out of Greece three years ago?"

The man gave a humorless chuckle. "Well, of course, we never know, do we, Mr. Stockton? But as always, we hope not. I can say that this time you won't be carrying delicate artifacts from historical sites, armaments or gold, so there should be no danger to your men. I hope that reassures you."

Somewhat, Garrett thought, but remained silent. It really didn't matter what it was, he didn't want to do it. Just a year ago, the thought of sailing for the Prince again would have excited him. He couldn't remember a time he wasn't ready to leave London within a week or two of arriving. Now, all he could think was that he didn't want to leave Julia. The thought of it twisted his gut. There was no doubt he owed the Prince more than he could ever repay, but he wouldn't leave Julia and her son for anyone.

"Right now, I'm not sure exactly which port you will sail into. That has yet to be settled. I should know within a month. I can tell you that your cargo will be animals."

"What?" Garrett grimaced.

"It's a long story but I'll try to make it brief. There's been private talk among some gentlemen who want to start a Royal Zoological Society here in London. Much in line with the one that's been successful in Paris. One of the men made the Prince privy to their discussions, and he became immediately interested in the idea. They've already started preparing an area and offered to help bring animals into London, and—"

"Wait, Mr. Brownley," Garrett interrupted. "I don't carry animals on any of my ships."

The man gave him a sniff of disdain. "I understand that you haven't done it before."

And not likely to now, Garrett thought. He wasn't in need of money, as he had been the first time he carried cargo for the Prince. Garrett had been to the Tower Menagerie. It was clear the animals weren't properly cared for and he had no desire to bring more to that facility.

"The Prince will have to employ another shipping company."

"Give me the opportunity to explain what the Prince has in mind, Mr. Stockton, before you make up your mind. Until now, animals have been caged for the benefit of people who want to look at them or poke them— not study them. I mean, who doesn't want to see an animal as large as an elephant or as tall as a giraffe? The purpose of the Royal Society will be to create a natural habitat for the animals so they can be studied. Not simply for the sport or enjoyment of mankind. You must realize this will be entirely different."

"Why don't they take care of and study the ones they already have in the Tower Menagerie?"

"Well, of course, the Prince wants to create this and be the first to do it. Have his own animals." Mr. Brownley sniffed again. "He doesn't want to redo what someone else has already started. This new organization he is considering will see to it that the animals will be treated quite differently from the animals currently at the Tower. As you should know by now, it doesn't matter what the Prince is involved with, he wants it to be done right and up to the best possible standards. He spares no expense to see to that. Both are the reasons I'm talking to you."

"I'm not interested."

"If you don't mind, I haven't finished, Mr. Stockton. The Prince wants the animals healthy and, shall we say, unbroken—the same way he wants every piece of china he receives from the Orient to arrive undamaged. He's heard the stories, as I'm sure you have, how animals are sometimes mistreated on long voyages. That is why he wants you. He trusts you to see that the animals will be taken care of properly by the men handling them and that they suffer as little as possible. He wants this Royal Society get started and be bigger than the one in Paris. The Prince's mission is always to do it grand or not do it at all."

"I'm not interested," Garrett said again. There was no doubt that he was once indebted to the Prince. But Garrett figured he'd paid the Regent in return several times over. He thought of Julia and Chatwyn again. He wanted to be with them. Chasing butterflies in the park or throwing a ball in the back garden. After all his years of traveling, Garrett was now feeling as if he'd come home. He wasn't leaving. "My sailing days are over, Mr. Brownley. And my shipping company won't ever be carrying animals."

"I'll take that as a maybe. The Prince wouldn't be asking you to do it if it was going to be easy for you, Mr. Stockton. The society in Paris seems to be doing quite well. Naturally, the Prince doesn't want to be seen as being second to anyone or anything. And there's no hurry for an answer as of now. Take your time and think about it. I'll be back in touch."

With his point made, Brownley rose and said, "I'll say goodbye and one other thing, Mr. Stockton. You can name your price. The Prince doesn't quibble about money when he wants something. And he wants you handling this for him."

Garrett watched the man leave. Mr. Urswick walked back into the room and closed the door.

"Have you started back to work on the ledger?" Garrett inquired.

"Yes. Once I decipher what he's using for the first letter of the alphabet and the number one and zero, I should start to make sense of the system."

"This is urgent, Mr. Urswick."

"I understand, sir."

Chapter 16

Julia and Brina stood just inside the kitchen door-way at the house in front of the school, staring at what was before them—a wide, oval-shaped fireplace with a small oven built into each side. The hearth, elevated about a foot, extended out from where the fire would be. An iron-framed cooking rack had been placed on it. Wood was stacked neatly on the floor. Pots and pans of varying sizes and odd-looking cooking utensils hung on the walls. Neither of the ladies had ever been in a kitchen. It simply wasn't a place a lady should ever find herself.

Especially if there wasn't a cook or a scullery maid in sight.

A sizable worktable stood in the middle of the room, and much to Julia's relief, a bowl filled with cabbage, potatoes, celery, and other vegetables had been placed in the center of it. Three arched doorways led to three separate and narrow rooms: a dry larder, a wet larder, and a pantry where china, crystal, and cutlery were stored. That was about the extent of Julia's knowledge of the kitchen.

She and Brina had decided this was the perfect day to cook. There was a fair in Hyde Park. Julia had given Mrs. Lawton the day off and enough money to enjoy all the exhibits and foods. She was extremely appreciative. That would give them plenty of time to cook the food and clean up so no one would ever know they had been in the kitchen.

But the best thing was that Julia hadn't seen Mr. Pratt for an entire week. She had no idea why he hadn't come back. She'd only felt grateful for it. She didn't know if the duke had had a change of heart after he sent her the letter saying the man would continue or if for some reason Mr. Pratt had decided the job of taming Chatwyn was far too difficult. No matter which, Julia was pleased the lessons had stopped. She had left Miss Periwinkle strict orders to come get her immediately if the man should happen to return.

"If I didn't know better," Julia said, her gaze resting on the filled bowl in the middle of the table again, "I'd swear Mrs. Lawton knew we were going to be making vegetable soup."

"What do you think she will she say if we use the vegetables? She's bound to wonder what happened to them."

"I doubt she will bother either one of us about them," Julia said, pulling two white, crisply starched aprons off a peg near the entranceway and handing one to Brina. "However, if she asks, I'll tell her the truth.

That I gave it to the school. Since that is exactly what we plan to do, it won't be a fib."

"Good. We've settled our first problem of the day." Brina tugged the neck of the apron over her head and fitted it around her body. "Where do you think we should begin?"

Julia's gaze made another sweep around the room.

"Let's start with the fire," Julia answered, tying the sash at her lower back. "Mrs. Lawton would never leave a fire burning knowing she'd be gone all day. We'll have to rekindle it."

Brina's brows pulled together in a studious way. "Do you know how to do that?"

"Of course," Julia said, feeling somewhat confident she could manage this part. "Not that I ever have. When I was a girl, at wintertime the maid would come into my room each morning to light the fire. I'd sit up in bed and watch her. Now, you can watch me so you'll know how to do it, too. First, let's get the cooking rack out of the way so I can begin."

With more effort than Julia had thought it would take, she and Brina lifted the rack and set it off to the side. Julia knelt in front of the ashes and started carefully brushing them away from the embers with the fire brush while Brina hovered over her shoulder. After she'd uncovered a sizable glowing bed of coals, Brina handed her three pieces of kindling. Julia placed them on top of the coals. She blew long, steady breaths until the first piece of tinder caught fire. Moments later the others were flaming, too.

By the time Julia rose from the hearth, the flames had taken hold and were blasting an enormous amount of heat into the room. Without thinking, she ran her hands down her apron, smearing it with ash and soot. "Oh, heavens to stars," she grumbled to herself. "I had no idea all that was on my hands. I was so careful."

She tried to brush it off, but that only made the marks bigger and longer. That's when she caught Brina smiling at her.

"Perhaps this isn't the time for me to tell you it's on your face, too."

Julia grimaced and took in a deep exasperated breath. "No, it isn't." She picked up the tail of her apron and wiped both cheeks. By the expression on Brina's face, she was only making it worse as well. "I'll wash up later," she insisted. "Let's put the rack back in front of the fire and fill the kettle and teapot so the water can start getting hot."

Once that was accomplished, Julia said, "The first thing we need to do is make the bread. While it rises, we can chop the vegetables and put them into the kettle. By then, the bread should be ready for the oven, and we can clean up the kitchen while it cooks. That sounds simple enough, doesn't it?"

"Perfect. I was thinking the same order of things. Thank you, Julia. This has me so hopeful. I've been feeling quite miserable about how little I do for myself and others. Already I'm feeling better."

Julia smiled. If only she was settling her own issues as easily as she was Brina's. "I'll get the things we need out of the dry larder while you find a recipe book."

Brina nodded and went in search of a recipe while Julia gathered a tall canister filled with flour, a large bowl, a salt cellar, and a cake of yeast a little larger than a teacup saucer. Mrs. Lawton was very organized, so everything was easy to find. Julia carried it all to the worktable and laid it down.

"I've searched every cupboard, drawer, and shelf," Brina said, lifting her hands in frustration as she rejoined Julia. "I've looked under things, behind things, and inside things. I can't find a recipe book of any kind. Not even a little piece of paper that's been written on."

"That seems odd. There has to be one. Mrs. Lawton is an excellent cook. I'll help you look."

However, after following Brina's path and turning over everything in the kitchen and the dry and wet larder at least twice, Julia was ready to accept defeat when Brina offered, "We'll have to do it from what you remember by watching when you were a little girl."

Julia's throat tightened a little. "I never managed to do that. Bread was made the first thing every morning. I never came belowstairs before sunrise."

"They make bread that early?" Brina questioned as much with her expression as her words.

Julia put her hands on her hips and studied the ingredients before her. Suddenly she felt the gravity of what they were about to attempt and the reason for it—so that Brina would know she could do the work should she decide to join the sisters. This task had seemed so much easier when she was just thinking about doing it. Now that it was time to do the deed, she wasn't as sure.

Inhaling deeply, Julia swallowed down her hesitation. "Well, it can't be that difficult, can it? Cooks do it every day. I know it doesn't take a lot of yeast or salt to make bread rise, so let's see how much flour this bowl will hold and we'll go from there. I'll put everything in and you stir it all together."

Julia took the top of the tin to pour. The flour fell to

the bowl with a heavy splat and poofed flour all over her and Brina.

"What did you do?" Brina asked coughing and waving the white cloudy mist away.

"I don't know." Julia started laughing. "It's all over your face."

"It's on yours, too," Brina added with a snicker of amusement. "And in your hair."

Julia brushed her hand across her hair.

"Now it's worse." Brina smiled.

Julia laughed softly. "So now I'm covered in soot, flour, and ash. I'll clean up later." She looked down at the bowl. "I don't think that's enough flour to fill a pan. I'll add more."

They both looked down at the bowl as she tilted the canister again. A double handful of it plopped on top of the first pour and it dusted them again.

"Are you doing that on purpose?" Brina questioned in disbelief.

"Of course not," Julia defended herself, and put the canister down with a clatter. "Do you think I want flour all over my face and hair? Look, it's even on our sleeves."

"All right," Brina answered in a calmer voice. "As you said, we'll wash up later. Let's get this made so it can rise."

After discussing at length the amount of milk, yeast, and salt they should use, they began.

It didn't take long before the mixture in the bowl became a white sticky paste that was clinging to the sides of the bowl and the spoon in wet clumps.

"This is getting too difficult to stir and it won't hold together," Julia offered. "I think we need to stop the milk and add more flour."

"I'll pour this time," Brina said confidently, "and you stir."

"Yes, of course," Julia agreed with a roll of her shoulders. "You need to know how to do it all. It will be good practice for you."

They changed places and Brina lifted the canister. She gently shook out the tiniest amount. Julia stirred. The effort was repeated until Julia said, "I think we have enough. Let's spoon it onto the table and then you can knead it."

"Me?" Brina asked, looking down at the wet sticky flour.

"Of course, you. We're doing this for you. Put your strength into it."

They scraped the mixture onto the table. Brina squeezed her hands into fists and the dough squirted through her fingers. Seconds later the dough started sticking to the table and then to her hands in knobby clumps. Julia added more flour but the consistency didn't get better.

"What happened to it? I can't get it off." Brina tried to wipe the dough from her fingers and ended up, sending more of if flying.

"There's only one thing to do." Julia walked over and grabbed a pan off the wall. "It doesn't matter how it looks or feels. It's how it tastes that matters. Let's get it into the pan so it can rise."

"And say good riddance," Brina whispered under her breath.

After the dough was in a pan sitting on a table near the fire, and their hands were washed clean, it was time to cut the vegetables. They decided to clean up the flour from the table and floor after the vegetables were in the kettle.

Surely making soup had to be easier than making bread. There would be no measuring or sticky stuff to worry about.

Julia saw steam coming up from the kettle on the cook rack. "The water's hot."

"It's getting hot in the kitchen, too," Brina grumbled, wiping her forehead. "I think you made the fire too big."

"I knew we had to have enough heat to cook the food," Julia argued. "There was nothing to be done about that." It surprised her how testy one could get while cooking.

By the time they finished chopping the cabbage, two potatoes, three onions, and several mushrooms, they had three large bowls of vegetables and one medium-size kettle of water boiling.

"Why does cabbage become so much more once it's been cut up?" Brina asked as she looked at the mountain of food. "What are we going to do with all this?"

Julia had no idea but agreed it defied logic that something that looked relatively small could turn into a mammoth mound. But then, who would have thought baking bread could be such a chore, or that two little cabbages could look like they would feed Wellington's army once they were chopped?

"Should we fill another kettle?"

"It will take too long for the water to heat." Julia was ready to finish this and get out of the kitchen. "Let's fill this one to the top with as many vegetables as we can get in it. We can take the rest of it over to the school and *they* can cook it tomorrow."

"That's a better idea." Brina gave Julia a grateful smile.

Julia looked over at the bread and gasped. It had risen out of the bowl and had fallen over the sides of the pan and onto the table.

Brina looked at Julia and together they said, "Too much yeast!"

Julia took in a deep breath, determined not to let making bread get the best of her. "We'll fill more pans and bake it."

Finally, the bread was in the oven and the vegetables in the kettle. "The school will have enough bread for a week," Julia said, washing her hands in a tub of water.

"Soup, too," Brina added, dabbing a towel to her forehead. "I suppose we should clean up, but I would really rather sit down and have a cup of tea first."

Julia surveyed the table, sticky with drying flour and dough, and littered with bits of cabbage, potato, and onion peelings and greenery from the celery. She thought she might never want to eat again. Especially if she had to do the cooking. It was too much work, and she simply didn't want to eat that badly. And she had as much experience cleaning as she had cooking—which was none.

"I need something stronger than tea," Julia said, brushing a fallen strand of hair behind her ear. "I need to be fortified before I attempt cleaning that table. Port is a fortified wine. There's an open bottle of it in the drawing room."

"Excellent idea," Brina agreed.

After a few minutes, a few laughs, and a few dry bits of humor about how they looked, Julia and Brina were well on their way to finishing their second glass of port. Tiny glasses emptied quickly.

When their chatter about the enlightening experience faded away, Garrett crossed Julia's mind and she started feeling somber.

"I didn't tell you, but Garrett and I have kissed and touched and much more," Julia said softly.

Brina sat up straighter in the settee. "I thought as much, but didn't want to pry."

"When we were together it was hurried, frantic, but so magical I can't stop thinking about it or stop wanting it to happen again and again even though I know the dangers of getting caught or getting in the family way. Either one would ruin my life with my son and that's what I'm working to protect. My mind keeps saying, *Be sensible. You have so much to lose,* but my body, my heart keeps telling me what he makes me feel is worth the chance."

They were quiet for a few moments before Brina leaned back against the settee cushion. She then drained her glass, placed it on the table in front of her, and asked, "Do you love him?"

"Sometimes I think I must, but I really don't know. I desperately want to be with him again and feel those earth-shattering sensations. Yet there are the issues with the duke. And there's the matter that Garrett is an adventurer. He could sail away again at any time and leave me with a broken heart."

"Do you really think that's the kind of man he is?"

"I don't know the answer to that, but I do know he doesn't usually stay in London very long. You've heard the gossip about mistresses and leaving young ladies with broken hearts."

"I think the sea has been his only true mistress," Brina said. "He has been good to help you with finding the duke's documents and trying to understand the ledger. I don't think he's going to sail away."

"I can't be sure," Julia answered.

"Then you must enjoy the time you have with him. Before the duke returns, before Mr. Stockton leaves."

"That's what I've been thinking, too." Julia swallowed hard and set her glass on the table, too. "What about you, Brina? If you go to live at Pilwillow Crossings, you will never have the possibility of being kissed again. Never have that feeling as if you're walking on air again."

"That's what I've believed since Stewart died," she said thoughtfully. "Now, when I hear you talking about how Mr. Stockton makes you feel, I wonder if I'm sure."

"You must be—" Julia suddenly felt as if her stomach jumped to her throat. Was something burning? She turned and looked toward the doorway and sniffed.

"The bread!" Brina exclaimed.

They rose and raced each other down the corridor. Their elbows knocked, shoulders bumped, and skirts swished as they passed the dining room, the breakfast room and stopped inside the kitchen doorway.

Smoke billowed from the ovens on either side of the fireplace. Liquid from the soup was sputtering and bubbling over the top of the kettle and puddling on the floor. The stench of charred bread mixed with the harsh odor of burned wood and cooked food swirled in the air. Julia opened a window, grabbed a towel and started fanning the gray cloud.

"I'll get the bread out of the oven. You take the soup off the rack."

Julia couldn't see into the oven to reach for the pans. She fanned harder.

"I can't lift the soup by my—ouch!"

"Are you burned?" Julia asked.

"Only a little. It splattered on my hand. I'm all right, but the handle's too hot. The kettle is too heavy. I need your help."

Julia swung toward Brina. The ovens were going to continue to smoke until she got the bread out of them, but she was afraid Brina might hurt herself. She needed to help her first. Julia wrapped her cloth around one end of the handle of the kettle, Brina the other. They were trying to move when she heard booted feet running down the corridor.

Garrett.

He rounded the doorway and stopped, instantly taking in the situation. "What in the name of Hades are you two doing?"

"How did—"

"Not now," he ordered. "Stand back before you catch your dresses on fire or get burned."

Julia and Brina stepped away and watched him lift the scorching hot kettle from the rack as if it were empty and place it onto the far side of the hearth. He then pulled a bread paddle off the wall and slid it into the oven, bringing out the pans and tumbling them into the tub of wash water.

The damage of what almost happened flashed before Julia's mind. She was furious with herself for what she'd allow to happen. What made her think she and Brina could cook anything? They could have burned down the house! Why did her best intentions always seem to turn out wrong?

The smoke was clearing. Garrett looked at Julia and Brina. His brow furrowed deeply. "What the devil are you two doing in here? Where's your housekeeper?"

Julia swallowed hard. It was a rather awkward position she was in. As was often the case with her impulsive ideas, she'd landed herself in a predicament that was proving more difficult than she'd believed it would be. And it appeared there was going to be no easy way to get out of it.

"Hello," came a girl's voice from the back door. "We saw smoke coming out of the window. Is the kitchen on fire?"

Julia heard quick footsteps which was followed by two girls from the school. They stopped and looked at the soup and flour all over the floor and the leftover vegetable trimmings scattered across the worktable, and then their gazes settled on Julia.

"Mrs. Lawton is going to be mad at someone when she sees what's been done to her kitchen, but it's not going to be me she's mad at."

Chapter 17

"This is all my fault," Brina said softly, a stricken expression on her face.

Everyone's eyes turned to her. She stood solemnly with her smudged chin high. Julia appreciated her friend's kindness in wanting to take all the blame but she couldn't let her.

"Nonsense," Julia said firmly. "It's mine for even suggesting we should try to cook when neither of us know the first thing about it. I'm the only one responsible for this horrible mess."

"But you did it for me. You were only trying to help me and I fear I can't be helped." Brina looked from Julia to Garrett to the two wide-eyed girls standing in the doorway. She then turned and walked out the door.

Julia glanced at Garrett. He gave her an understanding smile and quirked his head toward the door. "Go.

She needs you. I'll make sure the fire is put out." Julia's heart seemed to lift in her chest. She wanted to rush into Garrett's arms and thank him for his understanding. Instead, she hurried after Brina and caught up with her in the vestibule, picking up her gloves, reticule, and bonnet.

"Brina, wait. There's no reason for either of us to be upset about what happened. In fact, nothing terrible happened today. We didn't burn down the kitchen—just the bread. I'm sure many cooks, even the best cooks, burn the bread from time to time. We must look at what we did. Not at what we didn't do. We made soup." Julia laughed softly. "Think about that. You and I cooked a pot of soup. Everything's going to be fine."

Brina kept her eyes focused on her hands, lying so still on the table where she'd gathered her things. "You don't understand. It's not the bread burning or the soup pouring all over the floor. It's Sister Francine that has upset me. She was right when she said she didn't think I was up to the task of being a part of Pilwillow Crossings."

Julia's heart softened even more for her friend and she laid her hand on top of Brina's. "I won't hear that from you. You can't know what you are capable of accomplishing on just one try. Be as reasonable and kind to yourself as you are to others. We didn't know what to do. We'll try again, and next time—"

"No," Brina said earnestly. She looked up at Julia with eyes as bright as a summer day. "The really horrible truth about myself is that I didn't enjoy making the bread. How can I help others when I feel that way?"

"I'm sure it's a natural reaction for anyone the first time," Julia insisted. "I didn't enjoy it either. We've never been allowed in a kitchen to know what to do or how to do it. You can't revile yourself for how you feel, what family you were born into, or how you grew up."

"But how can I serve others, feeling as I do? The fact is I am the useless and pampered lady Sister Francine took one look at and saw."

"You are not useless. Don't say that about yourself. And I didn't suggest we try to cook just to show you that you couldn't do it. I actually thought we could do it. I had no idea it would be so difficult."

"I know. It showed me there's a difference between just standing in a line and handing food to people with a smile or a soft word—which is the only part I'd seen—and how much work there is to do before you can give people that comfort and kindness. I honestly don't know if I'm up to it. I thought I was until you helped me try it."

"Brina, I'm not going to try to talk you into anything or out of anything. That is your decision. I do think it would have been so much easier for us if we'd been learning with someone who actually had a recipe and knew how much flour, yeast, and milk to use. Or maybe if I hadn't suggested port instead of tea. Perhaps we wouldn't have let the bread burn if we hadn't started talking about Garrett and my feelings for him."

"That is the only sane thing we did."

"But you can't make your decision on this one attempt. You are a strong, capable person, whether or not you can make flour into bread, and you have many accomplishments. Most anyone can become discouraged when they are first trying to handle a situation they aren't accustomed to. I know that feeling very well."

Julia picked up the hem of her apron and affectionately started wiping Brina's cheek. "My dear friend, you cannot go home with flour all over your face and with that apron covering your dress. Your bonnet will cover your hair until you get to your dressing room."

Brina looked down. "Oh, you're right. I forgot I had it on." While she untied her apron, Julia helped brush her sleeves.

As soon as she laid the apron on the table, she picked it up again and said, "What am I thinking? I have to help you clean the table and floor."

"No, no." Julia grabbed the apron from her grasp. "There are two girls in the kitchen who probably know more about cleaning than we ever will. I'm going to put them to work."

"That doesn't seem fair. I helped make the mess. It's only right that I do my part to clean it."

"If you stay, there will be so many of us in the kitchen we will be running over one another. Please go and think on this decision you must make."

A resigned sigh passed Brina's lips. She then lifted her chin and shoulders. "What about Mr. Stockton?"

"I'll put him to work, too," Julia said with a smile. "The soup is so heavy we could have never carried it to school. I'll ask him to do that for us. I'll ask the girls to crumble the burned bread in the garden for the birds. Everything will be washed and put away in no time. The kitchen will be as Mrs. Lawton left it—minus a few vegetables."

"Julia," Brina said softly. "Just as I have some vital decisions to make, so do you."

Her friend's words seemed to seep into Julia's soul. She knew. Julia picked up Brina's gloves and reticule and gave them to her. "Go home. We'll talk about all of this again soon."

After seeing Brina out the door, Julia turned and

caught a glimpse of herself in the mirror. She tried to rub the soot off her face and the flour from her hair. But no amount of primping was going to make her look any better. She dropped her hands to her sides. There were more important things to do than make herself look better.

Julia walked through the doorway of the kitchen and stopped. Everything was clean. She glanced all around the room. Garrett was rising from the area where the soup had spilled over beneath the cook rack, a cloth in his hand. "What are you doing? How did you get everything clean so fast?"

"The girls helped by wiping the table. I just sent them back to the school with the uncooked vegetables."

"Thank you. I didn't intend for you to help clean."

Garrett smiled. "Why not? One of the first things I had to learn when I went to sea was how to scrub the deck. If you're going to sail a ship you have to know how to do every chore. I've already banked the fire and taken the bread out of the pans. They're soaking in the tub."

"I'm glad you saved something for me to do."

He nodded as his eyes stared intently into hers. "I'm going to take the soup to the school and then I'll be back."

His roguish smile and the way he said *I'll be back* caused Julia's heart to flutter.

Garrett picked up the kettle and headed out the door. He seemed to always be coming to her rescue. But she knew he didn't mind. He was such a strong but patient man. She thought of all the young and beautiful young ladies who had been at Lady Hallbury's party. Garrett could be riding around Hyde Park with any of them today. But he was here, helping her clean up the kitchen. A peacefulness settled inside her.

After she'd scrubbed the pans and had put them back in place, everything was tidy—except herself, of course. She poured fresh water into a basin and splashed it onto her face, letting the coolness trickle down to her neck and chest. She thought about what her life would be like if she were fully free to be her own master and not at the mercy of what the men in her life wanted her to do. She wanted to know what it would be like to have no fear her son might be ripped from her arms for the slightest infraction. What would she do first if she were truly free?

Her thoughts went immediately to Garrett. She'd invite him over to have dinner with her. Just the two of them sitting at a table, dining, sipping wine, and talking. She saw them sitting together on a rug in front of a fire, playing in tall grass with Chatwyn, and lying entwined together on crisp, cool sheets.

"Julia."

At the sound of Garrett's voice, she straightened and turned away from the basin with water dripping down her face and hands. "I didn't hear you come back inside."

Garrett walked closer to her and asked, "Where is the housekeeper?"

"I sent her away for the day so Brina and I could have the house to ourselves. We wanted to know if we could do something as simple as bake bread and, well, you can see how that turned out. How did you know I was here?" She looked around for a towel but didn't see one. She started wiping the water from her face with her hands.

"I saw Miss Periwinkle and Chatwyn in the park.

She wouldn't tell me where you were but when I asked Chatwyn he spoke right up and told me you were at the school."

"Of course, he wouldn't know not to tell. You were very clever to ask him. And I had to let Miss Periwinkle know in case Mr. Pratt arrived after I left. I told her to come tell me immediately. I don't know why but he hasn't come over for several days now."

"You won't have to worry about Mr. Pratt for a while."

"Oh, but I do," she answered. "The duke said he wouldn't make a decision on dismissing him until after he assessed him."

"I know," Garrett said softly, stepping even closer to her. "So I took the decision out of the duke's hands."

"What?" she gasped as hope and fear rose in her chest. "What did you do?"

"Nothing harmful, I assure you. I simply had him put on a ship that was sailing to America."

"You had him abducted?" Julia's body tensed.

"I didn't think he'd go willingly, but believe me, he wasn't hurt in any way. When the man arrives in New York Harbor he'll be told he was mistaken for someone else. He'll be given a generous amount of money to compensate him for the error that was made and put on a ship back to Southampton. From there he can hire a coach back to London. When a person is on a long journey and dependent upon the wind and the sails, he tends to learn a lot about patience and forbearance. I thought that might be a good lesson for the tutor."

For a moment or two, Julia's emotions warred inside her. Garrett had taken a man against his will and sent him to another country. But then she thought of Mr. Pratt's bulging eyes as he stared at Chatwyn with seething anger and from clenched teeth ordering him to stop clinging to his mother and sit still in the chair like a man.

"Thank you," she whispered to Garrett. "You did well."

Garrett smiled and moved even closer to her. "I did it for Chatwyn. I agree with you, Julia. He's too young and active to be under the direction of a man like Pratt. Remember, I met the man. He may not have laid a hand on Chatwyn, but it was only because you were there. In time he would have. I'd do what I did again to keep Chatwyn away from him."

Julia suddenly felt calmer. "Yes. Sometimes it's necessary to do the wrong thing for the right reasons. That's one worry I can put out of my mind. Now tell me, do you have good news from Mr. Urswick?"

"Not yet, but I'm still hopeful. But Mr. Ashfield has almost finished with the documents. They should be ready soon."

"That's good." She wiped more trickling water from her forehead down the side of her face. "Even if we don't have the ledger, I can present the duke with the copies and tell him I have the originals and the ledger. That should be enough to make him give me my freedom."

Garrett placed the palm of his warm hand to her wet cheek. His touch caused a shivery tingle to shudder through her. "Let me do this for you." He smoothed his hand all the way down her neck to her collar. His touch was purposeful, yet soothing.

For the first time since the fiasco happened, Julia trembled. She was so glad he'd come over and just at the right time. It was if he'd somehow sensed she needed his strength. She closed her eyes and gave in to the restful reassurance that he was there for her. With gentleness, he dried her forehead with the pads of his fingers. He pushed her fallen damp hair away from her face and behind her ears. He then lowered his face to hers and kissed the corners of her mouth, below her eyes, and the tip of her chin before lifting his head and looking into her eyes. He was teasing her, making her want to feel his lips on hers.

Julia couldn't remember a time of being so completely comforted. "You didn't tell me why you wanted to see me today."

He placed the tips of his fingers under her chin and lifted it ever so slightly while his thumb caressed her bottom lip. "Surely you know by now that I don't need a reason to want to see you. I simply want to see you."

His words thrilled her. Her stomach quivered deliciously and a teasing warmth tightened her breasts.

"However," he added, while lightly threading his fingers through the side of her hair, and making a few strands fall from her chignon. His hand then slipped around her still damp neck and gently pulled her closer to him. "I did have another reason for coming today."

A small puff of breath escaped past her lips as she whispered, "I knew it."

Garrett slid his arms around her waist and caught her up against his chest. "I have the money from the sale of the fabrics for you."

"Yes, that is what I wanted," she said, knowing her words could be referring to his embrace or the sale. She knew they were for both. "That's good news. Did you get a good price for the sisters?"

He kissed down her cheek again and over her jawline to nestle his nose in the warmth behind her ear. His strong hands massaged up and down her back.

Curls of pleasure moved inside her. "I think they'll be very pleased."

"Brina and I will plan to take it over one day next week. If she—" Julia trailed off her sentence. She realized she had no idea what Brina's feelings were right now concerning Pilwillow Crossings or what they would be next week.

Garrett seemed to sense the change in mood. He lifted his head again, and asked, "If she what?"

"Nothing." Julia shook her head and looked straight into his eyes. "It's a private matter for her that I can't share. But if you don't mind, I do have another favor to ask of you."

"You can ask anything of me, Julia. Being with you makes my life interesting. You are an adventure for me. I never know what you are going to do or say, but I'm ready for whatever you want."

His words pleased her more than he would ever know. "I would like for you to take the money and give it to Brina for me."

Garrett's hands stilled on the back of her shoulders. "Julia, I have no interest in Mrs. Feld."

She smiled and wove her hands around his neck. "I know that. She knows it, too."

He eyed her warily. "You have to admit it's a rather unusual request when she's your best friend and I have the money in my coat pocket ready to hand to you right now."

"I know." Julia sighed. "I have a very specific reason for asking you to do this. She has a difficult decision to make. It may make no difference at all in her determination, but it might help her to further reason out what it is she needs to do. It would mean a great deal to me if you could see your way to do this and not ask further questions."

"I'll see it's done."

His answer made her heart full. "Thank you."

"Do you feel better now?" he asked huskily.

"Yes," she whispered. "It seems you have now rescued me twice—from a tree and from a smoking oven. Now if only—"

Garrett's lips came down on hers, cutting off her sentence. The contact was delicate and feathery. Shivers of anticipation swirled through her.

Julia closed her eyes and reveled in his slow, languid kiss.

Chapter 18

Julia abandoned caution and fear, freeing herself of the concern she'd felt when they were in the duke's book room in the middle of the night. Right now, there would be nothing in her thoughts but Garrett.

It wasn't yet midday and they had all afternoon before the housekeeper would return. She wanted their coming together to be natural, flowing, and reverent. Julia led Garrett up the stairs to one of the bedchambers, where he locked them inside. But there was no changing nature. Their kisses and touches were just as eager, jubilant, and frantic as they had been the first time they were together. Neither of them could deny the desperate release their bodies demanded and wait until they were undressed. They braced against the door and kissed and touched until she trembled and he shuddered in the aftermath of their frenetic passion that left both of them breathless, happy, but nowhere near satisfied.

Only then did they disrobe. They wanted more. Julia pushed the coverlet aside and they lay down on the bed together.

The air in the room was cool. She shivered until Garrett stretched out his body, facing her, and gathered her close in the warmth of his embrace. He ran his hand down the plane of her hip, and then up to her waist, over her breasts, and back down to follow the same path all over again.

"I've been waiting for this," he said. "Me and you together. Alone. On a soft bed. With hours, not minutes, to be together."

"I've wanted it too, but there was always the worry—"

He kissed her softly, cutting off her words. "There are no worries right now. Just you and me."

She smiled. "Then kiss me again and again."

Garrett captured her lips in a deep passionate kiss. Julia moved her hands over him. His body was hard, lean, and magnificent to look at in the bright light of the afternoon sun shining through the windows. His skin was warm, smooth, and taut. She felt power in the breadth of his shoulders as her hands skimmed along their width. Muscles in his back and upper arms were perfectly defined and tight. His hips were slim and the swell of his buttocks firm.

Garrett became familiar with Julia's form, too. She'd ached for his touch, and that ache was eased when his hands glided down to her breasts, feeling the roundness before sliding down her ribs to her waist where he caressed the indention and pulled her even closer to him. His open palm moved over to her inner thigh and he touched her softly. He seemed to know where to touch her, what she wanted and needed without her saying a word. Each seductive stroke on the center of her womanhood was exhilarating, intoxicating, and deeply moving.

His fingers were gentle and sure as he quickly brought her to the peak of satisfaction once again and then allowed her to bask in the irresistible finish before he rolled her on her back and rose over her. She whispered his name over and over again, and each time he answered with a tender, "Yes."

Through their kisses they shared short breaths, sensual gasps, and long satisfying sighs. There was nipping, hovering, and deep kisses that bound them together in the sweet ecstasy of joining their bodies as one again. Their coming together was more passionate each time. Quick intakes of breath turned into soft sighs of wanting as his lips closed over her breast. Sensations of pleasure tumbled, swirled and rotated inside her. She savored each movement, each sensation. As if understanding her blissful torment, Garrett lingered and fed her hunger of wanting to be touched and adored, pleasing her all the more.

His embrace was at times gentle and possessive, and at all times persuasive that she was the one he wanted and treasured.

At first their lovemaking had been controlled and leisurely as their lips brushed, their hands clasped. Their bodies melded together smoothly, firmly, perfectly. His touch was magical, ethereal, and heady, sending waves of euphoria searing through her.

But all too soon, once more came the urgency. The abandonment of precious moments and reverence for spinning, mindless flashes of blatant, selfish pleasure.

Once again she was filled with extraordinary sensations that ended in delights too gratifying to be put into words. Julia welcomed them all. So did Garrett. The tremor of his muscles, the depths of his breathing, the intensity of his gasps as he whispered her name told her all she needed to know about how he felt.

Even as they rested, Garrett continued to softly kiss her lips, her cheeks, and the hollow of her throat. It was comforting and complemented the perfect contentment that had settled over her.

The afterglow of their coming together bathed Julia in a sweet feeling of contentment as Garret shifted his body and once again lay on his side. He cuddled her into the circle of his arms. She smiled, harboring no regrets for being with him again. Time with him was glorious.

She sensed he felt as she did.

They lay in silence filled with languor and memories of what passed between them. But now came the reality of how she felt and what Garrett meant to her. She'd told Brina she didn't know if she loved him. Now she knew she did. But would they ever be together again after today? Would she defeat the duke so she could be free? Would Garrett set sail again soon?

"Was Kitson a good husband?" he asked as his hand softly caressed her upper arm and shoulder.

Julia hadn't expected those to be the first words to pass between them after their love-making. His question didn't shock or dismay her. She actually understood his reason for asking. Curiosity was one of life's riches and was generally bestowed on everyone. Though some more than others. Since he had broached the subject, it gave her the opportunity to ask him a question that she had been pondering since they first met.

"Was the sea a good mistress?"

He chuckled, and said, "You made your point, my lady."

Without knowing why, she added, "I can't say I was in love with Kitson when I married him, but I feel no dishonor in that. We knew we didn't love each other, but to us our marriage seemed almost necessary. It gave us both what we wanted. I was free of the older viscount and he had defied his father. As happened, Kitson and I ended up being well suited, with neither of us demanding much from the other. And even though the duke never believed me, I properly mourned his son."

"Why would he doubt you?"

"Why wouldn't he? His second wife left him when Kitson was about seven because she could no longer abide his stringent command of her. I think because he didn't choose me for Kitson, he has always felt I'd one day run away, too. But I would never leave my son."

"That I know. It should have always been your decision who you married."

That's what Julia wanted. To make her own decisions. She kissed Garrett's lips and then smiled. "Were you and the sea a love match?"

He hugged her tighter. "The sea, no. The adventure, yes. It was a good life. I accomplished what I set out to do, what my father couldn't do."

"You can buy the house your father couldn't."

"Yes. It symbolizes a past, and a way of life I want to tear down. That a man can be a tradesman and a gentleman."

It didn't matter that he'd just given her an exquisite glimpse of heaven on earth once again or that he now held her cherishingly; Julia's heart constricted. She squeezed her eyes shut at the thought of him leaving London after he gained possession of the house. She remembered he'd told her he came back to see his friend get married and to buy that house. Now that he had breached the barrier of her defenses, she wanted him to remain in London.

Garrett kissed the top of her head a couple of times, and then she heard a chuckle rumble in his chest.

Julia's brows rose and she propped herself on her elbows. She gave him a teasing glare, and said, "I don't think this is the time for laughing, Mr. Stockton."

He shoved his arm under his head, and he stared right back at her with amusement handsomely displayed in the width of his smile and sparkle in his eyes.

"It is your fault."

"Mine? Whatever have I said to make you laugh after—after—well, while I'm lying here with you like this?"

"My apologies." He reached over and pushed her hair to the back of her shoulders. "I just kissed your hair and it tasted like flour."

Julia laughed, too. "You are a horrible man to remind me of that."

"You are beautiful. Your spirit of loving is beautiful. Even with flour in your hair and—"

She pushed at his chest and laughed again. "You are a beast. I should toss you out of the bed onto your rump."

He rolled to his back, pulling her down on his chest. His arms circled her waist and squeezed her close.

"Go ahead and try it if you think you are stronger than I am."

"Well," she said with an impish grin, letting her fingers glide easily across his chest. "I find I don't want to right now. I rather like you where you are and want to enjoy this feeling for a little longer."

"I want to enjoy it much longer. Marry me."

"What?" she asked breathlessly and then laughed, though she could see that Garrett was serious.

"I'm not like other men who might have sought your hand or heart, Julia. I don't want you for just an hour in the afternoons, or for a day or two during the week. I love you and want you for life. I want to marry you."

Julia swallowed hard. His words filled her with such joy she suddenly, inexplicably felt like crying. She never cried.

"No," she whispered, pushing away from him. "I love you, too, Garrett. I want to be with you like this. Sharing our love and desire for each other, but I don't want to marry. I want to be free. I want to know what it will be like to handle my life by myself without my uncle, my husband, or the duke controlling me. But it doesn't mean I don't want to be with you. I do."

His eyes swept lovingly down her face. "I would never control you as the duke has. You and Chatwyn would be safe with me. If you marry me you'll never have to worry about the duke again. I will never let him hurt either of you."

She thought of what he'd done to Mr. Pratt and she smiled. "I believe that, and it's not you that I don't want. It's marriage that I don't want right now."

He looked as if he might argue with her again, but

then he smiled, too. "All right. We won't talk of marriage. We'll only talk of love."

Garrett gentle pushed her to her back and rose over her. His lips came down on hers in a searing kiss.

Chapter 19

Garrett walked in the drizzling rain with only his heavy cloak and hat to protect him. He'd spent more days and nights than he could count on the deck of his ship with rain slashing so hard it felt as if it might cut into him. Being wet and cold didn't bother him. During his first long voyage, he'd discovered he could live on very little food and fresh water and live with few possessions. An early autumn rain wasn't likely to bother him.

Wiley had sent around a note asking Garrett to meet him at the house on Poppinbrook Street at four. As luck would have it, that house was only a street over from where Mrs. Feld lived. He decided to stop by to see her on his way to meet Wiley. Somehow his friend had found a man who had a key. He and Wiley were going to have a look inside.

It was still important to Garrett to take possession

of the house, tear it down, and build another, but helping Julia and what she wanted had become more important. He had faith in Mr. Urswick's abilities to eventually break the code. Fate had a strange way of dealing with people sometimes. He'd taken his father's ship to sea to build a company so he could buy anything he wanted. But now, the only thing he wanted was to live with Julia and her son.

A carriage passed him at a fast pace, but Garrett hardly gave notice to the wheels spraying his boots and cloak with water that had puddled on the sides of the roads. He was thinking about Julia and nothing else mattered when she was on his mind. He'd awakened this morning wanting her by his side, wanting to snuggle her warm body next to his, kiss her lips, the hollow of her throat, crook of her neck, and curve of her shoulder. The few hours they'd had together yesterday weren't nearly enough to keep him from wanting her.

He could understand her reasoning for not wanting to marry again, but that didn't mean he agreed with her or that he liked it. All she said was true. Men had complete control over their wives, their children and their possessions. Someway, he had to make Julia see he wouldn't be that way. It obviously was going to take time. He would protect her and Chatwyn, but he would allow her the freedoms she sought whether or not Urswick deciphered the code and Julia could condemn the duke for the explosion.

Just thinking of her lying in bed with him took the chill off the rain and made him warm. She was receptive and passionate to his lovemaking. He was certain she loved him. Only him and that she wanted to be with only him. But she wasn't ready to marry. He had to give her time to come to that realization.

Garrett had accomplished what he set out to do when he left the life of a gentleman. He'd never have to rely on an allowance from a relative, and neither would his sons, nor their sons. But now he'd found that he couldn't live without Julia.

He hadn't come back to London wanting to renew his life as a gentleman but now, because of Julia, he did. He hadn't expected his first day back in Town, he'd meet someone and then not want to look at another woman, but that's what happened. With her he wanted a home, not a house; a wife, not a mistress; an old dog, not a young one. And he wanted Chatwyn. He liked the rambunctious little boy.

Suddenly a thought occurred to Garrett that tightened his chest. Did Julia fear he would go on another journey, sail away, and leave her a sea widow? Was that part of the reason she didn't want to marry? The whispers of the wind had called to him when he was a younger man but he knew he could never leave her, even if they called to him again.

One thing he was certain of: it wasn't another man in her life that was making Julia reluctant to talk about marriage. She'd held back nothing when she was in his arms and he knew she wanted no other.

Another carriage approached and, this time, slowed. The driver offered a ride, but Garrett waved to him and walked up to the entrance of Mrs. Field's house and hit the iron plate with the knocker. While he waited for the answer, he removed his hat and knocked off the excess rain before resetting it on his head. He swung his cloak from his shoulder and shook it before folding it over his arm so that it would be ready to hand to the maid.

"May I help you?" the robust housekeeper said upon opening the door.

"I'd like to see Mrs. Brina Feld."

"Who might I say is calling, sir?"

"Mr. Garrett Stockton."

"Just a minute." The door closed behind her.

Garrett's thoughts went back to Julia.

Something was going on between Julia and Mrs. Feld. It didn't bother Garrett that he didn't know what it was. Friends had secrets they kept from others. But Garrett would like to know why they had been in the kitchen in such a state. Why had Brina rushed out almost in tears, and why did Julia want him to bring the money to her?

He liked Mrs. Feld. She was stunningly beautifully. There was a fragile look about her that would make any man want to protect her—but that was as far as his feelings for her went. He had desire for only one woman. He used to think the best times in his life were seeing new things or doing something he'd never done before. Now, he knew the best time in his life was being with someone he loved.

The door swung open again, and Garrett saw a different woman, but he knew immediately who she was, Mrs. Feld's mother. He'd seen her at various parties and balls over the years. She was almost as beautiful as her daughter. Just an older beauty. They had probably been introduced at one time, but he couldn't say he knew her. Judging by the air of haughtiness in her expression, she wasn't likely to give him the opportunity to do so. He was all right with that.

"Sir," she said, "my daughter isn't accepting callers today."

She must have thought he was there to pay a courting call on Mrs. Feld. Her tone was dismissive. It wouldn't have mattered to Garrett, except that Julia wanted him to do this.

"I'm here to deliver a message from Lady Kitson Fairbright."

"Mr. Stockton," Mrs. Feld said as she came up beside her mother. "What a surprise to see you. Please come in out of the rain."

Garrett walked into the house, handing his cloak and hat to the housekeeper. "Thank you for seeing me, Mrs. Feld."

"I'm glad I looked out the window to see who was at the door," Mrs. Feld answered. "I told Mama I didn't want to see anyone today, but I am delighted to talk to you. I know that you and Mama have met before, so there's no need for introductions."

He nodded to the lady and said, "Yes, a few years ago."

"Please join me in the drawing room, Mr. Stockton."

"After you, ladies," he offered.

Mrs. Feld's mother started down the corridor, but her daughter quickly said, "I will see him alone, Mama, but thank you for offering to visit with him as well."

The lady seemed to turn into a statue in front of Garrett's eyes. "But, dear, I think I should—very well, I'll leave you to your privacy. I'll be in the music room if you need me."

Mrs. Feld ushered him into the drawing room. "Come stand with me by the fire. You're probably feeling a bit chilled from the rain."

"I'm comfortable, Mrs. Feld. We can sit, if you prefer."

She gave him a soft, sweet smile. "You appear to

me as the kind of man who is comfortable in whatever situation he may find himself, Mr. Stockton. I can appreciate that. The closer we are by the fire, the less chance of Mama hearing our conversation. She means no harm by it, but she does like to eavesdrop on me from time to time. One would think I'd never been married as far as she and Papa are concerned. In this house, I'm still treated as their little girl."

"I'm sure they have your best interests at heart."

"They do. I appreciate it and haven't minded their attentions these past few years. Not overly much, anyway. I don't know if you remember, but I was married for only a very short time."

Garrett nodded.

"I heard you say you have a message for me from Julia."

"It's more than just a message." He looked at the doorway and didn't sense anyone lurking. "I suppose there's no delicate way to give you this." He pulled a heavy coin purse out of his coat pocket and extended it to her. "It's the money from the sale of the fabrics. For the sisters."

Her countenance didn't change nor did she reach for the velvet bag. "You're confusing me, Mr. Stockton. Why would Julia want you to bring it to me and not give it to her?"

"You will have to ask her to answer that. I tried giving it to her. That's why I went over to the house by the school when you were—" He watched her brows knit toward each other and her smile tightened. That day in the kitchen was obviously not something she wanted to talk about. "She asked that I bring this to you and I agreed. She didn't give me reasons as to why.

Only that it was a private matter between the two of you. I am only doing what she asked of me."

That answer seemed to please her. Her forehead relaxed and her features softened. "She wouldn't have told you even if you had pressured her."

"I would never do that." He extended the purse closer to her. "I want only to please her, Mrs. Feld. I hope you'll take this so I don't have to let Julia know that I failed my mission."

"Yes, of course, I'll take it." She walked over and wrapped it in a shawl that was lying on the settee. "Don't let Julia's secrecy about this bother you, Mr. Stockton. I've found that there are some things I must hide from Mama. This is one of them."

He nodded his understanding.

Mrs. Feld joined him in front of the fire again. "I'm glad you came over so I could thank you for helping us in the kitchen. I was distraught about what happened. Things didn't go as I'd hoped."

"Everything in the house was taken care of before I left. You have no cause to fret about anything."

"Thank you for that. I'm glad you were there to help Julia. I don't know what we would have done had you not arrived. We didn't even know to use the paddle to take the bread out of the oven. I suppose it's really quite sad. We're taught how to manage staff in the kitchen, plan menus for dinners and dinner parties, but not how to actually prepare the food. There are just some things Society feels that ladies of quality shouldn't know how to do, and cooking is one of them."

"I'm really not one to speak about the rules of Society, Mrs. Feld. I doubt many gentlemen have broken as many as I have."

She laughed. "I think I should learn how to break more of them myself. I liked you the minute I met you, Mr. Stockton. I can see why Julia has been so taken with you."

Garrett smiled but felt it was best not to say anything. He had no idea how much Julia had told her friend.

"What Julia didn't tell you about me is that I have been considering joining the Sisters of Pilwillow Crossings. Julia was helping me learn how to cook so I could tell Sister Francine that I knew how to do something other than play the pianoforte and do a fine stitch of embroidery—neither of which would be useful at the abbey."

Garrett had sensed a sadness in Mrs. Feld when he first met her at Julia's house. Now he realized it was more than sadness. There was also a controlled restlessness in her, too. He hadn't noticed it the other times he'd been around her because his focus was always on Julia. Now that he was looking at her more closely, he could see it. Like Julia, Mrs. Feld also wanted to break free of something. He wondered what it was. Her mourning perhaps?

"No, she didn't tell me about that."

"I've sworn her to secrecy, as I must now hope you will stay silent, too. My parents would never understand my thoughts and I would rather not burden them since I have no clear answer yet."

"You have no cause to worry about me talking with anyone about your private matters."

She nodded. "I was sure of that and realized I didn't want you and Julia to have any secrets between you. Not any of my making, anyway."

"Tell me, Mrs. Feld, do you think joining the sisters

will settle your disquiet and give you the peace you are searching for?"

"I thought that at one time. Now I'm not so sure. I don't know where I'm suited anymore, Mr. Stockton. I do want to help people in need, but Julia helped me realize I am woefully ill-equipped to be of much service to the women who are at Pilwillow Crossings."

"There are many ways to help the downtrodden without making it a lifetime commitment."

She seemed to think on what he said before looking at her shawl and nodding. "Do you mind if I ask you a personal question, Mr. Stockton?"

Garrett had no idea what she might ask, but he said, "Go ahead."

"Did you find what you were looking for during your many travels?"

"I found the fortune I was seeking, Mrs. Feld, and in doing so discovered it didn't bring contentment, only the brevity of happiness. After traveling around the world, I've now found that what I really wanted was right here in London after all."

"Perhaps you had to visit all the other places to realize that. Thank you for telling me."

"Life is not without its challenges no matter where you are. It's all in how you handle them."

"I think I'm coming to that conclusion myself. I hope you don't mind, but Julia told me of your interest in each other. You disturb her greatly. In a good way. Not that she needed it, but I told her I approve."

"I'm glad she confided in you. No one means more to me than Julia."

"You're going to be able to help her with the duke, aren't you?"

"Yes," he said confidently. He didn't intend to fail.

One way or another, he would free her from the duke's control.

"Thank you for bringing the donation and for your help last Saturday and today. I hope to see you again soon."

Garrett nodded.

The drizzle had become a heavy mist as he left Mrs. Feld's house. He made the short walk over to Poppinbrook Street and slowed his steps as the white house came into view. Though it was in the most expensive area of Mayfair, it was a simple home. No fancy arched entrance or iron gates. Just a flat front house with three steps up to a plain door. In his mind's eye he envisioned the kind of house he'd dreamed of building there. Big, impressive, and expensive. He took a few more steps and stopped.

A chuckle rumbled in his chest. He didn't care whether he tore down the house or left it standing. He didn't care if he built a new house or lived in an old one as long as Julia and Chatwyn lived in it with him. Being with them was what mattered to him now.

Wiley stood under the short overhang and waved to him. It pleased Garrett that Wiley had taken an interest in helping him with the house.

"Why does it seem as if I'm always waiting on you?" Wiley asked good-naturedly as he shook Garrett's hand.

"Because you usually are." Time wasn't something you paid a lot of attention to when you were on a ship.

"I didn't mind today. Miss Osborne has returned. I visited with her yesterday afternoon."

Garrett smiled. "That is good news."

"We hope to take a stroll in the park within the next day or two. I'll let you know so you can join us."

"You know I will, but only for a short time. I don't want to intrude on all your time with her."

Wiley nodded. "I've already unlocked the house and had a look around."

"Who did you get the key from? I assume if you'd found Moorshavan, you would have told me."

"I still haven't heard a peep about where that man might be. I got the key from your cousin, the earl who sold him the house. It dawned on me that he might have one he hadn't given to Moorshavan so I rode over and asked him about it. He looked around and found it." Wiley held up the large key.

Garrett clapped Wiley on the shoulder. "I'm glad you thought to ask him about it."

They entered the vestibule and Garrett looked around. He didn't recognize it as the front room he'd entered during the first twenty years of his life. It was much more expensively decorated. A large, gold-framed mirror hung on one wall, and a long, colorful tapestry on the other. Heavy velvet draperies covered the windows. Gone was the small, aged painting of Hyde Park and the Serpentine. The small table where he would lay his hat each afternoon had been replaced by a long side table with intricately carved wood. Fancy brass candlesticks had been placed on each end.

Garrett huffed out a low laugh. "If I didn't know better, I'd say we were in the wrong house."

"It doesn't look much like the house I remember coming to either," Wiley admitted.

They walked down the corridor, and Garrett stood at the entrance to the drawing room and looked inside. The shape of the room was the same. The fireplace and windows were all in the same places, but like the vestibule, nothing in the room was the same. Not the

furniture or rugs, not the color of the walls, or the
things hanging on them. The worn settee, the large
comfortable chairs, and simple straight-leg tables had
been replaced with gilt-covered wood and fine silk
fabrics.

"If we can find Mr. Moorshavan and talk him into
selling, and you decide not to tear down a perfectly
good house, you will probably want to have the draperies, paintings, and a few other things in the bedchambers changed. The bedcovers and pillows are made
from fabrics that have nude scenes on them. Some of
the paintings on the walls are quite explicit. There's
artwork sitting around, statues and figurines that,
well—there's no doubt he was running a brothel in this
house. Did you want to go abovestairs?"

Garrett shook his head. "I'll take your word for what
it looks like." He wasn't a man who let things seep into
his soul. He just handled things—as he had with Pratt.

It wasn't things that made a person happy or successful. It was contentment with what you had. His
father never wanted the house. He was content with being his cousin's guest. Garrett looked over at Wiley and
remembered how he smiled when he talked about Miss
Osborne. He was content to have her back in London,
looking forward to their nuptials. That's what made
people happy. Not what you had but what you felt.

"What are you going to do if you don't find
Mr. Moorshavan?"

"I'll find him," Garrett answered. "Let's get out of
here."

Chapter 20

Julia paced around the back garden while Chatwyn played. The rain had stopped, so she decided to let him outside in the wet grass and heavy mist. The duke would never have allowed him to do it—especially with the early autumn air having such a chill. But thankfully the duke wasn't in London yet. She was making the decisions for what her son could and could not do. It had been rewarding to have him all to herself and not have to share him with the duke.

Chatwyn was a strong, healthy child and had really never been sick a day in his life. She knew if he changed his clothing as soon as they went inside he shouldn't catch a chill. Not being able to go out for a couple of days had made Chatwyn irritable. He ran and shrieked from one end of the house to the other. Julia was patient—most of the time. Though she was feeling the strain of not hearing from Garrett.

He'd told her the documents were almost ready, yet he still hadn't brought them over. It wasn't that she didn't trust him with the deeds. She was fearful something had happened. An ink spill to ruin half of them. They may had been stolen, or gotten wet. Maybe the duke was having her watched and he had absconded with the documents. She had imagined all sorts of things that could have happened. She just wanted them in her possession so she'd know for certain nothing had gone wrong.

Julia threw the ball to Chatwyn and he chased it. He threw the ball to her and she chased it. He rode his wooden horse and squealed for her to watch him. They played until they were both out of breath before she sent Chatwyn into the house with Miss Periwinkle to get dry.

She was dragging the wooden horse to the rear of the house when she heard the side gate open. Turning around, she saw Garrett walking toward her, holding the butterfly net in his hands but not the leather packet she so coveted. It was elating to see him but disheartening that she still didn't have any evidence on the duke.

He walked up to her, took hold of the wooden horse, and placed it next to a bench. Laying the net beside it, he said, "I know you don't like for me to come to the duke's house, but I wasn't expecting to see disappointment on your face when you saw me."

Julia leaned against the wet house. "There is always a chance the duke will hear of my visitors, but that's not the reason I'm disappointed. I was expecting something a little more important than the butterfly net."

He joined her against the siding and crossed his hands over his chest and one foot over the other, seeming more relaxed than she was. "That net is very important to me. Because of it, I met you."

His words softened her heart a little. "I am happy about that, too," she admitted. He made her happy, but the fact remained that he was free and she wasn't.

"I didn't come just to bring the net."

Her heart skipped a beat.

He moved a little closer to her. "I also came over to tell you I took the money from the fabric over to Mrs. Feld yesterday."

"Oh," she said softly, her hope fading as fast as it had appeared. "How was she?"

"She's pleasant but somber."

"Yes. I had thought she might be. I sent her a note after our cooking experience, but she hasn't responded to me. I know she is having a difficult time right now."

"Mrs. Feld reminded me of myself when I first left London. She's restless and searching for something. I had the feeling she doesn't know what she's searching for."

"Yes," Julia answered, looking directly into his eyes. She had always been impressed by his intuitiveness. "She is searching, and it worries me that I haven't been able to help her. If I don't hear from her by tomorrow I'll go see her."

"You might like to know that she entrusted me with her thoughts about joining the Sisters of Pilwillow Crossings."

Julia straightened and faced him. "Did she? That surprises me greatly. It's a very private matter and not something that can be told. If it gets out, she could be ruined or have—"

"Julia." He reached out his arms and circled her waist. He spread his legs and pulled her up to him as he rested his back against the house. "She trusted me enough to keep her secret. I think you know you can trust me to keep it, too."

She smiled and laid her forehead against his chin. It was warm. The circle of his arms was comforting. "Of course I can." Lifting her head she looked at him. "But why are you talking about Brina and butterfly nets? I'm worried."

"You're right," he said, with a twinkle of amusement sparkling in his eyes. "I knew I came here for a different reason."

Garrett pulled the sides of his cape around Julia and hugged her up close to his chest as his lips came down on hers with soft, sweet passion. His lips were cool and moist. She leaned heavily into him and accepted his warmth and comfort. Unconsciously, her arms wove around his neck and her fingers laced through the back of his damp hair. Their kisses were richly sensuous and deeply satisfying. She gave of her heart in every touch, every gasp, and every sigh.

His lips moved across her cheek, leaving a trail of moist kisses over her jaw, down her chin to where her cape fastened at the hollow of her throat. She pressed tightly against him, making her achingly aware of every masculine contour of his body.

But all too soon Julia remembered where they were and knew that Miss Periwinkle or Mrs. Desford could come looking for her at any moment. She drew away from him. His cloak fell away and she said, "No more excuses. I want to hear about documents and ledgers."

He nodded. "That is the real reason I came over. Mr. Urswick is working night and day but right now, he is not hopeful."

Julia inhaled deeply. She thought she was prepared for that answer, but those were hard words to hear.

"But there is some good news. The copied documents are finished." He brushed his cloak aside and reached into the inside pocket of his coat and handed the leather packet to her.

Her stomach tightened and her heart fluttered erratically in her chest. Julia felt such relief, she did the only thing she knew to do. She rushed Garrett and kissed him again. "Thank you. Two such simple words seem so inadequate but thank you."

She took the packet and held it to her chest. For all the coldness that was represented inside, the leather was warm.

"I have the originals safely hidden in my office."

She smiled. "In a hidden compartment under the floor where your desk sits?"

"In an iron chest I bought in Turkey a few years ago. Without the key, it would take a cannon to get into it." Garrett put both his hands on her shoulders and gently pulled her to him again. "I'm serious when I say you only having the original documents without the ledger deciphered will sway the duke. It will be too easy for him to say he was only holding the deeds for someone else. I don't think we will ever find Mr. Eubury or Mr. Moorshavan. I believe it's exactly what the duke said. They aren't real people. Only men paid to register the deeds or manage his properties. Without the ledger to prove that the duke had monies coming in from the properties, I don't believe he will be swayed by anything you say."

Julia's throat felt dry. She couldn't give into the hopelessness Garrett was suggesting. "It's all I have."

"No." He brushed a strand of damp hair away from the side of her face. "I have another way to help you."

"What?" Julia suddenly felt a strange moment of panic. "If you had some other way to help me, why are you just now telling me?"

"It was something that occurred to me today while I was with Mr. Urswick."

"What are you talking about?"

He slid his arms down to her waist and tightened his hold around her once more. "We know the duke can sway every judge and magistrate in England but there is one place we can go where I have control."

"Your ship?" Julia pushed away from him. "Garrett, I can't sail away with you. Live the life you have lived going from one country to another. Never having a home. I couldn't do that to Chatwyn, and I would never leave him."

Garrett's eyes turned dark and stormy. "Julia, I would never ask you to give up Chatwyn. What kind of man would I be if I asked you to give up your son for me? I'm not a beast, though the duke might well be. London is your home. My home, now. But Chatwyn is your son. Not the duke's. His rule over you has to come to an end." He took hold of her upper arms and held his gaze steady on her. "Do you love me?"

"Yes. You know I do. I have risked losing Chatwyn to be with you. You must know I love you."

"And I love you. I would do anything for you."

"I can't marry you, Garrett. That would not keep the duke from taking Chatwyn away from me. The courts would allow the duke to maintain guardianship over Chatwyn."

"The duke may know all the judges in London, but

I will beat him at his own game. I have the Prince's ear."

She tried to tamp down the flicker of hope that rose in her chest. "What do you mean? You aren't thinking of putting the duke on one of your ships and sailing him to China, are you?"

Garrett's lips twitched with a bit of a smile. "I hadn't thought of that, but while I meant it when I told you I'm not afraid to go to prison for you, snaring the duke in the dark of night is not what I have in mind. What I will do won't harm the duke. Not physically, anyway."

He brushed a hand down to her shoulder and gave it an affectionate squeeze. "The duke is a good friend of the King but it's the Prince who is in charge of England right now. He is the only person who can exert control over the duke and force him to do anything. The Regent has the power to make all of Society snub him, smear his name, or take away his lands, and his power. And it just so happens the Prince wants me to do something for him and I can name my price for doing it. My price will be yours and Chatwyn's freedom from the duke. The Prince can make that happen."

"Yes, I remember," she said anxiously. "You have sailed for the Prince. What does the Prince want you to do?"

"Bring a shipment to London."

"That's all?" she asked, concern causing her to tense. "It must be something dangerous for you or illegal."

"No." Garrett reached down and kissed her lips softly. "It's not illegal or dangerous. It's something I didn't want to have any part of no matter the price, but I'll do it for you."

"You are worrying me. What is it?"

"He wants me to bring animals from Africa to London for a special organization he and some other gentlemen want to develop called the Royal Zoological Society."

"What?" Julia suddenly felt chilled. She pulled her cape tightly around her neck as a gentle rain started to fall. "He wants you to carry animals in your ship?"

Garrett nodded. "That practice is barbaric. Keeping them in cages for months on end to get them here. And then for them to live all their lives in a cage—no. I'm glad you declined such a horrific assignment."

"I will do it now, Julia. I must. He is the only one who has power over the duke. Mr. Urswick has failed and the courts will do nothing. This is our only chance."

"No," she said vehemently. "I don't want you to do something so dreadful. I went to the Tower Menagerie once and I know how the animals are mistreated."

"Animals do have a place in Society. If you've been, then you know what a lion sounds like when it roars. You can tell Chatwyn every day about the deep, frightening vibration of sound that comes from a lion, but he will never understand unless he experiences the sound for himself. He needs to see how tall a giraffe really is and how big an elephant is."

"Then I will take him to Africa so he can see them," she countered.

"I've been assured this new society the Prince is sanctioning will be different from the Tower Menagerie. The Prince wants me to do this for him because he knows I can be trusted to see the animals are fed, their cages are cleaned, and they are properly cared for. That's why I can name my price and my price is for him to see that the duke doesn't take your son."

"No, you simply can't do it. I will show these forged

documents to the duke and he will give me my freedom. I don't want the lives of all those animals on my hands. I'll find another way."

"How? There is no time left. You said the duke was better. He hoped to be traveling here soon."

"Maybe the Prince will do it for you for all the times you've carried shipments for him in the past. At least ask him."

"I will do anything for you, Julia, and I will do this, but the Prince is the type of man who usually forgets what you did for him yesterday and is only interested in what you are going to do for him today. The Prince assured me the Royal Zoological Society is building natural habitats for the animals and that this Royal Society will be nothing like the Tower."

"Would you want to live in a cage?" she asked, incredulous that he'd even consider doing such a dastardly thing to animals, no matter the reason.

"Domestic animals are caged," he argued as fiercely as she had.

"They aren't," she insisted.

"Then tell me what is a paddock, Julia? What is a chicken coop? A pen for hunting dogs?"

"That's different."

He smiled. "Different, are they? Is it the names that make them different? Is it the size? You are living in a cage, Julia. Can't you see that the duke has you caged, too?"

His words were so truthful she felt as if he were cutting her with a knife. The pain was sharp and piercing. She brushed out of his arms again. She had always loved animals. It was heartbreaking, but she loved her son more. "I understand," she whispered. "Thank you for the documents, Garrett."

Julia turned away from him and ran up the back steps into the house. At the back door she laid the leather packet on a table to take her damp cloak off. From the front of the house she heard boots thumping on the floor and then a voice. The duke's voice.

He was back.

Chapter 21

A shiver shook Julia, and then another. She slowly
laid her cape over the packet and wrapped it inside the folds of the damp wool to hide it.

Her mind whirled with thoughts. Had he seen Garrett? Did he know about him? Had the duke come to take Chatwyn away from her?

Julia walked down the corridor and into the drawing room on stiff legs and numb feet. The duke stood by the fireplace warming himself. He was much thinner than when she had seen him last. She'd never seen his shoulders stoop before. There was a sickly pallor to his skin, and his thin face looked gaunt. For the first time since she'd known him, it appeared as if he'd aged considerably.

"Duke," she said, and curtseyed, hoping that she wasn't visibly shaking as much as she felt her insides trembling.

"Lady Kitson," he answered with a nod. "You seem out of breath."

She swallowed hard. That hardly touched the way she was feeling. "I am. I just came in from playing outside with Chatwyn."

"You allowed him in the garden in this weather?"

"It's hardly a storm," she said cautiously. "Just a misting rain. Though, it may be raining harder now." She hugged the wrapped packet of documents to her chest so tightly the knuckles on her hands had turned white. She tried to loosen her grip so he wouldn't notice but she couldn't seem to let go.

"Where is my grandson?"

"I just sent him upstairs with Miss Periwinkle to change his clothing and shoes. You know I'm always so careful, just as you instructed, to see that he doesn't catch a chill. It's been raining for a couple of days now. He was quite irritable and needed to get out of the house for a while. He is now getting into dry clothing, so he should be fine." It irritated Julia to have to explain in detail how she took care of her son. "You still don't look well, Your Grace. Would you like to sit down?"

"I'm not well. I'd like to go up to my chambers and rest, but I want a brandy and to see my grandson first. Then I must go to my book room. There are some things I need to take care of in there."

Julia felt as if she might faint. She knew exactly what he wanted to do in his office. What was she going to do? She held the fake documents in her hands. Should she drop her cloak now and admit that she'd stolen the real ones? Should she wait until he went into his book room and confront him there?

Yes, that seemed the better idea than the drawing

room. And truly she needed more time to recover from his return. She knew it was inevitable but still a shock that it was now. She needed all the time she could get to calm herself. Now that she was going to actually confront him.

The duke sat down in his favorite chair by the fire, and said, "I don't know where the butler is. He's never around when I need him. Pour me a brandy and then bring my grandson down."

Julia looked around for a place to put her cape. She laid it on the secretary and then placed a book on top of it, hoping Mrs. Desford wouldn't come in, see it, and want to put it away.

She poured brandy for the duke and one for herself. She seldom drank the strong spirit, but this afternoon, she needed more fortification than just her anger and fear to get her through what she had to do. With her back to the duke, she put the small glass to her mouth and drank the entire dram. It burned all the way down, but she managed to hold in her cough.

After a few deep breaths, she walked over the duke. "How are you feeling?" she asked, hoping her question would distract him so he wouldn't see her hand shaking.

"Only somewhat better."

"I'm sorry to hear that."

"The fever is gone and I've decided that whatever it is that has beset me hasn't killed me yet, so it's not likely to any time soon. I've heard there's a new physician in Town and that he's quite good. I'm going to see him tomorrow."

"Yes. I remember you telling me that before I came to London."

"Perhaps he can do more for me than the present

host of men I've had at Sprogsfield seeing to my well-being."

"It does seem as if it's time for you to seek another opinion. I'll get Chatwyn for you."

"Before you go," the duke said. "I stopped getting daily letters from Mr. Pratt over a week ago. Do you have any idea why?"

She tensed. "No."

"You didn't think it necessary to mention in your letters to me that Mr. Pratt had stopped giving the lessons?"

"No. I assumed you had finally listened to my pleadings and dismissed the man. I was happy he wasn't coming."

Picking up her cape, she took it with her and quickly stuffed it behind a pillow on the settee in the vestibule before going to the top of the stairs and calling for Miss Periwinkle to bring Chatwyn.

Her little boy was shy at first and didn't want to leave her side but he soon remembered his grandfather and was asking the duke to chase him around the settee. Less than half an hour later, Chatwyn was sent back to his rooms. The duke was too weak to play with him for long. When he walked down the corridor into his book room, Julia's heart sank. The duke was in no shape to move the heavy desk, but she had no doubt it would be only a matter of time before he called in one of the healthy young footmen he brought with him from Sprogsfield to move it and retrieve the missing documents.

She just kept thinking that she'd hoped for more time alone, more time to be with Garrett, to be with her son before she had to confront the duke, but her time had run out. The brandy had helped to calm her a little and allowed her to start focusing on what must be done. There was such great risk in what she was about to do. The duke could throw her out of the house and forbid her to come back. He could take her son, leave immediately with him, and never let her see him again. But usually with great risk came great reward. She had to be strong and bluff the duke into thinking she had the ledger and it was being decoded.

Garrett crossed her mind again. Without him she would have never gotten this far. That he wanted to continue to help her filled her heart with such love for him. She didn't want animals to live in cages, and she no longer wanted to live in one either. She had to break free. Unwrapping the cloak, she took out the packet. It had never felt so heavy. With a deep settling breath, she held it tightly behind her back. Lifting her shoulders and her chin, she walked down to the book room doorway and stopped at the entrance. She didn't speak.

Her legs trembled. Her stomach quaked. The duke sat behind his desk looking at a letter he'd taken from his stack of mail. For a moment, she truly didn't know if she would be able to go through with this. But then she heard Chatwyn's squeal of delight and her shoulders lifted.

She didn't know when the duke first saw her, but she walked into the room and stopped in front of his desk. Her body, heart, and soul told her that just as it had been with Garrett, this was worth the risk.

"Your Grace," she said.

"I am tired, Lady Kitson, and I thought I bid you good day."

"You did." Her voice trembled. She took in another deep breath and shored up her courage. "There's something I've been wanting to say to you for a long time."

"Some other time, Lady Kitson. I'm in no mood for more talk."

"What I have to say needs to be said here and now. Though you always doubted me, I wanted you to know I did mourn for your son after he died. His death grieved me deeply, and I'll always be sad that he didn't live to see his handsome son be born and grow up. He was a good husband to me and I, in turn, a good wife to him."

The duke's stare was icy. "Lady Kitson, I said I am tired and not going to discuss this with you."

There was so little movement in his cold, thin face, he could have been a statue talking to her. She almost faltered. His stoic roughness had always intimidated her. But not today.

"I'm not finished, Duke," she said, giving him an icy stare of her own. "Chatwyn and I have lived under your roof, your commands for four years now, but it is time for us to be on our own."

"Now see here. I won't allow you to talk to me this way."

She felt herself grow stronger as she gripped the packet so tightly her hands hurt. For once, he wasn't going to stop her. "You have no choice. I'm not finished, Your Grace. I will no longer agree to your stringent demands on me. From this day forward—" She halted for a moment and sucked in a deep breath. "From this day forward, Chatwyn and I will live on our own and you will release enough of my inheritance to see that our lives will be comfortable and befitting the life of a duke's grandson. In return, I will see to it that Chatwyn will know he is Kitson's son. I will tell him what a good and courageous man his father was, but we will no longer be accountable to you for anything we do or for anyone we see. Do I make myself clear?"

The duke rose from his desk and placed his hands heavily upon it as he leaned toward her. His dark-brown steely eyes seemed to pierce her, but she held strong. "You have just made a grave error in judgment, Lady Kitson."

"No, you have." She brought the packet from behind her and placed it in front of him.

His expression was filled with disbelief and he straightened. "How did you get that?"

"That isn't important. What is important is that inside you will only find forgeries of the documents you've been hiding. I have the originals that were registered in the Courts at Westminster. I only made copies so you would know for sure I had each one of them. You have forced my hand and I had to lower myself to your level and steal them. You have taken control of my son away from me for your own selfish reasons. So you have left me to play the game your way."

He jerked up the packet, opened it, and thumbed through the pages, letting them fall one by one to the desk and scatter on top of it.

Julia kept talking. "I know about the company where the gunpowder led to an explosion that killed all those people, and that you did nothing to help them. I know about all the nonexistent men who own your companies and brothels. I know it all because I heard you and your solicitor discussing them."

He threw the empty leather packet on top of the desk. "You dared to eavesdrop on my conversations?"

His arms were shaking and his eyes bulging. He was angry, but so was she. "No, I didn't have to. You walked right past me and didn't see me. I have proof you are not the saintly man you proclaim to be, and I will reveal your secret and make all this known to Society if you ever come near me or my son again." She spread her hands out over the strewn papers.

"What have you done?" He grabbed up the leather packet and looked inside it again. "Where's my ledger?"

"I have it."

Julia turned and saw Garrett standing in the doorway behind her. Her heart suddenly felt as if it might beat out of her chest. Her body felt as if it might have frozen in place. He was the last person the duke needed to see. What was he doing? Was he was going to bluff the duke, too.

"But of course it's in a safe place, where it will remain." Garrett walked over to stand beside Julia and put a sheet of foolscap in front of the duke. "I admit it wasn't easy for my man to figure this out. It was very clever and difficult. This is only a copy of the first page, but you can see enough to know that your code has been broken, and this lists most every company and house you have in these records. Including dates and amount of monies you received from each of them."

Julia couldn't hold in a loud intake of breath at hearing Mr. Urswick had been successful.

"Who are you?" the duke asked, his face, his arms, and his hands shaking from rage.

"The rogue who will see to it that you leave Lady Kitson and her son alone."

The duke picked up a handful of papers that were scattered on his desk and threw them at Garrett. "Get out of here. This proves nothing. And what could you do about it if it did? Who cares if I make money off the two things I detest most—gaming houses and brothels?"

"Gentlemen, Duke," Julia said. "Most men enjoy both but for years they have listened to you say you are above such evil pursuits. What do you think Society will feel about such a pious man, such a wealthy man as you profiting from them while you malign them?"

"Tell the whole of London. No one will believe you, but if one should, he won't care," he muttered contemptuously.

"Do you really want to take that chance?" Julia asked. "I realize that as a duke you are immune from prosecution in any form. But as a man who gains from his self-made reputation as a man who is everything kind and good and the model for how one should conduct his life, this will make you go down in the history books as one of the most evil and uncaring men in history. How will you like that? Your likeness alongside the worst cheaters in England. What will your sons say? Your daughter and her children? What would the Prince say if he knew you were the man who owned the building where the gunpowder explosion happened and not the fake person to which it was registered? And you stood by and did nothing to help in the aftermath."

"You wouldn't dare," he murmured menacingly, shifting his cold gaze from Julia to Garrett.

"I'm going to give you two days. If I don't hear that restitution has been made and money has been paid to the families of the victims in the Manchester disaster, I will be distributing copies of all this to every door in Mayfair."

The duke looked from Julia to Garret again. Rage and disgust were evident in his features. "I always knew you were just like my cheating wife. I take care of you and show you how to live properly for your son and your husband and this is how you repay me. You turn on me for a younger man who probably hasn't a penny to his name."

Julia glanced at Garrett. His calm expression of determination hadn't changed since he'd come. His quiet assurance gave her all the courage she needed. "You forced my hand by your rigid unbending rules and suffocating ways. My mind can't be changed. Your reputation can be destroyed and everyone will whisper about you when you walk by or you can do what is right for the town of Manchester and for me and Chatwyn. It's up to you how you want this to end."

The duke crumpled and fell back into his chair, winded and jerking. "Brigid was never good enough for me," he said in a raspy, slurring voice. "She betrayed me with other men before she ever married me just as you betrayed your husband. But she got what she deserved and so will you. After the wastrel she ran away with had wagered away all the money she stole from me, he left her hungry and penniless in a wet ditch." The duke chuckled low in his throat as he rested his head against the back of the chair. "No one knew she ever came back to me, but she did. She was destitute and wanted my help. Just like you will one day. And I'm not without mercy. I gave her what she deserved. I opened a brothel and forced her to work there. I was amazed at how profitable it was. That's when I realized I could make money from the two things I hated most. Gambling and loose women."

"You are a despicable wretched soul," she whispered.

"Go. You'll come crawling back one day. Just like she did."

"I think you've heard enough," Garrett said to Julia.

She nodded. "What are you going to do?"

"Stay here with him to make sure you get out of the house without any problems."

Julia turned back to the duke. One of his hands jerked and one side of his mouth was slack, but he was laughing and mumbling in a whispered breath. It was clear he wasn't well and he might have suffered a fit of apoplexy.

"I'm going upstairs to get my son. We'll be staying at the house at The Seafarer's School. I'll send for our things tomorrow."

The duke tried to rise. "You can't—"

Garrett held out his hand toward the feeble duke. "I'm the one who's going to see that she leaves here with her son. And I'm the one who will stop you if you try to prevent her."

Julia looked at Garrett. She met his gaze and tried to tell him how much she appreciated his help, how much she loved him. His support had given her all the courage she needed. She looked at the duke again and for reasons she couldn't fathom, she felt a pang of sorrow for him. "I'll ask Mrs. Desford to send for a physician to tend to you." She then turned and walked out.

Sometime later, Julia walked into the house at the school with Chatwyn, Miss Periwinkle, her maid and York. An aching weariness had settled over her. Mrs. Lawton didn't seem surprised. Julia knew why when the housekeeper told her she had a visitor. Mr. Stockton was already at the house and waiting for her in the drawing room.

Chapter 22

Julia swallowed hard and drew in a strong uneven breath. She wondered how Garrett had made it to the school so fast. She'd wanted to see him. She started taking off her gloves. There were questions that needed to be settled.

"Thank you, Mrs. Lawton," Julia said. "After you finish helping prepare the rooms, you can retire for the evening. I'll see Mr. Stockton out and lock the door before I go abovestairs."

"Yes, my lady."

After laying her gloves and cape aside, Julia took off her hat and placed it beside them. She then removed the pins from her chignon and shook out her long hair. It tumbled and pooled down her back and around her shoulders. A strange feeling settled over her and she didn't know if she felt like laughing or crying. She was now free to be herself. That meant she could wear her hair down in front of a man in her own home if she wanted to.

And she did.

The drawing room was washed in the golden glow of lamplight. Garrett knelt in front of the fireplace, bringing the flames back to life. York stood guard beside him as if watching to make sure he did everything right. Hearing her walk in, Garrett rose and laid the iron beside the wall. They faced each other across the distance, neither of them speaking for a few moments. She felt mesmerized by him and the loving emotions he stirred inside her.

"Is Chatwyn all right?" he asked.

"Yes," she answered, appreciating Garrett for asking about her son. "On the way over I told him he was going on an adventure and he was excited about that."

Julia walked farther into the room and York wandered over to her and brushed against the side of her skirts. She reached down and patted the hound's head a couple of times and rubbed behind his ears. That seemed to be enough attention. He turned around and wobbled back to the fireplace and laid down.

"How did you get here so fast?"

"As the bird flies. Your carriage had to go around all the streets. I cut through the middle of them." He smiled softly. "And I might have entered a few back gardens and jumped over a fence or two."

She laughed softly as she looked at him, standing with his back to the fire. "You brought Mr. Urswick's findings just in time. I believe the duke felt defeated tonight." Garrett nodded. "You do know it's the gentleman who is supposed to save the damsel in distress, don't you?"

Admiration shone in his eyes. The potent sensuality of how his gaze swept across her face comforted and thrilled her. "I do, and you did save me. But how did you know the duke was there?"

"I saw his carriage while I was leaving. I knew you would confront him before the evening was out, so I went back to the office to tell Mr. Urswick to contact the Prince's man and tell him I would carry the animals on my ship and what my price would be. Urswick told me he'd finally broken the code, but he'd only had time to translate the first page."

"We only needed one." She walked over and stood in front of him and enjoyed the feeling that a heavy weight had been lifted from her. "Thank you for everything. I couldn't have broken free of the duke without you."

"I wanted to help you the moment I first saw you," he said, his voice husky. "It took you a long time to trust me."

"The risk of getting caught was so great I had to."

"I know and you were right to take such care. What you said to the duke was courageous, eloquent, and passionate. No one could doubt the truth of your words or their meanings. You were riveting."

She watched his face and moved even closer to him, thinking she'd never get tired of looking at him. "Yes, I was," she agreed, needing the affirmation that she had defeated the duke. "I knew the time had come to stand up for myself, Chatwyn, and for what I believed was right."

"I know the duke was captivated by every word you said. He is a sick old man. I don't think he has any recourse but to accept your demands. I think we'll be reading soon that the owner of the Eubury-Broadwell Gaming House will be helping the people who were injured in the explosion." His voice stayed low and gentle. "I would like to take credit for how this turned out, but the truth is, you saved yourself."

"So this means you won't be bringing animals to London in your ships?"

"I have no reason to now. If the duke changes his mind and tries to take Chatwyn away from you, we will revisit that option."

"I was deeply touched by your willingness to go against your principles and bring the animals to London in order to help me even though I couldn't bear the thought of you doing it."

Garrett placed his hands on her shoulders and caressed down her forearms and back up again. His touch was tender and inviting.

"I stand by my argument that there needs to be a controlled and safe place for animals where they can be properly cared for and where children can go and see them."

"And I may be willing at some point to consider your argument and listen to the plans for this Royal Zoological Society that you say is forming for the better treatment of captured animals."

"I feel sure changes are coming in the months and years ahead. You know, one of the things I admired about you was that you never stopped being a good person just because the duke was mistreating you."

"Are you trying to say it was all right I stole his papers from him?"

Garrett's hands tightened on her shoulders and he moved his face closer to hers and looked deeply into her eyes. "My feelings for you haven't changed. I love you, Julia. I want to marry you and be a father to Chatwyn. I will be here when you are ready to talk about your feelings for me. I'm not leaving London. I'm going to be building a new life and a new house. I want you and Chatwyn to live with me in it."

Julia brushed her lips across his, giving him a tender kiss. "That's good to know." She slid her arms around his neck. His hands went around her waist and his arms encircled her, pulling her tightly to him. It felt divinely comforting to be in his arms again. She continued to stare into his dreamy golden-brown eyes, sparkling with lamplight, and asked, "Do you want to know what I want?"

"More than anything," he said huskily. "If the answer is me."

"I want to live by myself for a while and be courted by a gentleman."

He blinked and then smiled, tightening his hands on her back. "Courted? You want me to come to the front door and bring you flowers?"

"Yes, and take me on rides in the park, walks in the snow, dancing at balls, and skating when the Serpentine freezes."

"Maybe I never told you, but one of the things I wanted to do when I came back to London was meet a lady I wanted to court."

"Then we are in agreement."

"We are, but—" His arms tightened and he lowered his face closer to hers. "I hope this doesn't mean you want me to stand by and watch other gentlemen call on you, and that you'll accept attentions from them?"

"I don't know." She felt a rise in his breath as she made the statement.

"I am not good at sharing what I hold dear."

All pretense fell away from her. With a smile, she said, "You are the only man in my thoughts. Do you think you can keep me interested in only you?"

"I'll do my damnedest to see that I do."

"I love you, Garrett," she whispered softly as she laid her cheek against his chest. "I don't want other gentlemen to call on me. I only want to have some time to be free to enjoy my son and live on my own."

He kissed the top of her head and hugged her close. "You know I understand that feeling and accept it. I want you to know that I'm not going anywhere. I'm not going to leave you. I'll be here waiting for when you are ready for us to make a home together."

"Thank you for that."

Garrett's lips covered hers swiftly, fiercely, and possessively. She had no doubt he was settling his claim on her and leaving no room for anyone else.

Julia knew he was the only man she wanted today, tomorrow, and forever. She wanted to be his wife. And she'd let him know that.

Very soon.

Epilogue

Julia kept watching out the front window for Garrett. It was Christmas eve and she and Garrett were hosting their first dinner party as man and wife in the house at the Seafarer's School. The house on Poppinbrook Street was being renovated and should be ready for them to move into by spring. Garrett had decided it didn't need to be torn down. It needed to be lived in.

It was a bitter cold day but fires had warmed the room and the pleasing aroma of fresh-baked fruit pies filled the air. The staircase, the doorways, and all the tables had been decorated with greenery, berries, and ribbons that had been made into bows. From the far corner of the drawing room, Julia heard the violinist and cellist tuning their instruments. In keeping with the Christmas spirit of mistletoe and holly, and in celebration that she no longer had to wear a widow's garb, Julia had chosen a candlelight-colored gown with garnet-colored ribbons accenting the waist, sleeves, and hem of her skirt. Nestled around her neck were the three strands of pearls held together with a ruby clasp Garrett had given her the day they married.

He was late returning home. If only he would take a carriage to White's or wherever he was going as did most gentlemen, he'd be home by now. But no, the rogue preferred to walk everywhere he went. Julia didn't mind, most of the time, but their guests were due to arrive soon.

"Can we come out now?" Chatwyn called from the drawing room.

"No," Julia answered, turning her head toward the corridor. "Stay where you are. You must not spoil the surprise. I will let you know when you can come out."

When she glanced out the window again, she smiled. Garrett was striding up the walkway, the winter wind causing the tail of his cloak to fly out majestically behind him. She would never get tired of seeing him come home to her.

Unable to contain her happiness and wait, she rushed to the door and opened it. "You are late," she admonished, with no real irritation in her voice or expression.

He took off his hat and replied, "You are beautiful."

Garrett laid his hat, packages, and gloves on the table. He threw off his cloak and swung Julia into his arms and kissed her sweetly, before looking deeply into her eyes and saying, "Can we change the date of the party so I can have you all to myself tonight? You are so ravishing l don't want to share you with anyone."

She laughed. "I will be all yours after everyone has left for the evening. Now we must hurry." She pushed out of his arms. "Our guests will be arriving in less than half an hour, and you have to change, but first, Chatwyn and I have a surprise for you."

His expression softened and he pulled her back into his arms once again. "Are you?" His eyes questioned her. "Are you with child?"

"No," she gasped. "Oh, no. I'm sorry, my darling. I didn't mean for you to think that. That would be a surprise to both of us. It never crossed my mind you might guess I'm in the family way. Not only that but we haven't been married long enough for me to be with child."

His eyes narrowed and he quirked his head a little, looking doubtfully at her.

"Well, I suppose I could be, but never you mind about that right now—I'm not with child." She looked behind her. "Chatwyn, you can come out now."

Garrett reached down and kissed her lips, her cheeks, and down her neck. "You look delicious and you smell heavenly," he whispered.

"And you are misbehaving." She gently pushed out of his arms again. "Chatwyn, where are you?"

From down the corridor her son came walking out of the drawing room, leading an old gray Irish wolf-hound behind him. The top of the tall, lanky dog's head reached above Chatwyn's shoulder. His shaggy hair was thinning, and missing in some places. His big body was emaciated and his limp pronounced.

Julia's heart melted all over again as she watched the old dog. "We found him in the park today. He clearly doesn't belong to anyone so we brought him home for you. I know he looks shabby, but you can see he must have been a magnificent dog at one time."

"He still is."

Garrett couldn't have said anything that would have

pleased Julia more. "You have a new family, and now you have a new dog, too."

Garrett laughed and dropped to his knees as Chatwyn and the dog stopped in front of him. He first rubbed Chatwyn's head and said, "Thank you," and then he patted the dog.

"Do you like him?" Chatwyn asked.

"He's perfect. This hound might be old but he hasn't lost his noble posture, has he?"

"No," Chatwyn said, "but he can't see well. He keeps bumping into walls and furniture."

Garrett looked up at Julia as he cupped the dog's gray muzzle with one hand and rubbed his ears with the other. "He has soulful eyes, and he's just the kind of dog I need."

Julia's chest heaved. "I'm so glad you like him, too. He may not see well but he's gentle. I thought he'd look grand lying by your feet in the evenings when you sit down to read and have a brandy."

"All gentlemen should have a dog as grand, Julia. Thank you." Garrett glanced back to Chatwyn as York moseyed up and nudged his shoulder. He patted York with one hand and the wolfhound with the other. The two old dogs were already friends. "It's a good thing you found him when you did. He's skin and bones."

"I helped Mama get him home."

"I'm glad you did. What's his name?"

Chatwyn shrugged and looked up at Julia. "We don't know. Mama said he's your dog. You should be the one to name him."

"All right. That seems fair. What's your favorite name for a dog?" he asked Chatwyn.

"Bear because bears are strong and fierce like me."

Chatwyn puffed out his chest and made a growling noise.

"It just so happens that Bear's my favorite name, too. So his name is Bear."

"I've never had a dog by that name, but it is a fine name for him," Julia said to her son. "You can take him back to the book room now," she said to her son.

"Wait, before you go." Garrett rose and handed one of the packages he had brought to Chatwyn. "I have something for you, too. These arrived on one of my ships today. Open it."

Chatwyn tore off the lid of the wooden box. His eyes widened. "It's an elephant, and a tiger. This is a lion, and there's a giraffe in here, too."

"Your own menagerie of wooden animals to play with." Garrett glanced at Julia for approval.

She gave him an indulgent smile.

"What sound does a lion make?" Garrett asked Chatwyn.

"Roooar!" Chatwyn yelled.

Garrett laughed and looked at Julia again. "He needs a little practice. Perhaps he should hear a real lion roar some time."

"No promises," she answered in the same light tone. "I'm in no hurry."

"Take your menagerie upstairs," she said to Chatwyn. "Have Miss Periwinkle re-comb your hair and change your waistcoat. Our guests will be arriving any minute now and they'll all want to say hello to you before you're put to bed."

Chatwyn stomped up the stairs with his gifts. York turned and started down the corridor. Bear followed him.

Julia turned to Garrett. "You have very little time to dress before dinner."

"I'll make it," he said. "First I have something for you." He picked up the other package he'd brought in with him and handed it to her.

Julia smiled, knowing it was a book, but with the wide dark blue ribbon she couldn't see the title. She untied the bow and read, "*Quick and Easy Recipes for the Novice Cook.*"

"You'll note there are two pages bookmarked," he said with amusement in his eyes. "One is on the page that has a recipe for bread, and the other for soup. Just in case you want to try making them a second time."

Julia laughed. "You are terrible. You know Brina and I vowed never to try to cook again."

"I'm not so sure about that. You never cease to amaze me with all you do and try to do."

"That was very sweet of you. I would like to read through this and find out what we did wrong." She threw her arms around his neck and kissed his mouth. "Now I'm the one wishing we were going to be alone all night."

"Can we ask our guests to leave early?" he questioned.

"No, but we can hurry them along by asking Mrs. Lawton to skip the meat course."

He studied on that a second and said, "No."

Julia laughed. "I didn't think so." She gave him another quick kiss and said, "Now off you go or I'll be receiving our guests alone."

"One more thing, my love. How did it go when you went to see the duke today?"

Some of Julia's merriment faded. "He still can't

speak or get out of bed. Mrs. Desford said the doctor doesn't have much hope he'll ever recover."

"And how are you feeling?"

"Sorry for him. Chatwyn has asked about him and I think I'll take him over to see the duke after Christmas."

Garrett smiled. "Every day you make me happy that you fell in love with me."

Julia felt a deep abiding love for Garrett. "You make me happy every day, too."

Half an hour later the drawing room was filled with music and soft chatter. Brina arrived late and Julia met her in the vestibule. She looked happier than Julia had seen her in a long time. "I've been waiting for you to arrive," Julia said, "and you look so lovely. Come have a glass of champagne."

"I will, but before we join the others I wanted to tell you that I've decided I'm not going to join the Sisters of Pilwillow Crossings or any other abbey."

"I suppose it sounds heartless of me, but I'm glad to hear that."

"You are the least heartless person I know," Brina answered. "I think I could eventually learn to do the work that would be required of me but decided I would be of more help to them if I started a society of ladies who, like me, want to help in other ways. We could roll bandages for wounds, knit scarves and mittens. That sort of thing for the sisters to hand out to those who come. At first it seemed like such a small thing to do, but a scarf handed to someone who doesn't have one is not a small thing, is it?"

"No, it's a worthy thing to do. I'll be the first one to join your society."

Brina nodded. "I knew you would, but it will have to wait for a while and that's because I'm leaving for Paris after Boxing Day."

Julia held her breath. "What do you mean?"

"I've written to my Aunt Josette and asked if I could come for a visit, and I've heard back from her that she'd be delighted for me to come and stay as long as I wished."

"You know I'll miss you, but I understand. It will probably be good for you to leave London for a while and see her and Paris. I'm going to believe you'll be back in time for the Season."

"We shall see. Now, I'm going to take some fruit tarts up to Chatwyn before he falls asleep."

"Really, Brina. He doesn't need anything to eat this close to bedtime."

"I know, but I don't know when I'll see him again, so let me spoil him with a treat tonight."

"Of course, but you are coming back, aren't you? I mean we—the school needs you. The sisters need you."

"I'll be back. I simply don't know when."

Julia watched Brina go up the stairs and felt an arm slide around her waist. She turned and faced Garrett. "Is Brina all right?"

"Yes. She wanted to see Chatwyn. She'll be leaving for Paris in a few days."

His gazed lovingly caressed Julia's face. "I think that will be good for her."

"It will. I think she is finally ready to put the past behind her."

Garrett reached down and gave Julia a quick kiss. "It takes some of us longer to do that than it does others."

"Yes," she answered.

"I love you, Julia. I'm glad she is the one going to Paris and not me. My journeys have come to an end."

"Yes," she said. "You have come home."

"Merry Christmas, my love," Garrett said, and kissed Julia on the lips.

She thrilled to his touch.

Author's Notes

I hope you have enjoyed Garrett and Julia's story. It's always a joy for me to share the stories I create with you.

The Prince's role in wanting to bring animals from Africa to help aid and develop the Royal Zoological Society wasn't actually formed until a few years after the Regency in 1826 and it didn't receive its Royal charter until 1829.

During the Regency, ladies of Society had little to no knowledge of a kitchen or how to cook. Something as simple as making a cup of tea was always prepared by a member of the staff. Kitchens were still quite primitive and it didn't take much to make an oven fill the kitchen with smoke. It's safe to assume that most ladies of Julia's and Brina's status in Society probably had no practical knowledge of how to make bread or soup. Their lifestyles were lavish. They had maids and footmen to carry out all personal and household duties.

As an author of Regency fiction, I often find a way to limit the number of servants that are in the household because it keeps the story from getting complicated. Most readers of this time period know ladies had maids to take care of their clothing, comb their hair, and tie or button them into their clothing. If I wrote in as many staff as would be required for a member of the ton, it would be cumbersome.

Ladies in the Regency era were ruled by men. When a man wanted to marry a woman, he had to ask permission from the male head of the family, be it her father, brother, uncle, or cousin twice removed. After marriage, her husband directed her life and their children's. He controlled all her finances, including any property or funds she might have brought into the marriage.

As an author, I strive to weave the modern man who tries his best to understand what women went through into a historical hero, a man who must be helpful, respectful, and take responsibility for his good and bad behavior.

The premise of every story I write is that my heroine wants the hero to desire her more than anything in life and be willing to go after her and prove to her she is the only one for him.

I always enjoy hearing from readers. If you haven't read book one in my First Comes Love series, *The Earl Next Door*, I hope you'll look for it at your favorite local bookstore or e-retailer and be watching for book three, *How to Train Your Earl*.

You can email me at ameliagreyauthor@gmail .com, follow me on Facebook at FaceBook.com /AmeliaGreyBooks, or visit my website at amelia grey.com.

Happy reading to all!

Amelia